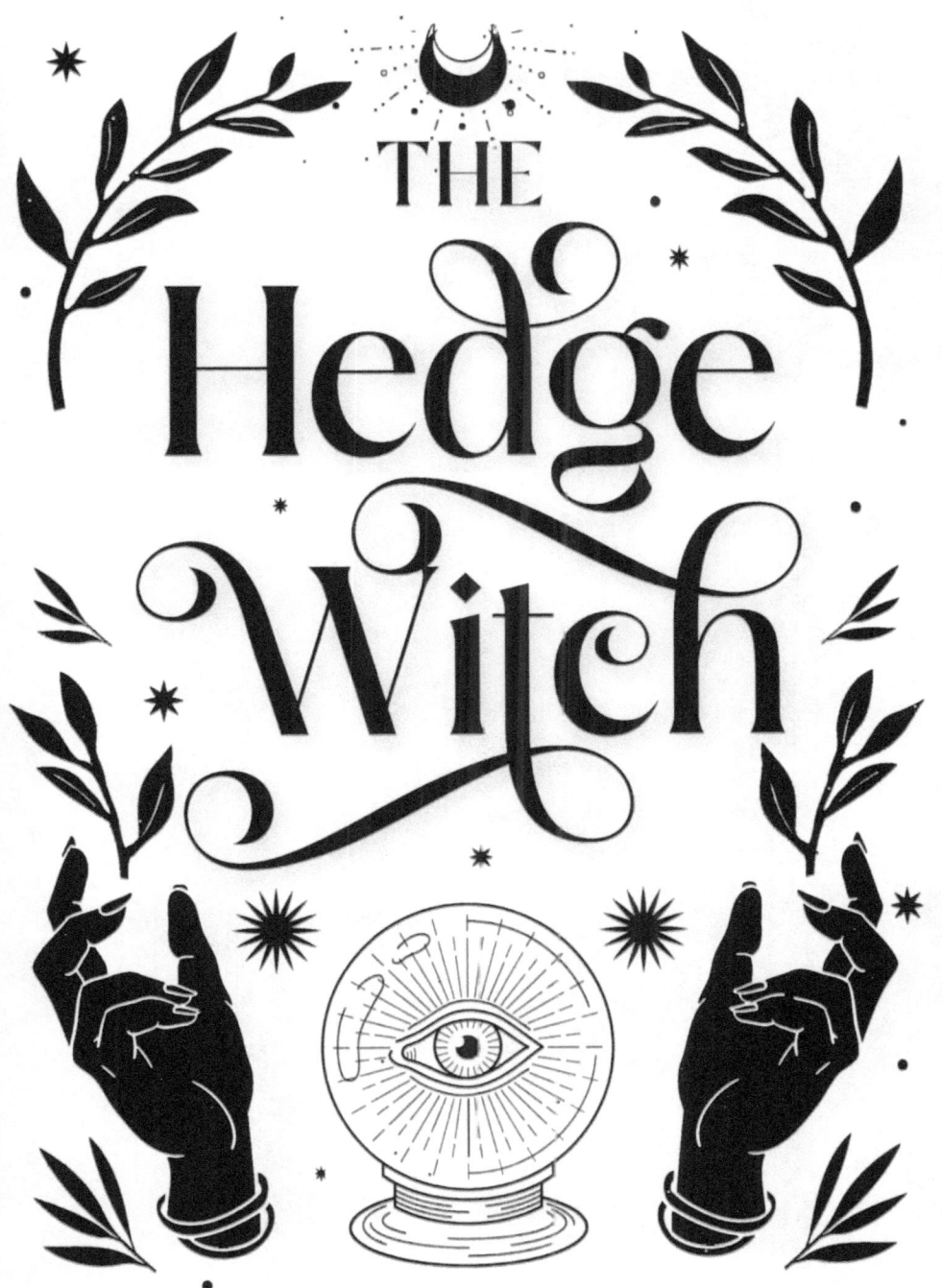

THE Hedge Witch

COLLEEN DELANEY

THE
Hedge
Witch

COLLEEN DELANEY

CITY OWL
PRESS

THE HEDGE WITCH
The Witches of Star Island, Book 1

CITY OWL PRESS
www.cityowlpress.com

Cover Design by MiblArt. All stock photos licensed appropriately.

Edited by Tee Tate.

For information on subsidiary rights, please contact the publisher at info@cityowlpress.com.

Print Edition ISBN: 978-1-64898-454-9

Digital Edition ISBN: 978-1-64898-453-2

Printed in the United States of America

To Dad

I would never have wanted you to read this, but I wish you were here to see me publish it. You would have appreciated Owen's carpentry skills. I'll miss you for the rest of my life.

Praise for Colleen Delaney

"Delaney casts a spell with the first in *The Witches of Star Island* paranormal series. The love story is endearing and the supernatural twists propel the story forward at an exciting clip. The ending leaves many questions unanswered... but Delaney's sturdy worldbuilding ensures this series has plenty of places to go. This is a strong start." — *Publisher's Weekly*

"Family relationships, soulmate relationships, past lives, and incredibly well done magical elements keep you turning the pages of this one." — *HJ Reviews*

"*Finding His Mate* is an interesting story in a dystopian future where different paranormal creatures rule the world. The characters are so damaged and so resilient, and the next book promises more of the same. Highly recommend for fans of shifter romance with fated mates, especially if darker backstories are your thing." — *Jaycee Jarvis, author of The Hands of Destin series*

"*The Hedge Witch* is a fast-paced and delightful read with a heavy dash of spice as well. I recommend this to fans of a good witchy romance, particularly if you enjoy a suspenseful plot to go along with it." — *Your Book Friend Blog*

Also by Colleen Delaney

THE WOLVES OF LUVEN

Finding His Mate

Waiting for His Mate

Stealing His Mate

Protecting His Mate

Aching for His Mate

THE WITCHES OF STAR ISLAND

The Hedge Witch

Bewitching Rosemary

Hauntings and House Witchery

Beltane

The bonfire was magnificent—untamed and elemental. Power vibrated off the flames in waves, cascading to the witches who built it. The sisters, witches of an ancient bloodline, danced with unrestrained joy under the protection of the smoke and ashes of their blaze.

Beltane was a night of the thinned veil, when wishes and spells were shouted to the celestial expanse before them. The witches danced and laughed while they casted, drinking sweet wine until their lips were stained red. The fire was bright and demanding, crackling, a shining spot in the dark of the night.

True darkness was found on this island, a spot in the ocean far enough from the mainland to be a world lit only by fire, moonlight, and starlight on this Sabbat.

They were witches by their blood, the product of generations of power, built and cut down, burned, yet surviving still. They were mastery and dominance, subtlety, and silence. They were the women of hearth and home. With abilities drawn from the feminine arts, passed down from mother to daughter for more years than any human could remember, they were creatures of complexity and simplicity, elaborate beings of luminescence.

Beltane was the heart of the sacred feminine bonding with the awakened masculine, a time for fertility, intuition, and the sacredness of love. They were unbound—all five of them—yet to have met their soul's mate in this lifetime.

The night was warm and windy, the salty air whipping their skirts into frenzies. Unlike others, their power didn't lie in water, but being surrounded by such a powerful force did magnify it occasionally. This night, it was as if lightning ran through their veins.

Not long after midnight, the five paused their dancing, caught up in a vision. They collapsed to the ground, forming a circle around the flames. Their hair was still damp from the afternoon rain, their eyes locked on the vibrating stars in the sky. The noise was deafening in their ears, but silent to any passersby.

An insistent voice called out in the dark. It demanded attention, respect, absolute obedience. They didn't know who owned the voice, whether it be an ancestor, a witch, or something more powerful than any of them could imagine. But they treated it with great reverence, bringing their palms to rest over their hearts as they stared and listened.

By Samhain,
Madness lays waste,
While each heart is claimed.
Endure your trials.
Build your strength.
Carry your craft.
Protect the bloodline.
It is your burden and your legacy.

They lay still for hours after the voice quieted, alone yet together.

The greening through the last harvest of the year would be a heavy time.

Chapter One

The Bay sisters' cottage was not the ideal environment for a peaceful, meditative tarot reading at nine in the morning on a Tuesday in early May. But Laurel woke up with a driving need to read her own cards, so she made do.

The house flurried with the activity of the four sisters who currently lived beneath the two-hundred-year-old roof that occasionally leaked in the upstairs bathroom during particularly violent downpours. Bodies clamored up and down the stairs, cabinets opened and closed with worrying frequency, and the door to the back opened and shut at least three times before Laurel had the chance to sit at the table.

"Do you absolutely need to have your cards spread out all over the dining table at this exact moment?" Rosemary complained as she walked by with four potted plants in hand. Now that it was officially true spring, Rosemary was busy as a bumblebee with her plants. Most of the indoor plants were being moved out for the warm months, giving them a chance to experience the sun in all her glory.

"Yes, I absolutely do need to have my cards out at this exact moment," Laurel retorted. "When I dream that I'm pulling cards, I do just that. I'll let you know if the spirits have anything to say about you."

"It better be that tall, bearded, and broad shouldered is on his way," Rosemary quipped. "I'm ready for some delicious soulmate action."

"More likely it's a disgruntled customer heading your way," Laurel muttered. It had been a week since their odder than normal Beltane. The Bay sisters were the witchiest of witches on holidays, but it wasn't every Sabbat that a voice from goddess-knows-where let them know that both love and doom were on the way.

Laurel straightened the velvet cloth she had laid in front of her, taking up about one-third of the table. She shuffled her cards three times, cut the deck, and placed them to her right. She set both palms on the cloth, closed her eyes, and—

"Coffee. Did someone make more coffee?" Sage, Laurel's youngest sister, pounded in through the back door, her boots clattering to the floor. "I swear to Nerthus, if someone finished the pot and didn't put more on, I'll—"

"Oh, for the love of *every* goddess, why are you all still here?" Laurel shouted. Usually, by the time Laurel sauntered out of bed to make her first cup of tea and scavenge whatever treats Lavender had left behind for breakfast, the house was silent and empty. This morning, though, three of her four sisters were home and taking up way too much space, both physically and mentally.

"Excuse us." Lavender crossed her arms in front of her chest and took a power stance. "But I took the morning off so I could get more than five hours of sleep."

"I'm off today," Rosemary chimed in.

"And I have been up since four-thirty in the goddamn morning transferring seedlings from the greenhouse and into the ground so this entire family can not only have access to fresh fruits and vegetables but also enjoy the income from the farmer's market we use to pay our electric and gas bill." Sage exhaled. She was a harvest witch. It was a rare breed, but Laurel did appreciate having a sister with the ability to grow the best tasting apples on the planet. "I'll be getting some coffee and exiting as soon as possible."

"Sorry," Laurel said, collecting her things. "I'll go upstairs."

It wasn't their fault. Laurel was rarely awake before eleven, and by then only Rosemary would be home and most likely tinkering in her garden. She could just as easily do the reading in her bedroom, but the light wasn't as good in the morning. Her window faced west, which made for some intense sunset spell craft, especially in summer, but was a bit dreary on cloudy mornings in spring.

"Before you go, it's almost tax time, and it's really the only bill you help out with—" Lavender began.

"I know, I know. I've got a big bachelorette party on Friday. I'll be rolling in cash and then give it all to you," Laurel called over her shoulder. She stomped up the stairs for effect, then shut her door a little more loudly than necessary. The din of her sisters' chatter hung in the background, but for the most part, she could find the stillness she needed here.

Laurel's room was cozy. A full-sized bed that had been hers for over two decades with a parade of pillows in black, silver, and deep mulberry velvet sat in one corner. She had a thrifted dresser that was once white, but she'd painted black when she was nineteen. Now, it was scattered with crystals and framed pictures of her family and her familiar. There was also a bedside table with three decks of oracle cards and a book on ancestral connections she kept meaning to read, and a desk currently used to hold clothes that were somewhere between clean and dirty.

She settled on the hardwood floor between her bed and the dresser. In the winter, she rolled out a wool area rug for her room, but the upstairs was a bit stuffy once the temperature hit the mid-fifties.

Laurel closed her eyes and inhaled, pushing away any thoughts that could affect her reading this morning. She didn't need Sage's exasperated voice niggling into her subconscious and throwing everything off.

"Find the light, and draw a circle around it," she muttered. She shuffled her deck three times, set it to the right, placed her hand on the velvet cloth and inhaled sharply. She held her breath at the peak, letting the energy build within, before bowing forward and exhaling loudly.

Laurel picked up the cards, drew three in front of her, but when she set the deck back, a fourth card slipped out onto her lap.

"Well, hello." She set that card to the side. It was something she would consider after looking over the original three.

Laurel was doing a traditional past-present-future draw. While she did practice far more complicated spreads, she didn't usually pull one of those out unless it was a special occasion. She'd done a horseshoe on the morning of Beltane, but the cards had decided to keep that weird prophecy to themselves and focus on her career instead.

She heard the front door open, and Verbena's voice joined the muddle downstairs.

"Focus," she reprimanded herself. Laurel homed in on the past card.

"Four of Wands," she announced. Laurel always narrated her readings, whether she was alone or not. It made sense for her to speak through the cards. "Harmony, peace. Sure, sure." It wasn't like she'd been living in bliss, sharing a house with three of her four adult sisters, but it was fine. For the past decade-ish, life had been relatively calm. And if she didn't have this completely paid-off house to share with her sisters, she would definitely need a job other than tarot reading, so life was pretty harmonious. She flipped the second card.

"The six of cups? What?" Laurel scrunched up her nose. That was a weird pull for the "present" slot. Usually, in her readings, the six of cups meant either there was something hidden in the past that needed to come to light or a memory that was bothering the querent. As far as Laurel knew, she didn't have any memories bubbling up that she needed to address.

She studied the image on the card—a character handing a cup of flowers to another, while five other cups surrounded them. "Maybe Rosemary is going to give me flowers?" Her sister was a garden witch, after all. She giggled. Even as an honest-to-goodness hedge witch, a card would pop up that stumped her. Sometimes, a very practical interpretation of the illustration was the best way to go. So, flowers it was.

"What do you have for me, future?" she teased. She flipped over The Wheel of Fortune. "Hm." She didn't like this card. It wasn't super "evil" or anything, but it was like throwing a dart at a board: the future would be what it would be, and apparently there wasn't anything Laurel could do to change it. Fate was in control now, and as a witch who heard a crazy voice, she understood it. But she didn't like it. The Wheel of Fortune was a fickle card. Laurel was affixed to the wheel, and it would turn her wherever it pleased.

"Now, who are you, so eager to tell me something?" She lifted the card that had jumped the deck.

"What the hell?" Laurel said, dropping it. The Tower stared up at her. "No, no, no. I know shit's about to go down, but not *you*. Misery? Burn it all down? Why are you here?" She looked at it briefly, then picked it up to shuffle back into the deck. She should reshuffle and start again. Maybe she hadn't been focused enough when she began. That happened sometimes, her brain would wander and then—

Soon, witch.

"What?" Laurel yelled. "Who said that?" She scrambled to her feet, knocking her deck across the floor, and clamoring to the top of the stairs.

"Who said that?" she called downstairs.

"Who said what?" Rosemary called up.

"'Soon, witch,'" Laurel repeated.

"What is soon?" Lavender asked.

"No! One of you said that. Or thought it. I wasn't trying but..." Laurel had the unfortunate ability of mind-jumping. She rarely practiced because entering someone's thoughts was unethical, creepy, and usually very disturbing for her, but sometimes it happened accidentally.

"Wasn't me," Lavender called back.

"Me neither," Rosemary chimed in.

"I'm thinking about a showing I have in a couple hours. Could it have been that? Or maybe Sage?" Verbena asked, coming around the corner to stand at the foot of the stairs.

"I don't know. Maybe." Laurel slumped down to sit on the hall floor. It didn't sound like any of her sisters. Or either of their neighbors. Laurel had never heard the thoughts of anyone further away than that. So, there was a voice in her head now, and it was connected to The Tower.

This was not how Laurel wanted to start her Tuesday. She got to her feet and sulked to the bathroom. A good long soak in the ancient tub with a handful of Rosemary's special relaxing bath blend was what she needed to face the rest of the day.

"Her eyes they shone like diamonds, I thought her the queen of the land, and her hair, it hung over her shoulder, tied up with a black velvet band," Rosemary sang as she harvested herbs from the garden right outside the kitchen. They kept the herbs closer than any other plants to the house, as they were used by every sister, and not only those inclined to gardening and cooking.

"So, come all you jolly young fellows, a warning take by me," Lavender joined in as she pushed through the screen door and walked outside. "When you are out on the town, me lads, beware of the pretty colleens."

Laurel sat on a small bench on the edge of the herb garden, sifting through the pile of freshly cut lavender, looking for the prettiest of the buds to keep fresh in a vase on her nightstand.

"Come on, Laurel, join in!" Lavender called. Laurel smirked at her older sister but did exactly that.

"Her eyes they shone like diamonds, I thought her the queen of the land, and her hair it hung over her shoulder, tied up with a black velvet band!" all three belted out, Lavender pointing at Laurel, who was currently wearing a black sports headband to keep the wisps out of her face.

"This ain't velvet." She laughed. "Nor will I be seducing young men at the bar this evening with designs on sending them to Australia." Laurel giggled. Rosemary's bath blend had done the trick. For the rest of the day, Laurel had cleaned her room, walked through the gardens, touched her roots up—pitch black of course—and shaken off the funk of her reading. Now, with a glass of red wine next to her and her sisters surrounding her, she was ready to have a good night.

"Well, I can hear Luke's dogs howling, so the Bay sisters must be singing." Sage grimaced. She walked out of the fields behind the smaller gardens, her hands and overalls covered with the grime of the day. "I need a shower, not a serenade."

"Shall we sing it again for you, Sage?" Rosemary winked.

"No, thank you." Sage hated singing, which was very un-witchy of her. She set her basket next to Laurel. "Carrots, kale, beets, and early strawberries. Do with it what you will, but I'll expect dinner on the table in an hour when I finally come out of my room." She kicked her boots off and left them on the back porch.

"So bossy," Lavender teased, carrying the basket inside. Sage was always bone tired in the evenings during the summer and fall. She did her share of cooking and helping around the house when she wasn't doing back-breaking work in the field all day.

"Laurel," Lavender called over her shoulder, "come help."

Laurel sighed but followed her older sister inside.

Lavender did the majority of the cooking because she was a kitchen witch so food in all forms was her forte, but occasionally, Laurel helped out with small things like chopping. Lavender had already been in the kitchen most of the day, testing out a new recipe for the bakery, a Flower Moon pie. It was appropriate for May and had bits of basil and tarragon mixed into the filling, as well as a few pansies on the border. Their whole house smelled like the height of spring.

"Why don't you de-stem the kale while I get the carrots in the oven?" Lavender suggested, immediately handing the basket over the Laurel. She took it, set it on the counter, and began the arduous task of pulling the ribs of kale apart from the leaves.

It was the full moon tonight so Verbena was coming over to eat, and Laurel would jump the hedge after dinner. She didn't travel into the Hedge World overly often, taxing as it was, so she couldn't do it if she had a reading the next day. Laurel would probably sleep for about twelve hours tonight to regain her psychic strength. Without a long sleep, she'd be useless as a diviner for ages. Then she'd eat a monster of a breakfast as soon as she woke up and start to feel normal again. But there was something about the full moon that magnified it all. She couldn't stay out of the Hedge World if she tried.

"After you're finished, pop the leaves in a bowl and give them a hefty drizzle of olive oil and then I'll season them."

"Sure," Laurel answered, half-listening, half-thinking about the Hedge World.

Laurel was a hedge witch, which meant dabbling in divination, visions of the future, accidentally mind-hopping, having access to an entire realm few witches did, and very limited healing powers. She had never taken the time to truly develop her healing skills, as she had a nauseous weakness when it came to pus, blood, and vomit. Her grandma had tried to convince her she'd make a great doctor when she was younger, but Laurel thought that was a bunch of bullshit. She was perfectly content to leave the doctoring to those who didn't want to have a good old-fashioned swoon whenever someone got a bloody nose. She also hated school and apparently doctors needed to go to school for an extra decade.

The Bay witches all had hearth and home specialties, with Verbena rounding out the group as an actual house witch. They'd inherited their powers through their mom's line; some witches managed to have only a magical father, but male lines of magic tended to be less powerful and genetically recessive, only showing up occasionally, like red hair. The Bays were one of the oldest magical families in North America, though their numbers were dwindling. None of their maternal cousins were magical, and their father had been a regular human.

Laurel finished with the kale and handed the bowl to Lavender before scooting out of the room. She did not want another job and would be content to lay on the couch until dinner hit the table. Laurel walked into the parlor where Rosemary sat and Verbana tidied and collapsed onto the couch.

"I saw Luke yesterday," Rosemary mentioned to no one in particular. "Friendly as always and looking handsome in his jeans and tight t-shirt."

Verbena didn't say a word, or even look up, but continued organizing the parlor. She moved different throw pillows to different surfaces, put the green door mat in the closet and got out the pink one, put a vase of roses that had been on the dining table onto the end table, and then took a step back.

"He is a handsome man," Rosemary continued, pulling a throw blanket over her legs. "Looks like the sort that would be a good lover."

Verbena dropped the pile of books she was moving off the coffee table and to the small bookcase. It landed with a thud that made Laurel jump, Lavender peek her head in from the kitchen, and Sage call, "What was that?"

"Rosemary!" Verbena seethed, bending down to retrieve the books from the floor.

"What? Nothing I'm saying is not common knowledge to the female population of Star Island." Rosemary leafed through a gardening magazine, dog-earing pages as she looked at them.

Verbena organized the books on the shelf, then turned to her older sister.

"The female population of Star Island thinks our neighbor and local barkeep, Luke Karnes, is a good lover? To the point that it is common knowledge?"

"Of course. If you would read any of those sex magic books I've passed along to you, you would know it too. The way he carries himself as he walks, his shoulder to hip ratio, the cowlick at the base of his hairline, the breadth of the palm of his hands, the shape of his feet, the fact that his fingernails are always trimmed, and clean—" Verbena put her hand up to interrupt Rosemary.

"Please stop." Verbena smoothed her white button-down shirt and fiddled with her necklace.

"I still don't know why the two of you—"

"Stop!" Verbena shouted, the bookcase rattling behind her.

Laurel raised both her eyebrows and sat up on the couch.

"Sorry," Verbena said quickly. "I didn't mean to do that." She took a deep breath, smoothed her shirt, and smiled. "I'm going to help Lavender get dinner on the table." She turned and fled the parlor.

"Rosemary, what the hell?" Laurel hissed.

"What? I didn't know she was going to get that upset."

"Still. You know she doesn't like to talk about Luke."

"What is her deal? It must be obvious to her if it's obvious to me. Why aren't they together?"

"I don't know, and I'm not going to ask." Laurel glared at her sister. Rosemary usually meant well, but she got in everyone else's business far too often.

"Fine, I'll let it be," Rosemary conceded.

"I'm jumping the hedge tonight. Want to watch over me?"

"Sure," Rosemary answered. "I have to cut some jasmine at midnight for a bridal bouquet sample I'm presenting tomorrow. I can arrange it next to you."

"Thanks."

"Dinner will be on the table in seven and a half minutes," Lavender called from the kitchen. "Wash your hands if you need to."

Laurel rolled her yoga mat out on the floor of her bedroom and arranged a candle at each corner. Sometimes she would jump the hedge in the attic, but tonight, Lavender was staying up late to work on her personal treasury of kitchen witchery, so her bedroom it was.

Rosemary lounged on Laurel's bed, headphones in and twisting twine around the stems of a bundle of flowers. Jumping the hedge wasn't particularly dangerous, but Laurel could never shake the nagging fear that she could get trapped there. If that happened, she didn't want hours to go by before anyone noticed, so a sister always watched over her. It was simple to get her out of there. Whichever sister watched over her could simply break the circle, extinguish the candles, and give her a good shake. She'd discovered that accidentally when fourteen-year-old Sage came bounding into her bedroom, tripped over her prone form, knocked over two candles, panicked, and doused the candles and Laurel with water.

Laurel lit the candles, slowly and with reverence: white for the element of air, playful and changeable; blue for water, healing and dreamy; brown for earth, stable and wise; and, lastly, red for fire, exciting and powerful. She carefully stepped onto her mat, took a deep breath, touched her toes on her exhale, then came to a seat. She sat directly in the center of the mat with her legs crossed into half-lotus. She knew exactly where to sit so that when she eventually tumbled onto her back—which happened nearly every time she jumped the hedge—she wouldn't knock over her candles or bonk her head on the wood floor.

When Laurel went to the Hedge World, it appeared to everyone else in the world that she was in a deep meditation. But the Hedge World was a real place, not one created in her subconscious.

Laurel let her eyes flutter closed and willed her mind into stillness. The first time she'd ever jumped the hedge, she was in high school and in the middle of her P.E. class. They were doing a unit on yoga and meditation, complete with flickering candles and total silence, and during savasana, Laurel found herself somewhere that was decidedly not the gym at Main East High School. She'd come to soon after, and her teacher assumed she had fallen asleep and didn't think anything of it.

Laurel took a few deep inhales and exhales and sought the Hedge World.

It was always there, like a small trapdoor in the back of her mind. Some days, she lit the candles, and it would simply appear, open and inviting. Other days, she had to search the recesses of her thoughts and dark corners of her mind for a tiny sliver of light to lead her in. But, either way, once she found the door, she always hopped right through. Whenever the door appeared, Laurel ceased to live in her body and lived entirely in her mind within the Hedge World.

Tonight, it didn't take long. The full moon that hung in the sky magnified everything in Laurel's brain, so in a few moments, she was through the door, and out of the human realm.

The Hedge World wasn't a place in the traditional sense of place. It was a realm, like where the fairies lived in the old British folk stories. Sometimes, Laurel wondered if the old faerie realm was actually the Hedge World, and if the people who wrote and told stories about it were witches who didn't understand their powers. Laurel was in no way an academic witch—she'd barely passed high school—but there weren't many texts on the Hedge World to study if she had wanted to dive deeper. As far as she knew, it was another plane only accessible to certain witches.

Only hedge witches and warlocks, and other beings with horns and tails and eyes that glowed under starlight, could access the Hedge World, and they were a rare group. Laurel had never met another hedge witch in her life, though her great-grandmother had been one.

Laurel wasn't quite sure yet what she was meant to *do* with the Hedge World. There were no secret libraries or schools of magical wisdom she had stumbled upon, and even if there were, she was hardly a star student. It was a pretty empty realm, in terms of structures built, and all the places Laurel had visited were rural. Maybe there was some grand point to her visits, but she was cool with wandering around for now. Exploring was fun and she was in no hurry to find a greater purpose to her magic.

Laurel walked through the door and stepped into the dense forest that always greeted her. It was a familiar place, even the first time she ever visited. There were tall evergreens, clusters of maples, the din of ever-present crickets, plus the occasional glow of lightning bugs. It felt like the forest on the outskirts of the town in Ohio where Laurel spent her childhood.

She often wondered if every witch had this gentle entrance to the Hedge World, if witches from France walked through a field of lavender, or those from the Sahara skipped over warm sand. Whatever the reasoning, Laurel always felt at home when she entered. As if whatever controlled the Hedge World considered the feelings of those who came.

She made her way through the forest, towards the other places to explore. There were meadows, a few huts she never dared to enter, and paths that led further than she could see. While she'd been hedge-jumping for fourteen years now, she hadn't explored every corner of the Hedge World, or even followed each of the paths that led out of this meadow. She had no idea exactly how big the Hedge World was. In her mind, it could have been the size of Rhode Island, Asia, or Jupiter.

Laurel turned down one of the paths she hadn't traveled before, wondering if the full moon might lead her somewhere interesting. This road was made of white gravel that glowed even in the failing light. The stone crunched beneath her feet, quickly drowning out the sounds of insects. Laurel walked slowly, occasionally passing another witch, and at one point passing someone that had both a set of wings and a tail but paid her no mind. She moved along, content to walk in silence, her eyes drifting from side to side. Her sisters had asked her whether she spoke to the people she saw in the Hedge World, but usually she did not. There had been a few times when she'd accidentally bumped into someone or helped a witch that stumbled, and a short exchange had followed, but other than that, she kept to herself. It felt weird making a friend in another realm. Especially because she had no idea who any of these people were.

Laurel never had a guide in the Hedge World. Her mom hadn't been a hedge-jumper, so she couldn't enter, and even if she had, she died a few months after Laurel's first foray into the otherworld. Maybe if she had someone to show her around, or explain the etiquette of the Hedge World, she would be more likely to talk to others. But for now, the Hedge World was a place she enjoyed alone.

The path eventually became duller until the white gravel completely disappeared, and the road was nothing more than beaten down grass. Trees sprung out of the meadow and gave way to a forest Laurel hadn't visited before. But she went on, curious as to where she was being led. The padding of her feet on the dirt became quieter, and she could tell she was close to swiftly moving water, the sound rising above all else, though exactly where it was, she was unsure.

Laurel decided to throw caution to the wind and left the path to find the water. She was nearly certain she'd never seen water in the Hedge World before and was baffled that there was suddenly a water source nearby. But she still had expanses to explore here. As far as she knew, there could be beachfront resorts here.

She ducked beneath low-hanging branches and pushed overgrown shrubs out of the way, climbing deeper into the woods, trying to find her way to the source of the rushing.

She was right; it was a river. The water hurried along as if there had recently been a deluge of rain—another occurrence she had never seen in the Hedge World. She glanced to her side, noticing another figure along the riverbank.

He was facing away, and from the back didn't look like anyone Laurel had ever seen before. His clothing was beyond odd, from a different time or place. He wore a plain beige tunic, and it had clearly been worn for days. Dirty leggings covered his legs, and his shoes looked like something out of a medieval painting. His brown hair was tied at the nape of his neck with a strap of leather.

Laurel reached out, drawn to his figure. She brushed her fingertips against his arm, then took a step back, suddenly afraid.

He turned to face her.

"Onfroi?" she gasped. Her mind raced. He was here. *How?* It had been... years? She couldn't remember how long. It felt like eons had passed since she'd seen his deep eyes.

It was him, her Onfroi. The man she had...loved? Laurel felt like her mind was meshing with another set of memories she couldn't quite access. But she knew he was hers. The Hedge World had brought him back to her.

"Amée? Enfin." *Finally.* He grabbed her waist and crashed their bodies together. Laurel jumped into his arms, her mouth finding his immediately.

He lifted her off her feet, devouring her. This wasn't their first kiss. This was the kiss of a lifetime. This was a homecoming. He teased her lips apart, his tongue tasting hers, stirring long-slumbered feelings awake. Laurel's mind raced and muddled in the immenseness of the moment.

Suddenly, she saw cold nights huddled together and days spent on a riverbank not unlike the one before them. She saw him beside her in a spring meadow and her heart swelled with the joy of finding him again.

Onfroi moved his mouth away from hers, trailing down her neck, reaching the neckline of her dress. Laurel vaguely remembered she had been wearing pajamas, but now she could feel her skirt, heavy and caught between her legs. It didn't feel foreign. It was a garment she'd worn hundreds of times before. When had that been? Laurel tried to search her mind for more memories, but Onfroi's mouth against her skin kept her from leaving the moment.

"Oú étiez-vous?" she breathed. *Where have you been?* She had missed him. She had needed him so much. What had happened? She would never have left him, and she knew he wouldn't have abandoned her.

Now that she had him, she could never let go. Onfroi was hers; he had always been hers. They were finally together again. After all those jumbled years of separation, Onfroi was here and in her arms again. They would never be separated. They had another chance—a chance for something greater and longer than before.

Their life came to her in spurts—a somber night beside the fire, a market on a sunny day, a terrible afternoon filled with smoke...

Before she could catch onto that memory, it flitted away like a feather in the wind. It didn't matter. Whatever had separated them couldn't do it again.

"Enfin," she breathed against his cheek. "Ne jamais partir," she commanded. *Never leave.*

"Jamais," he repeated. His arms wound around her waist, and he buried his face against her neck. "Mon petit oiseau."

She beamed with joy. Oh, her heart had missed this man more than she knew. But they were together now, never to be separated by...What was it? What had driven them apart?

"Rester," he begged, his grip on her becoming tighter. *Stay.* He pressed his forehead against hers, willing her to him. "Rester, Amée, avec moi."

She could feel her body being pulled away from his. She grasped onto his shoulders, but it was like holding ice. She shook her head, trying to fight the deep force trying to extract her from his arms. She didn't want to leave. She wasn't ready.

"Trouve-moi," she whispered as her body left his. *Find me.*

Laurel fell against her mat with a thud, her arms flailing out to the sides and knocking her candles over.

"Shit!" Rosemary exclaimed. She jumped off the bed and grabbed the candles before they could roll towards any linens and start a fire.

"Ow," Laurel moaned, rolling onto her side. Her head was throbbing. "What happened?"

"I don't know," Rosemary answered. She picked up the other candles and extinguished them. "You sort of fell over in a big way."

"Wait." The memories of the Hedge World came flooding back to her. "I need a piece of paper!"

"Right this second?" Rosemary still had the candles in her hand.

"Yes!" Laurel shouted. She played it over in her head. Onfroi, those weird clothes—they were speaking French. "Oh, goddess," Laurel's hands flew to her mouth. "He was my soulmate. That was my soulmate."

"What?" Rosemary threw the pile of clothes off Laurel's desk to get into the drawer. She pulled out a receipt and a pen and handed it over.

"I met my soulmate in the Hedge World." Laurel furiously scribbled down everything she could remember. Rosemary froze.

"Are you sure?"

"Yeah. It was him. But from a different life."

"Does that mean it's starting?" Rosemary slowly sat down in the desk chair.

Laurel nodded. She didn't want to commit to speaking it aloud, but it appeared the prophecy was beginning. And Laurel was up first.

Chapter Two

Owen Davies sat on a bench outside his apartment building, tossing his phone between his hands. He had a missed call from his cousin Morgan and was trying to decide what to do about it.

A normal person would simply call their cousin back. But Owen's cousins were anything but normal. Truthfully, neither was he. Owen was the first son of Meghan Davies, of the Davies Water Witch Clan. Morgan was the oldest daughter of Martha Davies, also of the Davies Water Witch Clan. Owen and Morgan were also not regular chatters, so if she called, it was either magical or extended family related, which wasn't any better. Their other cousins, and two of Morgan's three sisters, tended to get into trouble, both legally and magically.

Owen slipped his phone into his pocket and walked towards his truck. He had to be at work, and a conversation with Morgan would put him in a funk. Might as well wait until after the day was done. After he pulled up to the site, he jogged into the nearly finished house. He didn't like being the last one to arrive in the morning. He preferred to be first, but by the six cars already parked outside, he knew that wasn't happening today.

Traveler mug of coffee in hand, Owen found Mike, his best friend and fellow carpenter, leaning against the wall and grinning ear to ear.

"You look like hell," Mike said, slapping him on the back as he walked past.

"Thanks." Owen hadn't thought he looked that bad, but a missed call from Morgan at five-thirty in the morning had apparently done a number on his appearance.

"So, what's on the agenda today, boss?" Mike teased. The two had been best friends since middle school, but since their foreman threw his back out last week and left Owen in charge of the project, Mike had let him have it.

"Floors," he answered, letting the dig slide. "I'll start the living room. You and Jack tackle the kitchen dining area."

"You don't want help?"

"Nah." Owen liked getting in the groove that laying floors allowed. He'd put in his earbuds, start the work, and before he knew it, the room would be done. If he worked with Mike or Jack, he'd be listening to them jabber and the project would feel twice as long.

The day went by quickly, a blur of music and wood, a break for lunch with Mike and Jack, and the satisfaction of a job that was nearly complete. Tomorrow, they'd install the kitchen cabinets and appliances, and then they were done. The house wasn't quite finished, but Owen, Mike, and Jack didn't paint anymore. Owen would be off until another house popped up, or someone needed a small bathroom remodel or something like that. It was almost summer when business boomed. Living in Maine meant that the construction season was limited, so Owen had a lot of free time in January, but barely any in July.

Owen left the worksite a little after six and picked up a burger and fries on the way home. Normally, he would have gone to the gym and then grabbed something to make, or at least something with the appearance of healthy eating, but tonight he just couldn't be bothered.

He had a text from his brother, Aidan, asking whether he would be bringing a date to his wedding. The wedding wasn't until October, nearly six months away, but Aidan and his fiancée were over-planners. Owen was also certain Aidan asked so early because he couldn't imagine his brother bringing a serious date anywhere.

It was no secret that Owen didn't date. He didn't oppose the idea, and he did hope to one day marry and have a family of his own, but for the last few years, he'd been steering clear of the dating world.

Owen could tell very quickly whether he loved someone. Most witches and warlocks recognized their soulmates on sight. Owen wasn't quite a warlock though. He was a sonofawitch, a step below warlock, which had a pretty big range of abilities. Some of them, like his brother Aidan, had no magical powers whatsoever. But Owen could sense storms and if he concentrated hard, he could make them dissipate. But not like a hurricane or a tornado. Basically, he could get a light rainstorm to break up a little quicker than it would have. As far as powers went, it was dull. But whenever he kissed a non-soulmate, his heart felt like lead. He was convinced his particular powers extended to knowing when he was kissing the woman he was supposed to spend the rest of his life with.

He had tried to date seriously, even though he knew deep in his heart that he hadn't met his soulmate. When he was twenty, he had a girlfriend, Courtney, for a year. She was perfectly kind, attractive, and even a little funny. But, after a year, Owen couldn't kid himself any longer. He knew she wasn't his destiny, so he ended it. Courtney took the breakup badly, to the point that Owen decided anything long-term was off the table for him. It wasn't fair for him to put someone through a relationship with him, while knowing it would end eventually.

Owen texted his brother back that it was unlikely he would bring a date, but that he would have a firm answer for him by September first. If by some act of some god, Owen stumbled across his soulmate in the next couple months, he would be able to bring her to his brother's wedding.

He set his food on his small kitchen table—built for two but currently working well for one—and got out a beer. He was beat from work and thought a little alcohol might be exactly what he needed to sleep a little more soundly.

The apartment had two bedrooms, and he used the second as an office. While he was a carpenter by trade, doing the manual labor of house building, he dabbled in design. After finishing his burger, Owen brought his beer and went to his office, turned on some Bach, and sat in front of his drafting table. He was working on a craftsman style house that had been slowly coming to life in his mind the past year. He had the exterior done and was currently putting together the first floor. It would have two floors, a small, finished basement, three bedrooms, and a big porch. He wanted a place to eat outside when the weather was nice, and he wanted it to fit a table that sat six. Owen had his eye on a piece of land about twenty miles outside Portland that would be perfect. It wasn't on top of his family, but close enough that holidays and weekends would be easy. He was hoping he'd be able to finally purchase it by fall.

Tonight, when he began to sketch out the first floor, he changed his mind. For the past year, he had envisioned a kitchen-dining area open to a living room. But tonight, he thought he needed to add two additional separate rooms. He wasn't particularly sure why, but he let his hand follow the inspiration, knowing he could always change it.

Three hours later, his house now had a screened porch and a separate room off the kitchen. He thought it could be an office or something like that, but the house needed it. Otherwise, it would be incomplete.

It was close to midnight when Owen finally padded out of his office. He quickly brushed his teeth and stripped off his clothes and climbed into bed in his boxers. He never worked that late, especially when he had to be up early for work the next day. He switched off the light and fell straight to sleep.

Owen was at a river. He felt off. His core being felt the same, but this body felt different—lankier and sore. His joints ached as if he were an old man and his hair felt heavy. He was missing the nail on his thumb. He couldn't remember losing it, though it was a common injury for carpenters. He ran his hand over his head and was surprised to find that he had long hair tied into a knot at the nape of his neck. His clothes felt itchy too. He felt like he was wearing someone else's skin.

Someone touched his arm. He turned and his world lit on fire.

Amée.

His love stood in front of him. It was impossible. She was gone. They were gone, turned to bone and ash, and made anew beneath the earth. Yet, she was here. Was she haunting him? Was this a ghost long forgotten come to addle his mind?

He didn't care. He needed her, needed to touch her again. He pulled her body against his and relief washed over him. Her skin was beneath his fingers, and all was well. The entire world melted away to nothingness and there was only the two of them, pressed together.

She was here. Amée was here.

Owen jumped out of bed in a full sweat, his alarm blaring. He gasped for air and fell to his knees.

Amée. She was quickly fading from his memory, but he tried to keep her in the forefront of his brain.

"Amée with the wide eyes. Mon petit oiseau, my little bird. Amée. Small, raven-haired girl with eyes like stars and a voice like cool water. My love, my love, Amée." He scrambled to his feet, looking for his phone. He quickly opened his notes app and typed everything he could remember about her into it.

Onfroi. That was what she called him. He added it to the list. He was Onfroi, or at least he had been Onfroi. Onfroi who spoke French and hadn't bathed in months.

Owen collapsed back onto his bed, catching his breath. He ran his hand over his hair. It was shorn close to his scalp again, as it was before he went to bed. He checked his hands; all nails were present. He glanced down at his clothes; just boxers. He was back to normal.

Or at least, physically, he was back to normal. Mentally, his mind felt like it was sprinting a marathon.

His soulmate. It was her.

"What is wrong with you?"

"Huh?" Owen answered, setting his beer down.

"You're acting weird. You've been weird all day. Are you having money problems? We'll get put on another job soon," Mike pressed.

"I'm ok. Just distracted."

Mike may have been Owen's best friend, but he didn't know about his mom. He did know about the storm thing, but that was easier to brush off as a weird occurrence.

"You're beyond distracted. You need a vacation." Mike added and slapped the table.

"I don't remember the last time I went on vacation. Especially in the summer. We could get put on a job," he pointed out. Owen wasn't strapped for cash, but he wouldn't turn down work whenever it came his way.

"So? Owen, I'm looking at you, and if I'm being honest, you look awful."

"Thanks, man," Owen replied through a laugh.

"I'm being serious. You look like you need to sleep for a month. Maybe give yourself a week or two."

He mulled it over in his mind. He didn't like being too hot and most of the country was sweltering right now. There weren't many places cooler than Maine in the summer. Maybe he could go to Canada.

"Actually," Mike tapped his knuckles on the table, "Jack said his sister was looking for renters. She bought a cottage on Star Island a few months ago."

"Where the hell is Star Island?"

"By Nantucket I think? You gotta take a boat to get there. It's pretty far out in the ocean."

Owen exhaled. A remote island in the North Atlantic sounded nice. He could breathe some sea air, try to clear his head, recharge next to the ocean, and make a plan. He knew he needed to find Amée, but he had no idea where to begin.

Owen may not have known what the hell that weird dream experience was, but he knew that woman was his soulmate. He couldn't rest until they were together again. To a human man, it might seem corny, but he wasn't a human man. Owen Davies was a sonofawitch with a very magical family filled with powerful witches who did not fuck around when it came to soulmates. He'd been looking for her since he was a teenager, and now he had a face to go off of.

But he couldn't copy that memory of Amée into an image search engine and hope for an address. So maybe immediate obsession was a bad idea.

"That might be a good idea. You'll call me if a job comes up, though, so I can hurry back, right?"

"You're the only person I know who is planning on coming back from his vacation to work before he's even booked it. But, yeah, I will. Call Jack. Get it figured out. But first, get us another round."

Owen laughed and motioned for the bartender to come back. His phone buzzed against his leg.

> Morgan: I guess you aren't calling me back. You will be glad to know that no one needs bail money. You were in my vision a couple days ago, asshole. I'm glad you weren't getting hit by a bus or anything as you'd be dead. Anyway, you need to get yourself to a place called Solaris?Solarium? Solar something. I don't have a lot of details. But you've got shit to do there of a magical nature. Oh, and you're going to get laid so congratulations. Later, nerd.

Owen quickly slid his phone back into his pocket. He and Mike had been friends forever, but he only knew that his cousins got in trouble with cops on a regular basis, not that some of them had visions. Which apparently now included peeks at him having sex. Gross.

Looked like he'd be googling "places called Solaris" when he got home tonight.

Owen was wide awake. He didn't have work tomorrow, but it was still very odd for him to be awake at two am.

He wanted to see Amée. More than that, he wanted to wrap his arms around her again. Dreaming of her had sparked a deep ache in his chest that he couldn't shake.

He violently missed a woman he'd never met before. For all he knew, she was nothing but a dream, and he was losing his mind.

But she didn't feel like a dream, and he didn't feel like he was losing his mind. She felt important and monumental. He felt like he'd been drifting on the brink of sleep his whole life and now he was wide awake. He had a purpose now.

Owen hadn't told his mom yet. She was probably the first person he should have called, but he held back. She would throw a million spells and charms at him and look into the mirror to find her. She was his mom; she'd do anything to help him achieve happiness, but he wasn't quite sure he wanted to invite her into it yet.

Owen knew how he felt about Amée. He knew how his body reacted to her. If his mom looked into her mirror and saw whatever time they had been together, she might see things. Passionate things. Completely naked things. Things that apparently Morgan had seen. He wasn't a prude; he had been raised by a crazy liberal water witch. But he wasn't comfortable with his mom viewing him and his soulmate in the throes of passion, no matter what lifetime it was. For now, he was on his own. If he couldn't find her within a few months, he'd throw caution to the wind and let his mom help. He would probably end up mortified beyond belief, but it would be a small price to pay if she was able to find her.

Right this moment was one of the five times in his life he wished he was a warlock with real power. His entire adulthood, he'd been glad not to be swept into the world of magic. He was lucky; as a sonofawitch, he could walk the line between magical and non-magical very easily. But right now, along with whenever anyone bullied him under the age of twelve, he wished he could do something magical about it. Or at least recognize his soulmate if she was living in his building.

Owen opened the notes on his phone and read them again. On a whim, he opened his search engine and typed in Onfroi.

"Medieval French," Owen mumbled, reading the results. "That explains the itchy clothes."

It was a start. It didn't necessarily mean he knew Amée in medieval France, but that was the earliest it could have been. He closed his eyes and tried to picture her clothing. He hadn't been concentrating on it with her lovely face right in front of his, but if his memory served him, she wore a very plain, loose dress. Owen opened another tab and searched "Medieval French clothing." He was returned a collection of clearly aristocratic outfits. He was sure the soreness of his body and missing nail pointed to manual labor and scrolled past everything fancy.

Before he knew it, Owen found himself down an internet rabbit hole, and the sun was up. He'd been up the entire night obsessing over the woman from his dream.

He did need a vacation. Star Island was the place Mike recommended, but Morgan had said he was needed in Solaris, wherever the hell that was. He opened a new tab and typed in "Solaris USA," hoping that his cousin didn't expect him to fly out of the country to take part in some magic and have sex.

Owen nearly knocked his laptop to the ground with the first result.

Solaris: Star Island's tourist-friendly town. Click here for rental information.

It looked like Owen was going to Star Island and Solaris.

Chapter Three

"The Devil!" the maid of honor shrieked a mere eighteen inches away from Laurel's ear. "Cady! Cady! I got the Devil card!"

"It's ok!" Laurel tried to calm her. "The Devil doesn't mean what you think it means." She grabbed her hands. What the hell was her name? She searched her brain.

"Margot! Margot. The Devil card is not at all what we think of when thinking of the Devil." Laurel knew she should have used one of her more modern decks, but like most bachelorette parties, they'd insisted on an "authentic" experience and wanted the Rider Waite Smith Tarot Deck. "Basically, the Devil card means you're going to get laid. Or you should try to go get laid. It's like a sex and party card. More debauchery than the traditional Judeo-Christian idea."

"I'm going to get laid?"

"Most likely. Or get piss drunk out of your mind and have a blast? Just have fun this weekend. Don't think about any deadlines at work or whatever is waiting for you back in... Pittsburgh."

"Philadelphia." Margot corrected.

"Right, Philly. I always get Pennsylvanian cities confused." Laurel covered. "Do you feel better?"

"I think so. So, sex tonight. I need to shave my legs."

"Good plan."

Thirty minutes later, Laurel wrapped up her last reading of the group. The ten revelers were already each a few glasses of champagne in when she showed up so there had been some tears, a little bit of rage explaining, and a bride that looked like she was going to throw up the whole time she got her cards read. Not the least stressful party Laurel had ever been a part of, but it beat the time one of the bridesmaids confessed she was sleeping with the bride's brother. Who was already married.

But she left with a cool five hundred dollars in her pocket. Bachelorette parties made up the greatest chunk of her income, though she did have a couple of local regulars who saw her on a monthly basis. She had another big party in a couple weeks and, thankfully, she wouldn't be handing all of that over to Lavender.

Laurel hopped down the front steps of the rental cottage on the Centauri peninsula and grabbed her bike where it leaned against the railing. Star Island had five peninsulas (Centauri, Sagittauri, Polaris, Sirius, Vega) that gave it the janky shape for which it was named. Laurel lived on Vega, one point over from Centauri, so the ride wasn't too long.

She couldn't wait to go home and drink a huge cup of Wake Up Shake Up tea.

Laurel hadn't slept more than two hours straight since meeting Onfroi in the Hedge World. If she was able, she would have jumped right back into the hedge and searched high and low for her soulmate, but she was physically, mentally, and spiritually exhausted. There was no way she could handle going through that door in this state. She needed to recharge and rest, at least for a few days.

She should have spent her time off from work meditating and letting her soul rejuvenate from the trip to the hedge and prepare for her next foray.

Instead, she obsessed. As soon as she got home from the party and made herself a huge cup of tea, she went over her sketches of Onfroi. Over the past few days, she'd filled a small notebook with his likeness. Sometimes she drew him in settings that seemed like they were from distant memories, sometimes she drew small details, like the scars on his hands. He definitely worked with his hands. She could tell that from the rough feel of them against her neck and cheek.

Laurel tucked her sketchbook under her arm, grabbed her mug of tea and a scone from the plate in the kitchen, and headed to the attic.

The attic was their witch central. It was accessible only by a small staircase in Rosemary and Sage's closet, and there would be no reason for a non-Bay sister to end up there. It was a place where their witch flags could fly in the wind without the fear of a neighbor accidentally happening upon someone chanting, spellcasting, or in a trance.

She set her mug down on the small end table beside the plush emerald green chair and headed to the bookcases. When their mom died, they'd inherited her books, and their great-aunt June, the previous owner of the Bay cottage, had left a small library for them. There were spell books and bestiaries and countless encyclopedias of herbs and familiars and tools. A faint chalk outline of an eight-pointed star—a remnant of a spell Rosemary had attempted nearly three years earlier—stained the middle of the floor. Something about chanting over chalk made it difficult to remove. It was basically the dream room of every sixteen-year-old enamored with Stevie Nicks.

Laurel grabbed *The History of the Bay Witches* and plopped down in her seat. She shoved the rest of her scone into her mouth and cracked open the book. It was a huge tome that listed every witch (and some non-magicals) of the Bay line, beginning in 1134 AD when Matilda Bay decided to begin writing down her family history. The book had been rebound several dozen times, had paper added from a myriad of different time periods, and smelled like a mixture of dust, goat's blood, and ink. It wasn't Laurel's favorite scent.

Laurel usually avoided this book like the plague, which was explained in detail more than once how it claimed the lives of Bay Witches. Also she didn't love reading things like:

1362: Jane Bay accused of seducing neighbor; drowned in pond for witchcraft. While Jane did have an affair with her neighbor, Edward, she used nothing but her beauty to seduce him.

There were also lots of entries that were horribly sad, children being lost to disease, whole branches of the family wiped out in wars, and the inevitable burnings at the stakes. Reading the history of a magical family through the Middle Ages of Europe was hardly a light, happy read.

Laurel looked for any clues to her past as Amée. She wasn't sure if Amée was both an ancestor and a past version of herself, and so far, the books hadn't provided any helpful information. The Bay Witches were descended from a British/French line, so Laurel suddenly understanding some sort of French would make sense if she was a reincarnated version of an ancestor. But there were very few listings of French Bay Witches in the time period that Laurel had narrowed down from their clothing. Most of the French witches in the line didn't come into the book until the mid-1800's, and they all lived in cities. Laurel was almost certain she was dressed like a laborer from the medieval period, plus Onfroi's clothing had been stained with mud. It was possible they were city dwellers, but not in 1850. Also, none of them were named Amée.

Laurel closed the book and sighed. Looking through the disgustingly smelly copy of *The History of Bay Witches* had done nothing but depress her. There were no new clues about her past, which had been a long shot, but at least gave her some hope. Convinced there was nothing left to find there, she replaced it on the bookcase. There was one person who could help her, but she usually wasn't very helpful, especially when it came to past lives.

That particular Wednesday morning, The Immortal Cupcake, Lavender Bay's wildly successful bakery, was having a slow start. Laurel walked up to the storefront prepared for a line out the door, it was after all strawberry shortcake donut day, but was met with only two people on their way out. Laurel had a small group reading earlier that morning for a few women in their forties on a girls' trip, but now had time to badger her sister.

"You're done with the reading already? I figured you would go home and take a nap after your late night." Lavender commented as Laurel walked into the bright space. The bakery had a large case displaying the daily treats available for purchase, a seating area for those looking to enjoy their pastries with cups of tea or coffee in the store, and a large chalkboard with the day's offerings at the front. The white walls were covered in old recipes written in several different handwriting, bringing a dreamy quality to the shop.

"Can't really relax." Laurel slid onto one of the stools at the counter and set her bag on the floor. "Where did you find the past lives spell?" There was no use beating around the bush. Laurel needed to know about her past life and Lavender had completed the spell.

Lavender brushed a few crumbs off the counter. "Laurel, no. I can't stop you from doing it, but I'm not going to help you do it."

"Can you at least point me in the right direction?" Lavender had already done the legwork. It seemed unfair to make Laurel do it all over again.

"No! Seriously, no. I am not going to aid you in doing what is a supremely bad idea." Lavender got a lilac frosted donut out of the case and put it on a plate, sliding it across to her sister. "Eat something. Your brain is clearly not functioning at its normal level of logic."

"I will eat if you tell me why. Why on earth won't you tell me what book you used? Or better yet, the name of the spell? I promise I won't get you involved. We're on a deadline, remember? My soulmate showed up in the Hedge World. Shit's about to hit the fan."

Lavender exhaled loudly. Laurel didn't know a lot about what happened when Lavender looked into her past life, or lives. She'd been away at school when she did it, and within two weeks of the spell's completion, both their parents had died in a car wreck and twenty-year-old Lavender was going through the paperwork to be the legal guardian to three of her four younger sisters. There'd been no discussion of the spell after that, or basically anything other than how on earth the five of them were going to survive.

"Why would you want to see your past life? Spoiler alert: you die. And we're witches so you probably didn't die an old woman in your bed surrounded by grandchildren."

"I know I died." Laurel tried to fight the twinge of sarcasm in her voice. Lavender wasn't her mom but their murky relationship of both guardian and charge plus being sisters forced her to feel more respectful towards Lavender than Rosemary, Verbena, or Sage. "I'm not going to have a mental breakdown because I see my own death. I get it; I've been reincarnated, so clearly the past me is no longer living. Also, the Middle Ages were a very long time ago. I've yet to come across a witch who has managed to outrun death."

"You don't *see* your death. You feel it. You experience it. You'll come out of the spell knowing what it feels like to drown or be hung or shot or waste away from the plague or get gored by a wild boar. And if you got your leg sawed off on a Civil War battlefield, you'd feel getting your leg sawed off on a

Civil War battlefield. None of these are good feelings." Lavender busied herself putting together boxes of cupcakes, placing each miniature cake at the perfect position so the frosting flowers looked like a bouquet.

"How did you die?" Laurel had never asked her before. She didn't think any of her sisters had. She had a sneaking suspicion that Rosemary knew a little more than the rest of them, but she kept it to herself. For all her attempted meddling, Rosemary would take a secret to her grave.

Lavender paused her cupcake arranging and turned to face Laurel, wiping her hands on her apron.

"Blood loss."

"Blood loss?" Laurel repeated. It wasn't what she was expecting.

"Medically, that was my cause of death. At least in the life I saw. I have no idea if there were others because that one was enough for me."

"So, you know what it feels like to bleed out," Laurel continued.

"Yup." Lavender turned back to the cupcakes.

"What does it feel like?"

"Not good. Look, I can't tell you what to do, you're a twenty-nine-year-old woman. I know this man from the Hedge World has you in a tizzy, but I don't think it's worth seriously screwing with your mind and welcoming a new flood of memories into your brain to see how your past relationship played out. I'll give you a hint: it probably didn't end well."

Laurel regarded her sister quizzically for a moment. Lavender was a closed book as far as Laurel was concerned. She didn't talk about her life before their parents died, she didn't let Laurel read her cards, and she rarely spoke about anything other than her bakery and their sisters. Laurel was usually good at reading people, it came hand in hand with her clairvoyant abilities, but Lavender had always been a sort of puzzle she couldn't quite put together.

"Stop trying to see inside my brain, and go get some sleep," Lavender commanded, keeping her back to Laurel. "You're getting loopy. You had a dream about a guy who you are attracted to. Happens all the time."

"The Hedge World is not a dream—" Laurel began.

"Fine. You had a supernatural experience with a hot guy. Join the club. Now, go take a nap."

Laurel did take Lavender's advice and go home and take a nap. She ended up sleeping for seven straight hours and began to seriously consider that there had been something in the purple-frosted donut her oldest sister had given her. It was policy that Bay sisters ask before dosing relatives, but Lavender always held onto the idea that she was their guardian and sometimes guardian knew best. Even if Laurel was twenty-nine years old.

She woke up refreshed for the first time since meeting Onfroi, so while she was annoyed with Lavender, she couldn't be angry. After nights upon nights upon nights of tossing and turning or methodically reading every spell book in the library, it was heavenly to wake up in her bed after solid, dreamless sleep. It may have been five in the evening, and there was no way she'd be able to fall asleep, but hey, now she had a full night to research.

Laurel ambled downstairs, her hair piled in a bun and her deep purple robe floating dreamily behind her. She was wearing her favorite pajamas, a satin black top and short set. Laurel dressed like a witch, even for bed. It was only fitting that her nighttime wear reflected her true spirit.

"What are you wearing?" Sage was sitting at the table, unlacing her mud-caked boots. She was wearing a ratty orange t-shirt and jeans. Her nearly waist-length brown hair was pulled back in a braided bun, but about fifty percent of her hair had escaped.

"My pajamas." Laurel sauntered into the kitchen and put the kettle on. She needed a cup of tea and a meal. She felt like she had finally come out of the daze since meeting Onfroi in the Hedge World. She still needed to find him, and her resolve to look into her past life hadn't wavered, but she could see clearly now. If she wanted to work the sort of powerful magic that she was going to need, Laurel needed food, water, sleep, and sunshine.

"You look like how Hollywood thinks women dress for bed. I wear a clean t-shirt and granny panties. Or if it's cold, I throw on some flannel pants." Sage was usually up and out hours before Laurel woke up, and in turn was asleep hours before Laurel put on her pajamas.

"I'll take that as a compliment. I assume you meant to say I look pretty in my PJs." Laurel rummaged through the fridge looking for something to fill her belly. She found some leftover spinach and pea soup Rosemary had made a few days ago.

"I do not know why you feel the need to look pretty in your PJs. Your sisters are the only people who see you in them." Sage continued.

"Well, you never know." Laurel paused, holding up the container. "Do you know if Rosemary put anything in this? I'm ninety percent certain Lavender drugged me earlier today, and I don't want to double up on anything."

Sage stood up with an exhale and shuffled into the kitchen. She took the container out of Laurel's hand and smelled it.

"Spinach, peas, onion, chicken broth, basil, cilantro, and a squeeze of lemon. Provided she didn't chant while preparing it, I think the only thing you'll get is a full stomach."

"Thank you." As a harvest witch, Sage's sense of smell was unreal. She could decipher the difference between romaine and butter lettuce with her nose. It was a sight to behold.

Laurel heated up the soup and cut herself a large piece of French bread. "Where are Lavender and Rosemary?" she asked between mouthfuls.

"Rosemary went to the mainland and said she had to run into work after she got back. Lavender is working on a bachelorette party order. Apparently, they wanted naughty cupcakes, and she had to wait until closing to work on them. She couldn't have Mrs. Fitzpatrick clutching her pearls at the sight of a fondant penis," Sage deadpanned.

Laurel snorted, her soup nearly exiting her body through her nose.

"I do not understand the appeal of a fondant penis," she giggled. "At least make it buttercream. Fondant tastes awful."

"Agreed," Sage chimed. "Or be a little more creative. I have seven different vegetables in the garden at this exact moment that could be used for phallic representation. What about a crudité display? Eggplant, zucchini, yellow squash, bananas, cucumbers, carrots, parsnips...the list goes on."

"You should start a side business providing phallic vegetables for bachelorette parties and fruits that look like boobs for bachelor parties. It'd be a great addition to your stall at the farmer's market."

Sage cracked a smile. "I'm sure my clientele would adore me handing out cards to prospective customers. 'Excuse me, sir? You look like you could use a display of peaches, plums, mangos, or watermelon, depending on your personal preference.'" She shook her head. "I think I'll stick to selling my fruit and vegetables the old-fashioned way, with no sexual undertones that I know of."

"Hm, you're probably right. Keep the customers you have." Laurel finished her soup and bread and set to drinking her tea. It was Lavender's 'Lazy Evening' blend. It was a mix of almond, orange, and cinnamon and tasted like a warm summer night. Perfect.

By the time Sage ambled to bed, Lavender and Rosemary still weren't home. Laurel opted for an evening walk on their property to keep the clear head she had going.

The Bay Sisters not only inherited a lovely cottage from their great-aunt June but also close to ten acres of land in the center of the island. They held one of the five largest acreages on the island and the only one that wasn't a vineyard. Star Island had three vineyards that were popular destinations for weddings and bachelorette parties, and a fourth that was private. While Sage could have thrown her hat in the wine ring, she didn't care much for it. Sage liked growing fruits and vegetables for what they were. She didn't have the patience to process grapes into wine, and she wasn't a big wine drinker. To be a successful winery, the owners needed to be passionate about the product, and Sage preferred to be passionate about squash, apples, and tomatoes.

Laurel was still wearing her pajamas and robe, though she did slide on a pair of black flip flops before her evening stroll. It was nearly ten-thirty, but this close to midsummer, the sky was still slightly indigo rather than deep black. A few stars made their appearance, twinkling in their infinite distance.

Laurel walked past the herb garden, scents of thyme and marjoram wafting towards her. Rosemary tended to nearly every herb she had ever heard of, and Laurel was a witch; herbs came with the territory. There were all their namesakes, of course, lavender, rosemary, bay laurel, five kinds of verbena, and sage, as well as basil, parsley, dill, mint, oregano, tarragon, chervil, cilantro, catnip, borage, sorrel, chamomile...Laurel could go on, but the herbs were Rosemary's field. Laurel appreciated the benefits of herb magic, but she was by no means an expert in the field.

Past the herb garden, there were three different paths a witch could take in the evening. One led to Sage's orchard, a collection of apple, cherry, plum, and pear trees. The next led to the vegetable garden and greenhouse, which together took up over an acre. Rows upon rows of creeping vine plants, green peas, onions, potatoes, and everything one could dream of putting in a salad made up that part of the property.

Laurel wouldn't be taking either of those paths tonight. Instead, she chose the third path, the one that ran through the wooded area of the land, the perfect place for quiet skyclad activities, and home to Nyx, Laurel's familiar. She gave a quick, sharp whistle in the direction of the dense trees and waited.

A moment later, a foreboding dark figure glided out of the trees and landed expertly on Laurel's shoulder.

"Good evening, Nyx," she whispered to the great horned owl, giving her feathers a ruffle. Nyx hummed with approval, shifting her stance to stand closer to Laurel's cheek. "Fancy a stroll?"

Laurel and Nyx came together the first week Laurel lived here. She had still been reeling from her parents' death. In the space of a month, she'd lost both her parents, her older sister had gained custody, and they had moved to Star Island, hundreds of miles away from her home in Ohio. She had to switch high schools midway through her junior year, say goodbye to all her friends, and get used to living in an ancient cottage, rather than their 1980s colonial with a garbage disposal and central air. It was a lot to take in for an emotional sixteen-year-old.

On the fourth night here, she'd had a horrible fight with Lavender. Laurel accused her of lots of terrible things her sister in no way did, but Laurel didn't know what to do with her anger. She had finally stormed out of the house, after promising she would stay on the land, and ran until she reached the woods, then collapsed.

Laurel had cried and cried until she was a heaping pile of numb grief. When she finally looked up, there was an owl standing directly across from her on the ground. She'd never seen an owl on the ground, nor had she ever seen one so close. She had sat completely still, hoping she didn't frighten the creature away. After a few minutes, Laurel had reached a tentative hand out and the owl responded by waddling towards her until her hand rested on its head.

Laurel had felt something magical at the moment, a connection between her and the owl. She suddenly knew her name, Nyx, that she was four years old, and she had been waiting for Laurel. They were bonded that night.

"Would you like to visit the walled garden?" Laurel murmured, stroking Nyx's belly. She hooted loudly, a resounding yes.

The walled garden was Rosemary's crowning achievement as a garden witch. The stones were there when they took up residence, but the interior had been nothing but a snarled mess of half-dead vines and trees. Now it was glorious.

Laurel ducked through the ancient stone archway. They hadn't been able to find any information about who built the walls. In *The History of the Bay Witches*, it's mentioned the first Bay Witch came to Star Island in 1780 to escape the carnage of the Revolutionary War, but there was no mention of who constructed it.

The walls were lined with roses of all varieties. Blush pinks, striking reds, buttery yellows, and deep magentas decorated the archaic stone. Pebble paths wound through the garden around boxwoods and flowering trees to lead an observer to strategically placed benches. Laurel found her favorite bench, the one with the ram carved into the side, and took a seat.

The sky was dark now, no traces of the summer sun stained its immense black beauty. The stars were on full display, the moon a perfect half glowing down across the garden. Laurel took a deep breath and enjoyed the sweet scent of the roses. Nyx hopped off her shoulder and flew to the nearby dogwood. Laurel let her eyes close and exhaled.

It was winter. The flakes were fat and wet and stuck to her cloak no matter how many times she tried to brush them off with her reddened fingers.

Amée was downtrodden. She came from a good home, a family with love between them, and the woman had died leaving two small children with her distraught husband. She tried everything she could, but the fever broke her in the end, the intense sweat that would not stop. If she guessed right, at least one of the children would follow her in the coming weeks. The sweat was a terrible blight on the village.

In the distance, a solitary lantern swung in the storm. She smiled; he always waited for her. It wasn't wise to burn the fat all night, especially when she could be gone for days, but he always did. Onfroi led her home.

She stomped the snow off her shoes, trying to bring some warmth back into her feet, and pushed open the heavy door. It was well past midnight on this terrible night, but the fire inside still burned brightly. Onfroi sat beside it, and he jumped to his feet when she entered.

"Venez ici," he breathed, drawing her into his arms. *Come here.* He cradled her head against his chest, encompassing her with his warmth. She melted against him. She could always find solace in his arms.

"You are so cold," he continued, peeling the damp cloak off her body. "Come, sit by the fire. I will fetch you a blanket."

She complied, stripping out of her wet leggings and dress, tossing them over the table to dry overnight. She shuffled closer to the flames, reaching out her aching fingers.

He wrapped the blanket around her shoulders, then pulled her to the ground and cradled her in his lap.

"You take good care of me," Amée mumbled against his chest.

"You care for everyone else in the village. It's my honor to care for you. These cold, dark nights are the worst of them all. I wish I could do more to help you." He held her a little tighter.

"She did not survive," she lamented, her head resting against his chest.

"You gave her time, time enough for her husband and children to say goodbye."

"They will probably die too."

"You do what you can. You are not God." He brushed his lips across her forehead. "You give them hope."

Amée nodded and snuggled against him. She gave them something— time or hope—and she would be content with it for now. Tonight, she would hold onto Onfroi and let him warm her and feed her, and then when the hour became so late the sun began to rise, she would let him tuck her into their bed and she would finally sleep.

By God, she loved this man.

Laurel fell off the bench, her knees hitting the ground with a thud.

"Ow!" she cried out, shaking her head. She shifted to her bottom and stuck her legs out in front of her to examine her knees. They weren't bleeding, but she guessed twin bruises would appear in the next few hours.

Nyx hooted sharply, suddenly at her side with worried eyes.

"I'm ok," she soothed, "I think." Laurel rubbed her eyes. What had happened? She didn't feel like she had fallen asleep. She hadn't been in the

Hedge World. She felt like she had stumbled into a memory of her past life. She had no idea that was even possible.

She closed her eyes again, trying to bring it back to the forefront of her mind. Onfroi was there. He didn't use her name, but she assumed she was Amée again. The sharp pain in her knees brought her back to reality. She grabbed onto the bench and eased herself to her feet. She had about a quarter-mile walk back to the house, and she was going to be limping.

"What the hell?" she mumbled.

Chapter Four

Owen's mind was like a blizzard with hurricane-force winds. He tried to do anything he thought might remove it from that state, but so far, none of his plans had worked.

After going to the gym, cooking a huge breakfast, and showering, he decided to visit his storage locker a few miles away. He didn't have anything to drop off, nor was he planning to take anything out, but sometimes he liked to take a mental inventory of everything. It helped to have his designs fresh in his mind when he decided to make a new piece.

When he was making furniture, Owen liked to think of the life he would live when he used it and the person he might be living with. He'd hoped his soulmate would like it all, in a sort of faraway thought. She was always a blurry image in his daydreams of the future. After his dream of Amée, he had a soul to put to that soulmate. Suddenly, there was a lot more pressure to impress a medieval peasant woman.

The security guard waved and didn't bother to check ID as Owen pulled into a spot. He walked down the long row of huge garage-like lockers until he came to his, punched in his code, and opened the massive door.

A few years ago, Owen decided that it made more sense to rent a storage unit than keep filling his now office with the furniture he had made. When he first started making pieces, he kept them in his parents' basement, but he was too old for that. He occasionally sold a piece if he didn't feel like it fit with his vision anymore, but he still had a pretty good amount of furniture to fill his house someday.

His favorite piece was the cedar dining table he'd finished about eighteen months earlier. It had been a true labor of love, staying up late after long days on the job to sneak in an hour of work here and there. It had turned out perfectly, though, and worth every minute of lost sleep and every drop of sweat poured into it. Owen had it wrapped in padding and on its side in the corner. Most of his pieces were still wrapped from moving them here, waiting until he finally had a home for them. He couldn't fathom how it would feel to damage a piece after spending so much time with it.

He looked at the ornate headboard and footboard in the corner. It was for a king-size bed, but currently he slept in a queen. When he made it, he knew it would one day hold the bed he shared with his soulmate. Owen unwrapped the corner of the mahogany piece, just enough to glimpse some of his handiwork. He ran his hand over the intricate lattice-work he had spent days perfecting. He shut his eyes and only concentrated on the wood beneath his palm.

Amée, hair a mess, holding a baby in front of her face. She kissed her chin, nose, forehead, nuzzled her neck until she cooed.

"My tiny mermaid," she hummed, her fingers delicately running over the baby's back. "The sweetest baby in the world."

Owen released the headboard and jumped a foot back. His heart thudded against his chest.

What the fuck was that?

If Owen had thought it was difficult to keep his mind off Amée before, now it was even worse. He had no idea what he had seen. Amée was in bed, leaning against the headboard he had made with his own two hands. How was that possible? Owen wracked his brain. He guessed there was a chance he had made a similar headboard in a past life, and he was receiving some sort of memory. Of course, the alternative opened an entirely new realm of possibilities.

Was it a vision of the future? It made the most sense, supernaturally.

Owen had an easier time believing that he could suddenly see snippets of his future rather than him carving a nearly identical piece of furniture in the past. And she had been speaking English, and he was pretty sure the walls were regular walls painted blue.

Owen went home and did something he did not like doing.

He called Morgan back.

"You've reached Morgan Davies. If this is work related, leave a message. If this is personal, leave a message. If this is other, text me."

While a phone call between cousins could be classified as personal, Owen was pretty sure she'd consider it other.

> Owen: I have a magic question for you.

>> Morgan: Can't talk right now but can text. I'll delete conversation when we're through if you want.

> Owen: Thanks. Can new powers show up latently?

Owen watched as the three dots danced over his phone screen for a full two minutes before a reply finally came through.

>> Morgan: Not unheard of. What level of power are we talking? Suddenly able to shift the tides? Healing touch? A newfound connection to the moon? Breathe underwater?

> Owen: Visions of the future.

>> Morgan: Given our family tree, I would change my response from not unheard of to probable. Scary vision?

> Owen: No. Good. Don't want to get my hopes up though.

>> Morgan: Be glad it wasn't terrifying. My first vision was horrible.

> Owen: Anything I need to know?

Morgan: If you're getting too many, go see an herbalist to give you some nettle and strawberry paste to put over your eyes.

Owen: Are you being serious?

Morgan: I am. And tell your mom. She'll figure it out soon enough and has a lot more experience with visions than I do.

Owen: I will soon.

Morgan: Guess what? Millie got arrested this weekend. So I could have been calling about bail money before, but I didn't know she needed it yet.

Owen: Hell, what did she do?

Morgan: Technically, I think it was disturbing the peace. She scared the shit out of some tourists in Congaree National Park and they called the Rangers because they thought she was sacrificing animals. The Rangers called the cops, who arrested her. She wanted to spend the night in jail but used her phone call so we could chat. She doesn't have a phone right now.

Owen: Was she sacrificing animals?

Morgan: No! Millie doesn't sacrifice animals. Anymore. At least, not these. She had hung up a bunch of dead fish she'd found, plus a dead armadillo. And her familiar was next to her. It's an alligator.

Owen closed his eyes and rubbed his forehead. He'd always sort of hoped his soulmate was a water witch, for convenience's sake, but the more he got to know his cousins as adults, the more he leaned against that. A regular old human would be just fine.

Owen: Glad she got out of jail.

> Morgan: It wouldn't be a Sabbat without one of the Davies' girls getting arrested hahahaha

> Owen: Thanks again. I'll talk to my mom.

> Morgan: See ya.

Owen tossed his phone between his hands a few times, then got a glass of water, chugged it, and called his mom.

"Owen! How are you?"

He was always impressed that no matter the day, she sounded genuinely happy to hear from him whenever he called.

"I'm good. How are you and Dad doing?"

"Same old, same old. We went up to Margaret's for Beltane, had a nice quiet celebration for us old folks," she chuckled. "Lots of flowers and fire. Did you celebrate with your friends?"

"I've yet to make any friends who celebrate Beltane," Owen said. "Morgan invited me to her party, but it sounded a little too wild for me. I stayed home, lit some candles. Beltane-light."

Owen let a beat pass. He took a deep breath and let it all rush out. "Morgan had a vision that I needed to go to Solaris, which is a town on Star Island and then Mike suggested I go on vacation to the same place, and I had a very strange dream, and I think I also had my first vision."

His mom didn't answer, but Owen could nearly hear the gears in her mind turning over the silence.

"Mom?" he prompted.

"Tell me why the dream was weird and why you think you had a vision?" Owen could hear her rummaging around the house, probably powerwalking to find his dad.

"I dreamt of living a very long time ago. I was with my soulmate. That didn't seem like a normal dream."

"Not when your mother is a witch. So, you had a vision of the far past. Now, tell me about the true vision you had."

"I touched the bed frame I carved and saw the same woman, but she looked modern."

"Why did she look modern?"

"Her hair was in a messy bun, and she was wearing a tank top. Plus, the bedroom had blue walls." And the baby was wearing a cotton onesie, he thought.

"A baby?" his mom exclaimed.

Owen furrowed his brow and threw his gaze. The mirror that hung over his couch on the opposite wall had his mother's face in it.

"Mom! You are not allowed to mirrorgaze at me without asking." Owen spat. He hung up the phone and crossed his arms but turned to face her.

"Clearly, you weren't telling me everything, which I could tell. If you want my advice on visions, I would appreciate some transparency."

"Do not read my thoughts, Mom. I will break that mirror. I only brought it for emergencies." The last thing Owen needed was his mom peeking into his apartment whenever she felt like it and knowing exactly what he was thinking.

"I would say meeting your soulmate in a dream and then having your first vision at thirty-one both constitute emergencies." His mom sighed. "You've never had visions. Did we miss hidden powers when you were a kid?"

"I think if I had true water powers, I'd be able to control storms, not just sense them."

"Good point. I guess sonofawitch powers haven't been studied thoroughly."

"I'm going to take the mirror down and cover it with a blanket for a while. So do you have any advice?"

"Be careful!" She pointed her finger straight at him. "Morgan leading you someplace is never nothing."

"I'll be fine, Mom. Not a lot of people mess with someone of my height and stature."

"A metal witch could still throw a length of rebar through your torso." His mother raised both eyebrows. "Even with a water witch mother, a sea witch could carry you to the bottom of the ocean."

"Thanks for the visual." Owen grabbed the mirror by the side and laid it on the couch. "Glad the only sea witch I know is Morgan."

"I'm serious, Owen. Don't do anything stupid."

"I won't." He grabbed his throw blanket. "Bye, Mom."

"Bye, darling. I love you."

"Love you too." Owen tossed the blanket over the mirror, effectively ending the conversation.

Chapter Five

L aurel was buzzing. She'd managed to fall asleep at six am and stay soundly asleep until two in the afternoon, more firmly cementing her current nocturnal state. Maybe she'd be able to slowly get herself back on a normal schedule over the course of a week. Maybe not. It wasn't as if she needed to be on a normal schedule. She could sleep around tarot readings if she needed to.

She was in the attic researching like a banshee.

Laurel loved the turn of phrase "like a banshee." In truth, it didn't make a ton of sense. Banshees didn't do anything furiously; they sobbed and did laundry in rivers. Truly, Laurel was researching like a graduate student, but banshee sounded more fun.

She was newly determined to take a longer look at her past life with Onfroi. Clearly, *something* was giving her peeks into it. She didn't know if it was a spirit, a ghost, their own connection, a malevolent witch, or a god. But whatever *something* was responsible, Laurel was a woman possessed.

Their personal library held a collection of nearly a thousand magical books, and it was no easy feat to simply go through the table of contents of that many books. And the majority didn't even have a table of contents. Most of them were handwritten before the 1980s when witches could do things like use a word processor and home printer to make their own book.

So far, Laurel's favorite discovery was *A Compendium of Moderate Poisons, Bothersome Hexes, and Gentle Spellwork*. It sounded like witchcraft-light. She set that one aside to look through when she had time.

She had also turned to technology. A few years earlier, a particularly tech savvy witch from Silicon Valley created The Black Hat Haberdashery. It started small, like a message board for witches to connect with each other but exploded into a full-blown social media empire. There were groups for different kinds of witches (Laurel belonged to the "Working as Diviners" group and the Hedge Witch group), in-person meet-ups, and online events. Each witch had their own profile, and she'd met a few friends over the past few years.

Laurel had put up a question on the general past-lives board and had three promising responses and about a dozen warning her away from that path.

I love past lives! I died on the Oregon Trail in Utah and now it totally makes sense that I hated Salt Lake City when I went skiing there. I used Margery Marshall's spell—I have a copy of it somewhere in my store. I'll take a picture of it and send it to you when I have a chance to put my hands on it! – Paige A.P.

You just need an insane amount of thyme, like a huge pile of it. Dry it, use it to build a bonfire, sit close to it, and wait. Worked for me a few years ago. Who knew that I had been a beekeeper for the Médicis? I was so fancy! Have fun! – Daisy K.

Draw the symbol I've attached. Cut the palm of your hand and let three drops of blood drop into the center. Call out to Hecate to bless your knowledge, promise to raise your children to worship her, and you'll be in. You'll see more than you ever wished you'd see. First time on the Haberdashery. This place seems cool. – EvangelineTheBlackHeartedBitch

. . .

After those responses, Laurel figured she better either wait for Paige to respond or find her own spell. She didn't want to face Rosemary if she stole all her thyme, and blood magic was entirely off-limits for her. There weren't many directions her mother gave her before her death, but don't dabble in blood magic was emblazoned in her mind for all eternity. Also, Laurel super hated blood, so the idea of purposely cutting her palm gave her a deep sense of nausea.

Laurel heard the front door open and scrambled down the stairs. She was keeping up appearances with her sisters that two good sleeps had settled her mind on the matter and hadn't told any of them about her weird vision in the walled garden.

She snuck into the upstairs bathroom and quickly brushed her hair out. She still had it in the topknot she'd been wearing when she went to sleep that morning and she looked like a madwoman coming down from the attic to terrorize the occupants of the house. She washed her face for good measure, quickly ran into her room and threw on a black sundress, then walked downstairs.

"Why did you run out of the attic like an insane person and then bumble around upstairs for a few minutes?" Rosemary regarded her from the foot of the stairs. "Oh my goddess, do you have a guy up there? Were you getting laid?" she shrieked.

"A guy? Of course not. Rosemary, you know me, I don't hide guys upstairs." Laurel laughed.

"I thought maybe your Frenchman had shown up," Rosemary continued, walking into the kitchen. "I imagine, when he does, you'll need at least a few days to explore each other. I would recommend having sex under the full moon at least once during your first month together, the energy..." Rosemary shimmied her shoulders, "there's nothing like it."

"Thanks for the unsolicited sex advice, Rosie. I'll be sure to keep that in mind if my soulmate traipses through the front door: wait, don't tell me anything about yourself, take your clothes off. We need to screw under the full moon." Laurel grimaced.

"You will thank me when you do it," Rosemary giggled. "I'm famished. Care to take a turn around Sage's territory? I have a hankering for strawberries on top of waffles, and I'm sure she's got more than a few ripe enough for plucking. Or do you want to go clean up whatever the hell you were doing in the attic before Lavender comes home and does her weekly reading?"

"I'll be in the attic." Laurel dutifully headed back upstairs. If there was one person she didn't want to know she was still actively searching for a past life spell, it was Lavender. She didn't have any actual say over Laurel anymore, but she still felt pressure to please her. Damn that oldest-sister-legal-guardian power.

After cleaning up the books she'd left out and putting away the clothes that had been pulled out when she grabbed her dress, Laurel headed downstairs again. She was going to make baked lasagna with three kinds of cheese for dinner and it was going to be delicious. It was also going to have a hint of valerian mixed among the basil and oregano with some quietly whispered words to make sure no one interrupted her midnight research in the attic.

Right after midnight, Laurel heard Rosemary's book hit the floor. After Laurel, she was the most likely to stay awake long into the night, but that simple dose of valerian did wonders. Laurel tiptoed into Rosemary and Sage's room, slunk past their twin beds, and ascended the stairs, ready for something.

She still hadn't heard back from the witch, Paige, and she was getting anxious. She needed to know more about Onfroi and the life she lived with him. It was as if her mind couldn't focus on anything else until she had answers.

Were they married? Did they have children? Being a basic witch, Laurel had always pictured herself with a bunch of little mini-witches and warlocks running around while her strapping husband chopped wood in the backyard. Or organized spreadsheets on the computer. She wasn't fussy about the job he had as long as he was cool with lots of kids. After all, Laurel had four sisters. She liked chaos.

Laurel gathered that Amée had been some sort of healer, albeit not a very good one, from her vision in the garden. They appeared poor as well, though judging from their clothing they lived in the Middle Ages, and Laurel didn't think there were many people well-off in that time period.

Laurel approached the bookcases and started running her fingers over the spines. She had three books in mind that had caught her attention earlier, *Trips into the Deep Mind: A Guidebook*, *The Upside of Time Travel*, and *The Hodgepodge of the Witch Jane Goodman*. The last book's title didn't necessarily hint at past lives, but it was easily one thousand pages long. There had to be something in there.

She began with *Trips into the Deep Mind*. It held some promise at first, but the further she got, Laurel realized it was basically a book a witch from Virginia in 1850 wrote when she realized she could meditate. There were some chants and breathing exercises, but basically no actual magic. Laurel wondered if this would be better utilized in a Virginia library's local history section than in their magical library.

The Upside of Time Travel was about actual time travel, not looking into past lives. There were lots of spells and directions about how to travel through time. While this could be cool and informational, Laurel didn't have any idea exactly when or where she needed to go. She couldn't very well guess an exact day over the space of three hundred years in a country the size of Texas. Also, time travel sort of freaked Laurel out. She had a fear of being trapped in the past, and as a modern witch, the past didn't seem terribly friendly.

She glanced at *The Hodgepodge of Witch Jane Goodman* and cracked her knuckles. It was nearing one in the morning and if she wanted a good start by four-thirty when Sage woke up, she needed to get going.

"Amée?"

She looked up from the creek where she was washing her instruments. It was Onfroi, the boy with the kind eyes and strong hands.

"Bonjour," she answered, turning back to her work. She felt nervous around him. She knew he was important in her life, but in what capacity, she hadn't yet learned. For now, he was a handsome face who called her healer instead of witch and treated her with kindness instead of fear.

He sat beside her on the bank of the creek and submerged his own hands, thick with grime and spots of blood.

"Are you injured?" she asked, setting her tools to the side.

"Nothing out of the ordinary. Only from wear." He smiled.

She took his hands in her own, examining the calluses on his palms, the hardened tips of his fingers, and several blue nails. The blood was coming from a large splinter stuck between his thumb and forefinger. Amée bent forward and pulled the splinter out with her teeth, then turned to spit it into the dust. She dunked his hand into the water, running her fingers over his hands, feeling for anything else. When she worked on someone's body—gashes, broken bones, coaxing a baby through the canal—the whole world faded and Amée only saw how she could help. Onfroi's injury was minor, but that didn't make her focus any duller.

"Amée," he breathed.

She looked up. Onfroi was mere inches from her face, his expression nothing but longing. Amée felt her own heart quicken. He'd never looked at her like that before. Like she was something he wanted, something only for himself.

She enjoyed it.

"I love you." His wet hands came up to cradle her face, pushing stray pieces of her hair away from her skin. He brushed his lips over hers, just for a moment, then released her. "Come to me tonight, if you wish. I will be waiting." He pressed his mouth against her forehead and buried his hands in her hair.

By God, she wanted him. She wanted him like she wanted a meal after days of going without food, like she wanted rain in the middle of August. Onfroi was as imperative to her survival as anything.

"Onfroi," she whispered and reached for him.

Laurel jumped with a start. She'd fallen asleep with her face against *The Hodgepodge of Witch Jane Goodman*.

That was definitely a dream, but it felt like a memory. And her body was on fire.

She jumped out of her seat and put the books away as fast as possible. They were not in the places she had taken them down from, but she didn't care, nor did it matter. She rushed downstairs, quietly walked through

Rosemary and Sage's room, and landed in the kitchen where she poured herself an enormous glass of water. She needed to cool off.

It was only three in the morning. And sixteen ounces of water had done nothing to calm her. Laurel quickly ran to her computer to see if there was anything from Paige. Nothing yet.

Her soul was on fire.

Laurel looked at her options. She didn't have a safe way to look at her past life right now. These visions or dreams were driving her mad.

She needed to find Onfroi.

She needed to get back into the Hedge World.

Laurel padded upstairs to see if Rosemary looked even slightly awake. Lavender and Sage would be pissed as hell if she woke them up early, but Rosemary was a believer in love. She might be okay with Laurel waking her up.

"Rosie?" she whispered over her sister. Nothing.

"Rosie, are you awake?" She tried again and was met with a snore this time.

Damn. She couldn't in good conscience wake up her sister who had gone to sleep three hours earlier after being lightly drugged. By her.

She was on her own.

Laurel scurried to her room and unrolled her mat. She set up her candles and lit them with reverence. She hadn't gone into the Hedge World without someone watching over her since that first time. But she needed to tonight. She needed to see Onfroi. All she could do was hope he was at the river and get a chance to talk to him. Maybe this time she could get some information out of him about where he lived now, or what his name was.

Laurel positioned herself in the middle of her mat and fluttered her eyes closed. It took a little longer for her to find that door, but when she did, she felt her body slowly recline to prone before the sensations of her physical body were lost.

The Hedge World was different tonight. It was chilly, with a sharp breeze tossing her hair out of its bun. The sky was clouded, and no moon or glittering stars illuminated the white stone path. Laurel saw others there, but they kept their faces hidden from her by thick cloaks.

Usually the weather in the Hedge World matched that of home, and Laurel only had on a thin black sundress. She rubbed her arms a few times for warmth but set on her path. It was more difficult to find in the intense dark, but nevertheless, she was a woman on a mission. She needed to see Onfroi. She needed to figure out how to find him in their world. She had to get to the river.

The path was eerily quiet tonight; even the hum of crickets fell silent. When she was halfway there, Laurel felt a slow sinking feeling building in her gut.

She wondered if she should turn back, race home to the door and wake one of her sisters before going on. She glanced back, the path just as dark as the one that lay in front of her and strengthened her resolve.

Laurel was a hedge witch, and, by all the goddesses, she could handle a darkened path in the Hedge World. She was born to travel to new realms, rub elbows with ghosts, walk the line between darkness and light. Nothing scared her. Well, that wasn't entirely true, but she wasn't too worried about suddenly being thrown in the open ocean surrounded by sharks. The Hedge World didn't scare her. Magic didn't scare her.

She pressed on.

The air continued to get colder. It felt like summer had all but disappeared and a bleak January was on the rise. Laurel suppressed a shiver. She could hear the river. She was almost there.

She pushed through branches slick with ice, her feet crunching over the frosted ground. She nearly slipped but grabbed onto a tree to steady herself. She was so close. She could see the river through frozen leaves.

Laurel stumbled towards the bank, catching herself on her hands and knees before falling headfirst into the icy water. She gasped for air, then rocked back on her heels, steadying herself. She made it.

She glanced around, looking for Onfroi. He had to be here. She'd traveled so far. She needed to see him. She couldn't stand returning home without him.

She squinted; there was a figure in the distance. It had to be him.

Laurel got to her feet slowly, afraid she would step on a piece of ice and fall into the river. She steadied herself, then took a few tentative steps, trying to find solid earth. After a few feet, she lost her balance for a moment, then eased back to her knees.

"Onfroi!" she shouted, hoping to draw him to her. He turned towards her, clearly hearing her shout. She raised her hand to wave him to her.

He saw her.

She exhaled, relieved. He was coming to her. She had to keep her focus. Nothing would be gained if she could only kiss him and grab him and not say a word. No matter how much she wanted to, she needed to figure out how to find him in this lifetime.

"Hello."

Laurel jerked her head up at the figure before her. It wasn't Onfroi. It wasn't even a male. A woman in a black cloak stood before her. She pulled her hood down revealing a tumble of ice blonde hair.

"You look lost, little owl," the woman went on, kneeling so that her face was only a few inches away from Laurel's. She took a deep inhale and closed her eyes. "Oh, would you look at my luck." The woman smirked. "You smell like a Bay Witch." She grabbed Laurel's wrists, digging her nails into her skin.

"Let go of me," Laurel tried to pull herself away, but the other woman held fast.

"I've been looking for one of you," the woman continued, pulling Laurel closer to her. "What a find, what a find." She stared more intently at Laurel and pushed her hair away from her face. "Oh my, you're *just* the witch I was looking for."

In an instant, the woman's hands were at the nape of Laurel's neck, and she pressed their foreheads together. Laurel felt a flash of heat and pain sear her mind before disappearing as quickly as it came.

Laurel's hands were free and with all her strength, she pushed the woman away, knocking her on her back. Laurel scrambled to her feet and tore through the woods, scraping her arms on branches as she fled. She ran faster than she ever had in her life, her feet pounding down the white path until she reached a well-lit area. Suddenly, she was surrounded by the normal faces of the Hedge World. The temperature returned to summer as well. It was like the entire thing had been a dream within a dream.

Laurel didn't slow her pace and continued running until she reached the door.

She sat up with a gasp, nearly knocking over her fire candle. She got to her knees, extinguished the candles, rolled up her mat, and put everything away. Then she stripped out of her black dress and got into pajamas.

She sat on the edge of her bed trying to slow her heart rate. There was no way she was going to fall asleep now.

Who was that woman? Laurel assumed she was a witch. Occasionally, she saw something that appeared more magical, like that time a satyr had winked at her, but most of the Hedge World occupants were witches. Plus, she had looked human.

Laurel reached a tentative hand up to her forehead and ran her fingertips over the spot the other witch had pressed their heads together. She winced. It felt like she'd been hit with a baseball square in the middle of her forehead.

She shuffled to the mirror hanging over her dresser to get a better look.

Right in the center of Laurel's forehead was a fiery red symbol.

"Oh, shit."

Chapter Six

L aurel screamed.

It started as a muffled shriek. She clapped both hands over her mouth and tried to will herself to stop making noise, but she couldn't. The symbol on her forehead started to burn, then glow brightly, before it melted beneath her skin and disappeared.

Laurel heard a pack of feet clamoring into her room and within moments was surrounded by three of her sisters.

"What's wrong?" Lavender gasped. Even though her room was down a flight of stairs, she managed to be the first one in the doorway.

"Nothing," Laurel forced out. She knew it was a ridiculous lie. Even now, she was holding onto her dresser to keep her body upright. "Nightmare?" she followed up unconvincingly.

Lavender raised her eyebrow and entered the room. She flicked the light on and stalked the room like a big cat looking for prey. Rosemary and Sage walked in and sat on Laurel's still made bed. Damn, she should have thought to muss the sheets.

Lavender picked up one of Laurel's candles and felt the wick. Her fingertips came away covered in wax.

"Care to explain why this is hot? Were you in the Hedge World alone?"

She was caught. There was no way she could keep this from her sisters.

"Can we all get dressed and talk about what happened in about thirty minutes? I need a moment." Laurel looked at the line of three of her four sisters with concern in their eyes.

"Sure, thirty minutes," Rosemary answered for the group. "I'll make tea and call Verbena."

Around five am, Verbena calmly walked through the front door and joined her sisters at the dining table. She was dressed for work, in a tailored white dress and bright blue cardigan. Her hair was already straightened, and her make-up was precise and perfect. No one would have guessed she received a call in the middle of the night.

"Why are you dressed like that?" Rosemary asked, pushing a cup of tea towards Verbena.

"I always dress like this." Verbena furrowed her brow.

"Let me amend that. Why are you dressed like that at five in the morning?" Rosemary was wearing a t-shirt and shorts and her hair looked like one of her shrubs. Sage was wearing her coke-bottle glasses and her always braided hair was loose and curly.

"I was up when you called. I have a very specific morning routine that I go through every morning, so I was already awake, showered, and dressed. I did my makeup and left."

"Am I the only Bay sister who doesn't wake up for the day in the middle of the night?" Laurel bemoaned. The lack of sleep was wearing on her. She needed to get back on a normal schedule. And a cup of caffeinated tea. And a donut.

She needed a lot of things.

"You are the only Bay sister who has woken up all her sisters in the middle of the night," Sage responded dryly. "What the hell happened?"

"I'm going to begin by saying don't get mad at me," Laurel said slowly.

"No promises," Lavender answered. "Spill."

"You all know I've been a little preoccupied with finding my soulmate since meeting him in the Hedge World."

"Obsessed," Verbena interrupted. "Just say obsessed."

"Fine," Laurel conceded. "I've been obsessed with finding my soulmate.

I've had a few visions and dreams that I believe are memories from our life together." She decided to leave out her incessant searching for a spell to allow her to access all the memories of her past life for now. She didn't want to give Lavender too much to handle.

"I had to find him. None of you have met your soulmates, so I don't think you get how intense the feeling is," Laurel continued. "So I went to the Hedge World. I didn't want to wake anyone, so I went in by myself."

"Did you find him?" Rosemary prompted after a beat of silence.

"No. But someone found me." Laurel took a deep breath. "A witch, I think. She felt powerful. She said she'd been looking for me. And she touched my forehead with hers."

"And that made you scream?" Sage questioned.

Laurel shook her head. "When I got away from her and back here, I looked in the mirror and there was a symbol burned into my forehead. It disappeared right after I screamed."

"A symbol?" Lavender's voice sounded severe suddenly. "What kind of symbol?"

"I don't know, you know I'm not good at symbology." Symbology was one of the many subjects Laurel hadn't taken the time to study.

"Draw it." Lavender pushed her chair away from the table and rummaged through the kitchen until she returned with a pencil and a piece of paper. Laurel quickly did a sketch of what she remembered. It had been dark and disappeared quickly, but she did her best.

"I don't know what that is," Lavender said, peering over her shoulder. "Anyone else?"

Verbena, Rosemary, and Sage took turns glancing at the paper, but had no answer either.

Laurel slumped down in her chair, wishing she could melt into the floor and escape the judging eyes of her sisters.

"All right, here's what's going to happen," Lavender began. In times of crisis, Lavender's guardian status came out, and she took the reins. "Laurel, you're going to get back on a normal sleep schedule. You will be going to bed at ten in the evening and waking up at six. I don't want you up all night and sleeping all day anymore. You clearly make poor decisions when you are sleep-deprived and alone. This soulmate business has its fangs in you, and you're a mess. I only hope you didn't put yourself in danger."

Laurel could feel her cheeks redden. She didn't look at Lavender like a parent, but she still didn't want her angry.

"After everyone is done with work today, and every day until we figure this out, we'll be meeting in the attic here. We need to figure out this symbol, and who the witch was that put it there."

"Do you want me to check the Haberdashery message boards?" Rosemary asked.

"No. She could be on the boards, and honestly, she doesn't appear friendly."

"I didn't recognize her from the hedge witch group. There's only a handful of us," Laurel said.

"Draw the witch!" Rosemary exclaimed suddenly, soliciting a jump in Laurel. "Sorry, but I know a lot of witches. I have, like, ten thousand friends. If you can draw her, maybe I can figure out who she is."

"I don't know how much help that will be. She had a cloak on, and I was a little distracted. Her hair was blonde, though, really blonde. Like a Targaryen. Sorry." Laurel paused. "I'm sorry."

"It's ok, we'll figure it out," Rosemary answered quickly. The other three sisters didn't look as calm and didn't say anything.

Lavender locked eyes with Laurel. "Follow the rules. No more mistakes."

Laurel had seriously screwed up.

"So, evil blonde witch said both, you smell like a Bay Witch, and you're just the witch I've been looking for?" Lavender confirmed.

"Yes. And she smelled me."

"A lot of witches can use their sense of smell to identify other magical people. I think we are in the minority that we don't do it," Verbena announced while she scanned their copy of *Ancient Egyptian Hieroglyphs*.

"Are you saying we should start smelling people?" Sage responded, her voice even. "Because I think sixty to eighty percent of us have worked very hard to appear as normal as possible to the general public. If we take up sniffing strangers, it will be a step back."

"Why am I not necessarily normal?" Rosemary cut in.

"The fact that you knew I was talking about you and not about Lavender, Verbena, or myself is all the reason you need." Sage sighed. "I'm not good at this book stuff. Are you sure I can't, I don't know, plant an orchard of pear trees for protection?"

"If you think a herd of pear trees is the type of protection Laurel needs, then by all means start digging," Lavender began, "but I don't think I've ever come across a case of pear trees protecting a good witch from a bad witch."

Lavender was the most well-versed in the contents of the Bay Witch Library, though Laurel had done a good job getting new titles under her belt over the past week. They had made piles of the books most likely to have the symbol listed first thing that morning. The plan was to search those books first before raiding the entire library.

By eight in the evening, Laurel could barely keep her eyes open. She had promised to get her mind and body back on a normal sleep schedule, so she had been up for over twenty-four hours, minus the ten-minute catnap she'd taken with her face pressed against a book. She curled up in the cozy chair in the attic trying to stay awake, but after she dropped her book twice, Lavender called it.

"All right, let's go, sleeping beauty." She motioned to Laurel. "Time to take your tonic."

"My tonic?"

"Yes. If you think I'm letting you go to sleep when you could wake up in a few hours and jump back into the Hedge World or try to do a past life spell, you need to get your head checked."

"Lavender, I wouldn't. I'm too exhausted to do any spell work, and I don't want to make any more mistakes," she insisted.

"Sure, sure, but you're still going to drink the tonic to be safe. And it will block your dreams. No visits from your French boyfriend tonight."

Laurel's face fell. While she had no plans to do any spells or go into the Hedge World, she had been hoping for another peek into her past with Onfroi.

She couldn't help it. Now that she'd been in the arms of her soulmate, she ached for it. Even to see a glimpse of him could help ease the constant state of want she found herself in.

Laurel had never had a real boyfriend. She dated a couple guys in high school and went to dances and stuff like that, but she'd never felt anything past like for any of those guys. She'd never even lusted after them. Sure, she had let Billy Hurley feel her up a few times, but it hadn't stirred anything more than, "Hm. This is interesting."

Laurel saw Onfroi's face, and her world lit on fire. She wanted to kiss him and strip him naked and do things to his body that she didn't actually have any idea how to do. She also wanted to pledge her undying love and fidelity to him and maybe have between two and ten of his babies. Seeing Onfroi's face made her a madwoman.

Maybe a tonic was a good idea. Laurel probably needed to cool off if she was going to focus on this new foe and find out what sort of power the symbol that had burned her forehead had.

The next morning, after a solid night of dreamless sleep, Laurel sat on the shore at Vega point. She had slipped off her sandals and wore only her black bathing suit. Verbena was watching over her, of course, but further away from the water on a work call. Lavender still wasn't allowing Laurel to be alone, but she needed to recharge after such a traumatic experience in the Hedge World.

Different witches recharged their powers in different ways. Laurel was a bit of an enigma. As a hedge witch, meditation should have done the trick. But Laurel had a hard time straight meditating without accidentally wandering into the thoughts of family, friends, and neighbors, which made for some embarrassing moments. Once she was trying to recharge around midnight and had wandered into the thoughts of their neighbor, Luke, and the movie his brain had been playing of himself and Verbena had made Laurel want to scrub her eyes out with bleach. She couldn't look at Luke for a full six months after that. She even had a hard time looking at Verbena. Laurel knew it wasn't a memory, but, whew. It had been very specific.

As an Aries, Laurel could have been recharged by fire. She was a fire sign, after all, and did a lot of work with candles. But, whenever she was around fire, she felt a strong pull to do magic, but not to let herself be replenished.

Oddly, water did the trick. She could go into the ocean, walk along the beach, or, in a pinch, take a bath and be completely recharged. While Laurel wasn't looking to do any big spells anytime soon, she needed a pick-me-up in the magical sense today.

She left her shoes and cover-up on the stone beach and waded out into the cool Atlantic. The waves were choppy today, so she didn't stray too far from shore. Once the water reached her waist, she plunged beneath it.

Instantly, Laurel felt like a weight had been lifted off her shoulders. She relaxed and let the water heal her and replenish her being. Her muscles relaxed. Her mind went blank. It felt so good to be surrounded by the power of the ocean. She let her arms go limp and sway from side to side in the current.

"Enjoying yourself?" Verbena called to her as soon as she popped her head above the surface. Her younger sister had her shoes in her hand and her feet in the water.

"Yes, why don't you join me? I know your little Scorpio soul is dying to get in here," she teased.

"I'll stick with just my feet. I've got a video call with potential clients in an hour, and I need to look professional and not like I took a mid-day swim."

"C'mon, the island is all about mid-day swims! And you could not put your head under."

"You know as well as I do that if I get into the ocean, I am putting my head under. I will also swim for at least an hour, get all pruney, and miss my call with a developer who isn't interested in island life, only in profiting off it. I'll raincheck for tomorrow." Over the past few years, several developers had been coming to Star Island to convert the older buildings and homes into perfect vacation condos. While Laurel felt a little sad the population of the island was changing, change was inevitable. Plus, Star Island was gorgeous. Everyone wanted to vacation here.

"Okay," Laurel conceded. "Give me ten more minutes and I'll be ready to go."

Laurel had a headache. She had looked at thousands of symbols. She'd looked at Egyptian hieroglyphs, Greek and Chinese characters, Ogham, which was basically ancient Irish, and five different sets of Runes, and she hadn't seen a thing that looked like the weird tornado on her forehead.

The sisters were all in the attic, but in separate corners, absorbed in their own space. Lavender stood by the table, several books open, scanning each page quickly and turning the pages in succession. Sage was laying on her stomach lazily flipping the pages of whatever she had been assigned and Verbena had switched to a laptop and was searching symbol databases. Rosemary laid on the ground with her eyes closed, taking a break, and singing softly.

"T'was of the young captain who sailed the salt sea, let the wind blow high, blow low, I will die, I will die, the young captain did cry, if I don't have that maid on the shore, shore, shore—"

"Got it!" Verbena shouted. The other four sisters shot to their feet and ran to the corner Verbena had huddled herself into. She flipped the laptop around to show the group. "That's it, right?" She looked at Laurel.

Laurel looked at the red square bordering a swirl that ended in a circle.

"Yes! That's it. What does it mean?"

Verbena flipped the screen back to her and quickly scanned the paragraph. "It's Slavic...first appears after the meeting of the Rus and Germanic peoples. It unifies the past and the present and the living and the dead. Connects the soul with the body. Can be used to connect two souls." Verbena said the last part slowly, then glanced at Laurel.

"Okay, so that blonde witch branded my forehead with a symbol that connects us? Great." Laurel huffed.

"Maybe she's dead?" Sage offered. "She's a ghost that wanted to hitch a ride into the mortal world?"

"I don't think she followed me out of the Hedge World. Plus, she was very corporeal," Laurel answered.

"This is good," Lavender interrupted. "Now that we know what it is, we can work to reverse it. Rosemary, tomorrow I want you to search the message boards. See what you can find on this symbol. Don't ask, just look. Maybe a witch has already figured out a way to negate it."

"Will do."

"Laurel, let's go put together a cleansing tonic for you. Can't hurt to try to flush any foreign energy out of your body. Everyone else, go to sleep. We've got a lot ahead of us. Verbena, do you want to stay here tonight? Your room is still set up," Lavender added hopefully. While Verbena had left nearly a year earlier, the other sisters hadn't moved anything in her room, even though Rosemary and Sage still shared.

"I need to go home. I have my routines to keep," Verbena replied. "I'll be back in the morning. I have a quiet day." She closed her laptop and stood to leave.

"Verbena?" Laurel stopped her. "Thank you for finding that."

"Of course. I'll see you tomorrow."

There was a rift between the other sisters and Verbena, though Laurel didn't know why. She only knew that before she moved out, Verbena could scarcely stand to live in the Bay house any longer. She'd been a mess of pain and tears whenever she was there, like something beneath the surface was driving her slowly mad. But now that she had her own apartment, she could have meaningful relationships with all of them, and visit without incident. Whatever had been plaguing her at their cottage was leaving her alone now.

Chapter Seven

On the ferry to Star Island, Owen felt renewed. He definitely felt on the *right* path. Something was going to happen there, at least according to Morgan, and he would help facilitate it. The cool, salty air reinvigorated him with every deep breath. He skipped the small cabin most of the passengers huddled within and stood on the deck, relishing the ocean around him.

Owen may not have technically been a water warlock, but that didn't mean the changeable element didn't call to him. He'd grown up near the Atlantic, on the banks of a river, and spent his springs, summers, and autumns running barefoot through storms. Water flowed through him as much as blood. He came from a long line of very powerful water witches. Even Aidan, who didn't have a magical inkling in his body, loved a beach day.

Two hours after leaving the port in Massachusetts, the ferry entered the harbor at Star Island. Owen liked the look of the place. It had a maritime feel, an island of old, and didn't appear to have any tourist trap nonsense that he couldn't stomach. The last things Owen wanted out of this vacation was to be hassled by hustlers trying to sell jewelry and t-shirts.

He disembarked and retrieved the slip of paper from his pocket that had the directions to his cabin on it.

Emma, Jack's sister, had written to find Venus Avenue, take it north, then turn right at Proxima street, and then turn right again on Centauri Way. The cabin was at 52 Centauri Way and had an uninterrupted view of the Atlantic from the front porch, a full kitchen, an above average bathroom, and two bedrooms, one of which held a king-sized bed. The king-sized bed had been a relief. Owen was a large man. He measured in at six-foot-three and weighed in around two hundred fifteen pounds. He was bulky. He had the shoulders, biceps, and forearms of a man who did manual labor all day long and the legs of someone who could deadlift a bathtub if needed. And it had been needed exactly once when he found himself alone at a site and a bathtub in the wrong position. Owen had spent much of his adulthood sleeping in a queen-sized bed. He found that hotels often advertised a queen when in actuality they were providing a full. A king would truly be a vacation.

Owen meandered through town, taking in the quaint nature of it. He passed a bakery, a bar, a few restaurants, a post office, a library smaller than most storefronts, and a couple gift shops. It was clear that most of the people on the street today were tourists, given away by their shopping bags and New York accents, but not obnoxiously so. This would be a good place for him to relax.

Owen unpacked his bag at the cabin, which was much more luxe than he had pictured. Owen had thought that, while comfortable, he'd be in a regular old cabin. Instead, he was met with white bedding and towels, vases of fresh flowers on every table, a schedule of the cleaning service that came on Tuesday mornings from nine to eleven, a pile of beach towels and four beach chairs, and an assortment of mini toiletries lest he forget his own.

This was the nicest place he had ever stayed.

Owen liked unpacking rather than living out of a suitcase. He hung up shirts, stuffed his shorts, boxers, and socks in the drawers, and organized his two pairs of shoes in the front closet. He set up the bathroom to his liking, then wandered into the kitchen. The fridge had a fresh quart of milk, a carton of eggs, and a loaf of bread. Emma knew how to make a guest feel welcome. He'd walk into town in a little while and visit the market to get staples for the week. But for now, he would be checking out the front porch.

Owen situated himself in one of two rocking chairs framing the front door and breathed a sigh of relief. There was something about sitting in a rocking chair and staring at the ocean that made him unwind. Tension in his shoulders relaxed, and he propped his feet up on a small table and leaned back.

He let his mind wander to random thoughts. He might a grow a beard this week. He'd brought his razor but there was a dignity to growing a beard on vacation. It made him feel calm and collected. Sure, he was supposed to be hanging out here for some greater magical purpose, but maybe that purpose didn't start for five days.

Around three, Owen finally got off the rocking chair on the front porch, put on a pair of shoes, and walked into town. It was one of those perfect days; warm, but not hot, breezy, but not windy. There were no clouds on the horizon, and Owen could feel that the closest storm was over a hundred miles away and wouldn't necessarily head in his direction. It was a good day to be enjoying an island.

Once he reached Proxima, he followed the foot traffic until he was in the center of Solaris. He popped into the bakery and grabbed a coffee, then found a bench. He wanted to finish his drink before going into the market, and sitting in dappled shade watching people go by suited him just fine. The playful wind tossed the newly sprouted leaves in the trees, people walked by in their newly pulled out of storage shorts and dresses. Owen relaxed into his seat. It was a perfect late spring day.

"Hello."

Owen looked to his right. A young woman, wearing a bright yellow floral printed dress and a large sun hat was standing beside the bench.

"Good afternoon," he answered, turning back to his coffee. He wasn't in the mood to chat with a random woman, but she didn't leave. Instead, she stuck a hand on her hip and stared at him.

"Who are you?"

Owen regarded her quizzically. This woman was nothing if not blunt.

"I should say, I don't recognize you and you do not have the typical tourist look, so who are you? Did you move to Star Island recently? I pretty much know everyone on the island."

"Oh. No, I'm here on vacation for a couple weeks. I guess even though I don't look the part, I am a tourist." Owen looked away and gulped his coffee, hoping if he came off as uninterested, she would move along.

"Hm," she continued, sitting next to him on the bench. "You didn't tell me who you are."

"Owen." He wasn't entirely sure what was happening, but he thought giving her his name might soothe her enough to leave him alone.

"Rosemary. Nice to meet you." She looked him over a minute, a small smile played on the corner of her mouth.

"What do you do for a living? And before you remark that I haven't told you my occupation, I'm a florist."

"Carpenter." Owen couldn't help thinking that this woman was very odd, but strangely familiar. He didn't think he had ever met her, but started to wonder if she'd been a child actor and had a face that stuck with him. Maybe this woman had something to do with why Morgan had sent him to Solaris? He wasn't sure if that was a sign to stay or try to run away while he still had time.

"Perfect. I live with three of my sisters in an old cottage on the interior of the Vega peninsula. Oh, yeah, tourist. There are five peninsulas here, hence Star Island. Vega is the best. It's the northeastern one. Anyway, we've had a loose board in our front steps for over a year that needs to be fixed before someone breaks an ankle. Would you be willing to take a look at it? I'll pay you of course."

Owen knitted his eyebrows together. Did this woman introduce herself to him because she had a feeling he could fix her porch? Or did she usually ask random strangers to work on her house?

"Honestly, we only have one carpenter on the island and he's terrible." She shook her head. "I shouldn't say that. He's seventy-eight years old, and I feel horribly guilty making him bend over to fix this. He also chides me that I can't do it myself, but does he arrange his own flowers for his wife on their anniversary? No, he does not." She took a breath. "So, what do you say?"

"I guess I could take a look at it." Ugh, Owen was such a pushover. He should have said no, lady, I'm on vacation, I don't want to look at your porch. But that wasn't like him. If he could help, he would. Plus, he was here because fate sent him. Maybe fate wanted him to fix this damn porch step before he relaxed. Maybe he would be preventing some terrible accident and that's why he was on Star Island.

Improbable, but maybe.

"Perfect. You can take my bike."

"Your bike?" Owen eyed her. He was close to a foot taller than her.

"I'll raise the seat for you. My sister can give me a ride home in her car tonight. It's not that far that you won't be able to walk back, but the walk both ways is kind of long. The tools are in the shed on the east side of the house. I'll write down directions for you, but it's easy to get to. You'll be there in a snap. I can't tell you how much I appreciate this."

"No problem," Owen grumbled.

Fifteen minutes later, he was riding Rosemary's bike down a wooded dirt road towards a house with a broken porch step. Her bike had a woven basket, was painted in an explosion of flowers, and had a bell he kept accidentally knocking with his hand.

This was not how he pictured the first day of his vacation going.

He turned into the driveway of 100 Gazer Lane but kept pedaling. Rosemary had told him to ride all the way to the porch. Apparently, they had a long driveway. When the house finally peeked through the trees, his breath caught in his throat. The cottage was beautiful. It was old, sure, but he could immediately tell the owners had taken expert care of the property through the years. The house was painted a pale yellow and adorned with black shutters. There was a well-maintained stone path that led from the dirt driveway to the front porch. Beyond the path, the yard was a mess of wildflowers in all colors. Owen glanced to the side of the house; it looked like the property went on forever.

He walked the bike up to the front porch and let it balance on the kickstand. Then he inspected the steps. Within moments, he picked out the wobbly step. The step had lost a couple nails that needed replacing, but the wood still looked solid. It would be a quick fix.

He found the shed Rosemary had mentioned and entered. It was the most pristine shed Owen had ever seen. The interior was painted white, and every single tool hung on its own hook. There were empty pots and a small bag of soil on the potting bench, and a few seed packets were tucked into the windowpane. By the looks of the equipment, the people that lived here were big gardeners.

Owen found a hammer hanging up and a box of nails and within a few minutes, the step was fixed, and proven so by him jumping on it several times.

He stepped back to take another look at the house. It was a beauty. Personally, he tended more towards the craftsman look, but this cottage vibe fit the feel of the island. He was going to make a point to check out some of the older buildings while he was here. The cabin he rented was a new construction, as were the rest that lined Centauri Way. Those houses all looked like they'd been built in the last five years.

He picked up the hammer and extra nails and walked back to replace them in the meticulously organized shed. He did, then turned to walk back to the bike he'd left next to the porch, but something caught his eye behind the house.

There was a woman in the backyard. He saw a blur of dark hair move between greenery. Rosemary had mentioned she lived with sisters. This was probably one of them.

Owen knew he should get back on the bike and ride back to town, try to find that pushy woman and return her bike, and then go to the market. It was the responsible, non-creepy thing to do.

He chose the irresponsible, creepy thing to do.

Owen walked towards the woman wandering through the property. There was a garden right behind the house, and she walked between the rows and rows of what looked like herbs. Owen's mom wasn't a big herbalist, but they had a small herb garden in their yard growing up. He could differentiate between basil and thyme.

The woman ran her hands along the leaves, stopping to bring her palms up to her face and inhale. Her long skirt trailed behind her, brushing against the small shrubs.

Owen felt his pulse quicken. His fists balled, and his arms went rigid at his sides. He could only see the back of her, a mess of black hair piled on top of her head, a black skirt swishing as she walked, bare feet stepping through the plants. He followed her from a distance, his eyes unable to leave her.

She stopped, clearly sensing him or something. Her head cocked to the side, as if her ears were pricking at his movement. He paused and tried to let his arms fall loosely at his sides. He took a giant step backwards to give her a little more space. He attempted to look as non-threatening as possible. He was, after all, a huge male stranger prowling around her property. He didn't even know if Rosemary told her to expect someone fixing the step.

She turned and faced him, her brows pinched together and her hands on her hips.

"Who the hell—" she started but abruptly stopped. Her hands dropped from her hips and her eyes went wide as her lips parted.

"You," Owen breathed.

It was her. Amée. The woman from his dream. He found her. She was standing not twenty feet away from him, alive and looking much healthier than she had before. He shook his head in disbelief. Was it really her? Was she his soulmate? Truly?

That didn't make sense. He wasn't a warlock. He didn't have the ability to recognize soulmates. Yet, here he was, staring at this woman and thinking, this is the person. This is the woman of my past, my present, and my future.

He was relieved. A warmth spread through him. It was a mix of comfort, lust, love, and hope. She was here—with him. They were together. He wanted, oh, he wanted so many things. The first thing he wanted was to close the distance between them and pull her against him. If he kissed her, he'd know. He would know for certain if she was his.

He took two determined steps in her direction. He'd been waiting his entire life to wrap his arms around her and hold her close. She was here. She was his.

"Stop!" she shrieked, throwing her hands up. He froze.

Oh, shit. She didn't know who he was.

Chapter Eight

Onfroi was in Laurel's garden.

Well, it was him and it wasn't him. This version was taller, broader, cleaner, and even from twenty feet away, she could tell he had all his teeth. And those teeth were white. He was also wearing normal shoes and clothes.

Her soulmate was within her sights.

She couldn't speak, or move, or do anything other than stand completely still with her eyes about to pop out of her head. How did he get here? How did he find her? Did he make it a habit of wandering into random yards? Was fate slapping her across the face right now?

Oh shit, she thought. He's actually here now, so that Slavic witch is definitely going to try to destroy her or kill her or something dark and terrible.

He moved towards her, quickly and eyes full of purpose.

"Stop!" she yelled, then slapped a hand over her mouth. She couldn't... she felt like her entire mind was about to explode. If he came closer, she didn't know what would happen.

"Sorry," he said and took a few steps backwards. "I was hired to fix your front step by Rosemary. I'm—"

"Onfroi," Laurel nearly panted. His eyes flickered and one side of his mouth ticked upwards.

"You remember? You're Amée." Now he spoke with conviction.

"Yes. Or I was. But I remember. Some parts at least." Laurel turned her gaze to the rows of thyme in front of her. Part of her wanted to set the whole row on fire at that exact moment so she could see the entire past. These snippets were never enough. But now she had him in front of her. She didn't have to wait for dreams or a successful trip into the Hedge World.

Onfroi was standing in her herb garden wearing shorts and a gray t-shirt.

She glanced back at him, taking in the look of him. He was, after all, her soulmate. She ought to take in the sight of him.

He looked strong, like he could hoist a tree trunk over his shoulder and walk the length of a football field while doing so. His hair was black, like the ocean at night. His hands were huge, bear claws almost. She squinted and noticed they were banged up. His knuckles were bruised, and the skin looked toughened, like they'd taken a beating. Was he a boxer?

"Amée?" His voice was low and slow, like he was afraid she might run like a scared rabbit at any moment. But he didn't look like a wolf.

"Laurel," she corrected. "This time around, my name is Laurel."

"Laurel." He paused, as if he was taking the time to consider her name. "I like that. It suits you. I'm Owen, not Onfroi anymore."

"Not for hundreds of years," she mumbled, her eyes returning to the thyme.

He walked beside her, motioning for her to continue walking her path, but keeping the thyme between them. His thumb circled the tip of his ring finger incessantly. Good, she thought. He was nervous too.

"Have you always known? Always had the memories?" he asked.

"No, I didn't know until I saw you in the Hedge."

"The hedge?"

Laurel stopped. She forgot that her soulmate didn't know she was a witch. He probably didn't even know what a witch was or believe in magic. And he didn't seem to have any idea what the Hedge World was. She had to watch her mouth. Witches and humans were soulmates all the time, but navigating those relationships was difficult, at least at the beginning. She was going to have to take her time explaining it.

"The dream. I didn't know who you were until I saw you in the dream," she covered. "How did you find me? In the dream, how did you know to meet me by the river?"

He looked uncomfortable for a moment, like he was mulling something over in his mind. Laurel bent down and picked a handful of thyme, breathing its scent deeply, then popped a small bundle of leaves in her mouth. The spicy herb helped ground her. She needed to stay focused.

"I fell asleep, and I was there," he finally answered. "I do dream of rivers a lot. But never that one before."

Owen turned towards her. She looked at him closely this time. His eyes were dark brown, almost black, and clear. He had a small scar on the right side of his jaw. There was a hint of black stubble along his chin that would probably become a full beard in a few days.

"Amée," he breathed, his hand reaching for hers. "I missed you." He slid his fingers over her wrist. Her skin felt electric beneath his touch; the intensity overwhelmed her, traveling from her arm to her heart, to her head, until every inch of her body felt like it was about to be consumed by fire.

She jumped back, took three steps away from him, and tripped over a basil plant. Her entire body splayed out over the herbs. Her legs were trapped, tangled up in her skirt, and she had a bramble in her hair.

"Are you ok?" he asked, offering his hand to help her up.

"Nope." She shook her head, hard. She ignored his hand, rolled to her side, and got to her knees. "I need you to leave. Please. Please go, right now." She scampered to her feet and hightailed it to the screened porch. "Sorry, I need you to go. Right now. This is so rude. Sorry, again. It's too much, this is too much. I might faint. Or throw up." She was starting to hyperventilate. "I need...I need...I need." She stopped, her feet on the single step leading to the porch. She steadied her breath and closed her eyes.

What did she need?

"I need time," she settled on, and marched into the house, locking the door behind her.

"Did you get my surprise?" Rosemary peeked her head around the front door slowly, her voice full of glee. She raised an eyebrow when she saw Laurel. "What is wrong with you?"

Laurel was lying on the couch. Rather, the upper half of Laurel's body was on the couch while the lower half had slid to the floor about an hour earlier and she had yet to reposition. She moved her eyes from the bookcase they'd been staring at to her sister.

"Surprise?" Her brain could barely register that Rosemary was in the room.

"That man! He's yours, right? Your soulmate? When I saw him, I knew he was one of the soulmates, but not mine. It was so weird, like he had an extra layer of aura and it screamed 'I'm going to love a Bay witch!'" Rosemary looked back at Laurel. "Oh, did I screw it up? Is he Sage's? Seemed a little old for her," she rambled on, setting a bouquet on the coffee table in front of Laurel. "Those are for you."

"Rosemary, what the hell are you talking about?" Laurel let the rest of her body slide to the floor. Maybe the hardwood floors would ground her enough to form coherent thoughts.

"That was Onfroi, wasn't it? He sort of looked like the picture you drew, and I could feel it in my bones he was meant for one of my sisters, but I couldn't tell for sure which one. I'm surprised he isn't still here." She sighed. "When my soulmate shows up, I'm going to ride him for at least a day before I come up for food."

"Thank you for that visual." Laurel crossed her legs and leaned against the couch and shook her head out. "You sent him here?"

"Yeah, to fix the porch. That was convenient, him being a carpenter. What if he had been an accountant? I couldn't very well say, hey you! You're going to fall in love with my sister! Go deflower her right now!" Rosemary giggled. "So, tell me," her eyes flashed with mischief. "How was it?"

"How was what?" Laurel could not track a word of what Rosemary was saying. Her brain was still stuck on the fact that Onfroi, or Owen, had been in her backyard.

"Meeting your soulmate, sleeping with your soulmate, how was all of it? I've been dying to hear about what soulmate sex is like. Do you come, like, immediately?"

"Rosemary," Laurel rubbed her eyes and sighed. "I didn't sleep with him."

"What? Oh, you prude. You don't have to make him wait, you know, to make sure he sticks around. First of all, that idea is bullshit. Women should be allowed to sleep with whoever the fuck they want without worrying about what society will say. Secondly, he's your damn soulmate. He's not going anywhere."

"Rosemary, stop." Laurel rubbed the bridge of her nose. Right now, she would rather be having this conversation with any of her other sisters. Or with no one at all. Or maybe a therapist who specialized in past life reunions. Were there witch therapists? There had to be. She should look into it.

"I know you probably can't understand this," Laurel continued, "but it was very overwhelming. We talked for a little while, he touched my wrist, I tripped over a basil plant, and then fled into the house. Since he's not skulking around the yard, I assume he left."

"Who left the front door open?" Lavender called from the path. "We are going to get mosquitos in the house and that insect banishing spell smells like spoiled milk."

"Oh, thank all the goddesses," Laurel said, pushing up to her feet. She turned to Rosemary. "Thank you for your attempt at comforting me. I'm going to make a cup of tea and talk to Lavender."

"What? You'd rather talk to Lavender than me about your soulmate! Come on, Laurel. This is my wheelhouse! I've been training for this moment my entire life! This isn't fair! I'm the sex and love witch of this family, you know that. This is my moment to shine in my support of you."

"Which is exactly why I do not want to talk to you. I'm not the sex and love type. I need someone with a heart frozen solid to talk to at this moment." Laurel walked towards the kitchen.

"Hey, Lavender? Can we talk?"

"Good," Lavender said firmly after listening to Laurel's afternoon.

"Good? I panicked and hid from my soulmate. Why is that good?"

"You panicked and hid from a random man stalking you on our property. He was lucky you didn't call the police. Or shoot him. This is America."

"Lavender." Laurel took a deep inhale. "It's him. He called me Amée. He was Onfroi. But he's more handsome and stronger and smelled like he had showered this morning." Goddess, he had smelled good. Laurel fought the urge to moan simply remembering how damn good he smelled.

"Ok." Lavender waved her hand between them. "I don't need a breakdown of the reasons you find him attractive. But you did the right thing. Just because you know someone is your soulmate and you're in it for the long haul with them, doesn't mean you should jump into anything. Especially anything physical. Taking steps in a relationship is important. You shouldn't skip to the end because it's written in the stars that you'll be in love. Your soulmate can still hurt you." Lavender paused. "I should rephrase that. Your soulmate can still break your heart. In fact, your soulmate can hurt you more than anyone else you could ever date because of the connection you share. No one ever talks about the soul-crushing grief of being hurt by your soulmate."

Laurel stared at her sister, eyes bugging out of her head.

"What the hell, Lavender? You were supposed to calm me down. Now, I'm terrified."

"You should be. Being connected to someone forever is terrifying." Lavender raised both her eyebrows.

"I thought you were going to say something along the lines of, take it slow, no rush, get to know him. Instead, you're all fire and brimstone and broken hearts immediately."

"I think I did tell you to take it slow. That was in there. Look, if you want a rainbows and sunshine approach, talk to Rosemary." Lavender stirred her tea with her spoon, then took a deep sip.

"I did talk to Rosemary. And she's not rainbows and sunshine. She's all, 'get naked and have sex.' I need a happy medium between the two of you."

"Sadly, Laurel, that's you. Sounds like you might need to counsel yourself for a little while. Because Sage will tell you men are not worth the time, and Verbena has her own pile of...issues with the sterner sex."

"It's times like these I wish we had a few living aunts to ask advice. Or cousins. Or a magical mentor I trusted completely. Or Mom." Laurel bit the inside of her lip and looked down.

Lavender pulled her in for a quick hug and then let her go. "Sorry, sister. You're stuck with us."

Laurel decided to take her sister's advice and trust herself. She went up to her room, laid a silk scarf on the floor, and set her tarot cards on top of it.

"Let's do this," she mumbled to herself. "Four card spread. Tell me about Onfroi, I mean, Owen. His name is Owen. Tell me about Owen...last name to be determined." Laurel took a deep breath and exhaled slowly. "Find the light, and draw a circle around it." Laurel knocked on the cards, shuffled them three times, split the deck, and flipped the first card.

"Oh, for crying out loud." The Ace of Cups stared at her. This was the card for new relationships and the warm fuzzies that came with it.

She reached for the next card and flipped it. The Lovers. Of course, it was The Lovers, what else could it be? But...this card had multiple meanings, not all good. Sometimes it meant coldness between two people. Or that they needed balance. But, in her gut, Laurel knew that wasn't what it meant here.

Frustrated, Laurel flipped the last two over one after the other, eyebrows raised. Strength and Justice. Shit. It looked like life was about to become complicated.

She collected her cards and placed them in her pouch. She had done what Lavender suggested and asked herself. And now she had her answer.

The next morning, Lavender called a family meeting. She, Rosemary, Laurel, Verbena, and Sage surrounded the dining table, with a pile of Lavender's lemon basil donuts in the center. Since Laurel's mess began, family meetings were becoming a daily occurrence, but Lavender was truly helping shift the mood from gloomy to delicious with her baked goods.

"While there has been some distraction over the appearance of Laurel's alleged soulmate," Lavender began.

"Wait, what?" Verbena interrupted. Her eyes shot to Laurel. "Who the hell is your soulmate?"

"Um, Owen...something? I saw him for about two minutes."

"He's a carpenter!" Rosemary added. "We should make a list of stuff that we need done around the house. Do you think he does bathrooms? The grout upstairs could use an update."

"You know, I was a little busy losing my damn mind to ask him if he knew how to update bathrooms." Laurel clenched her teeth.

"Where's he staying? Does he live here? Is he on vacation?" Verbena asked. "What does he look like? The same as Onfroi? Holy shit, it's really starting now."

"As I was saying, soulmates aside," Lavender attempted to regain control of the conversation, "I was looking through *The Compendium of North American Magical Families* last night. I made a list of all the families with Slavic roots. There are only twelve. I thought we could split them up and do a little old-fashioned research into their normal lives. Maybe find out where they live, maybe we'll luck out and there will be a picture of the blonde woman who marked Laurel online."

"Good idea," Laurel said. It would be good to concentrate on something other than Owen for a little while. She needed a distraction if she wasn't going to turn this island upside down looking for him.

"Ok, but the next time you see Owen, it would be super nice if you were able to somehow work into conversation that we have a few handyman projects around the house that could use some attention." Rosemary smiled and bit into her doughnut. "Oh! Maybe one of us will end up with a mechanic. Or a pipefitter. Useful skills for all of them, I hope."

Chapter Nine

Owen watched Laurel flee into her house and lock the door behind her.

He stood completely still for a few minutes, then shook himself out of his stupor. She had quite literally fled his presence.

This didn't bode well.

He wanted to rush after her, talk to her, touch her, kiss her, and pray that something in his soul clicked that let him know *for sure* that she was his forever and ever. His feet were burning holes in the ground where he stood, aching to go after her.

He took a deep breath.

She was afraid. She asked for time.

He gave it to her.

He finished putting away the tools, tucked Rosemary's bike against the house, and began the long walk back to his cabin. It was around four miles, if he had figured correctly, but he didn't mind. His brain was doing all sorts of flips, races, and jumps, and a long walk might soothe the chaos bouncing around in his skull.

Amée was Laurel, and she was on Star Island. For a person with a magical upbringing, Owen wasn't overly obsessed with fate or destiny. He didn't think things like, if I had missed that stoplight, I wouldn't be stuck talking to a person I went to high school with right now. He believed many of the happenings of this world were coincidental.

But Morgan having a vision about Solaris, Owen then renting a cabin on Star Island, a remote spit of land in the Atlantic where a woman he had been dreaming about—a woman who had to be his soulmate, right?—happened to reside, then running into her sister who commissioned him to fix their porch? That wasn't a coincidence. That was fate giving him a kick in the ass. That was fate screaming into his ear.

"Laurel," he whispered, letting her name play over his tongue.

Owen let all the noise in his mind melt away and simply thought of her. She was gorgeous, that smooth black hair, wide eyes, her slightly upturned nose, and the face she made when she realized who he was; Owen could dream of that face for the rest of his life. He'd wanted to run his hands over her skin, make sure she was real and that he wasn't losing his mind. He'd wanted to do a lot of other things, like kiss her and hold her and spend the next five to ten weeks doing nothing but worshiping her.

He exhaled and rubbed his hands over his face.

He needed to get back to town and find her sister. Then, he could maybe get her phone number, or try to figure out a better time to see her again. He wasn't sure how to contact her without knocking on her door, and she hadn't reacted well to him being close to her person. Next time he saw her, she would expect him. Maybe he should write her a letter.

When he finally made it back to town, it was after five. He asked for directions to the florist, but they were closed, and Rosemary was nowhere in sight.

Without a plan beyond finding Laurel's sister, Owen settled on waiting until tomorrow to make a new plan. He turned to walk back to his cabin but saw a door propped open to the town's bar. He hadn't made it to the market yet, and he could use a drink.

Owen grabbed a seat at the bar and took a handful of peanuts while waiting for the bartender to get his order. It was more crowded than he imagined it would be on the island, but they were only steps from the harbor, with a ferry leaving in an hour. Most of the patrons looked like they were grabbing one last drink, or couple of drinks, before they hitched a ride back to the mainland. Lots of the tables were surrounded by backpacks and rolling suitcases.

"You need a menu?" the bartender asked after a few minutes.

"Nah," Owen answered, "I'll take a Rusty Nail and an order of whatever that guy's having over there." He stuck his thumb over his shoulder and pointed to a plate of mozzarella sticks, loaded potato skins, jalapeño poppers, tater tots, and wings.

"Combo plate. What kind of sauce do you want on the wings?"

"Something hot enough to distract my mind from anything else."

The bartender chuckled. "I'll get your drink."

As Owen enjoyed his beverage, the bar quieted down. The tables of tourists left, some of them sprinting to catch the evening ferry back to the mainland.

"If you leave right now, you could still catch the ferry," the bartender mentioned.

"In that case," Owen began, "I'll have a refill." He had destroyed the plate in front of him in record time. His mom had always teased him and Aidan about being members of "the clean-plate club" and tonight, he was the president.

"The wings do the trick?" the bartender asked, handing him another Rusty Nail.

"I think this might be a job for booze," Owen chuckled.

"I've got plenty of that. You staying the night?"

"Two weeks."

"Then I might as well introduce myself. I'm Luke." He stuck his hand out and Owen shook it.

"Nice to meet you, Luke. I'm Owen. And I might be staying longer than two weeks now that I think about it."

"How much longer?"

"I don't know, a while." Owen was a practical man. He was going to see where this business with Laurel led. Plus, there had been no sign of magical shit he had to deal with yet. He needed to stay long enough for that to run its course.

He told his mind to pump the brakes. He should probably get to a point where Laurel was comfortable being in the same room as him before he stayed longer than a vacation. But he was also a thirty-one-year-old man who was finally close to the woman he'd been looking for since he was sixteen. He wasn't going to run away from that.

"Is it our gorgeous scenery?"

"In a way." Owen sighed. He guessed a bartender was as good as anyone when it came to talking through his feelings. "There's a woman here."

"Ah, a woman. I should have made that drink a little stronger. Is she a local?"

"Yup."

"What's her name? I probably know her. I know nearly everyone who lives here year-round."

"Laurel." He paused. He didn't know her last name. He'd have to rectify that.

"Laurel Bay?" Luke stopped working and looked at him.

"Maybe. We didn't get that far."

"Dark hair, big eyes, wears all black, does tarot card readings for the bachelorette parties?"

Owen laughed. He didn't know if Laurel did tarot card readings, but he could imagine himself falling head over heels for a woman like that.

"Sounds like her."

"In that case," Luke stuck his hand out again, "I'm Luke Karnes. I live next door to the Bay sisters, and I have a feeling we'll be seeing a lot of each other. I know them pretty well." He smirked and shook his head.

Owen furrowed his brow. "Are you dating Rosemary?"

"Rosemary? Hell, no. God help the man who ends up with her, and I say that with nothing but respect for her. No, there's a bunch of Bay sisters, and I'm...close to a different one. Or I used to be," he laughed. Luke pulled out another glass and made himself an Old-Fashioned. "I think I deserve one of these tonight."

Owen exhaled.

After four Rusty Nails and the combo plate, Owen took a slow walk back to his cabin. The sun had set an hour earlier, but there were still touches of indigo in the sky. Luke lent him a flashlight to navigate the streets and recommended getting his own if he was planning to walk around at night. He also told him to rent a bike from Pat in the morning unless he wanted to rent a golf cart. Owen wasn't much of a bike rider, but he couldn't picture himself tooling around in a golf cart.

Tomorrow, he would go to town, rent a bike, visit the florist, and get Laurel's phone number from Rosemary, and probably get another combo plate from Luke. But tonight, he had to do something. And those four Rusty Nails had given him the stones to do it.

"Hey, Mom." Owen had promised he wasn't going to use his cell phone on this vacation. He still brought it, and the charger, just in case. He didn't know whether or not a job would come up so he needed to be somewhat reachable. But calling his mom had definitely not been part of the plan.

"Is everything ok?" his mom asked immediately. He'd let her know he was planning to unplug for his two weeks here. He had told her that so she wouldn't worry if his phone was off, but now he succeeded in worrying her anyway. And there was nothing like a vision from Morgan to put everyone on edge.

"I'm fine."

"Ok, good." A beat passed. "How's your vacation?"

"It's nice here. It's quiet and calm without being desolate. I'm sitting on my front porch right now, listening to the ocean."

"Oh, that sounds like a dream." She wasn't lying. His mom loved any house with a view of water. His childhood home looked at a pond, had a river running by less than a half-mile away, and was a twenty-minute drive to the ocean. His mom liked lots of water sources close by.

"You and Dad would like it here. Aidan and Sarah too. Maybe we could all plan something."

"You seem awfully sold on an island you've been on for less than twenty-four hours," his mom started cautiously.

"That's actually the reason I called." He inhaled deeply. "There's someone here."

His mom was quiet for a moment before asking, "Who?"

"There's a woman here. I think I might have found her."

"You found who? Wait, her? *Her* her? You found the mother of my grandbaby?" His mother nearly squealed.

"Um, at this point, she can barely stand to look at me for two minutes without panicking so grandbabies might be a while off. But to answer your question, yes. I may have found her. The important her."

"Tell me everything about her," his mom gushed. "Rhys!" Oh, boy, she was bringing his father in. "Rhys, Owen found his soulmate!" Pause. "On Star Island. I'm still trying to figure the rest out. Owen? Are you there?"

"I'm here, Mom. And I don't know for sure if it is actually her, but it feels like her."

"Owen Gruffydd Davies, you have never in your life called me and told me you met even a maybe. I have faith that this is her. What's her name?"

"Laurel."

"Beautiful. I love it. What's she like?"

"Honestly, I don't know her yet. From what I can tell, she's a little jumpy. But she's beautiful. Dark hair, big eyes, she's lovely. And I found out she reads tarot cards for a living."

"Ha!" his mom cackled. "I love her already. Are you seeing her tomorrow? Are you seeing her tonight?" Owen was certain he'd never heard his mom so excited by the prospect of one of her sons getting laid.

"Definitely not tonight. I hope tomorrow. But I'm going to hang up now. I think it's time I stared at the ocean for a few hours and let the magnitude of today wash over me."

"All right, my little storm chaser."

"Mom, I'm a foot taller than you."

"I carried you within my body; you'll always be little to me. But call me again with more details once you get a chance to have a deep conversation with her. I want to know everything about her. Laurel. I'm so happy you found her. Good night, Owen."

"Night, Mom."

Owen stayed on the porch until close to midnight, listening to the ebb and flow of the waves on the beach, watching the moon move across the sky. On more than one occasion, he swore he saw a shooting star, but satellites often confused him. Either way, in this dark world, he found Ursa Major and Minor, Heracles, and Lyra.

The next morning, Owen woke up with a mission. First, he walked to town and grabbed a coffee at the bakery. Then, he rented a bike from Pat.

Once he was caffeinated and had a mode of transportation, he went to the florist to find Rosemary.

Therese's Flowers was a much bigger store than Owen was expecting. There were less than eight hundred permanent residents on Star Island, and yet the florist took up three store fronts. He walked through the threshold and was immediately bombarded with the scent of roses. He glanced around the room, noticing that most of the bouquets included deep red and pale pink roses. He should get Laurel flowers. He wished he had some memory of a favorite bloom of hers.

"May I help you?"

Owen looked up at a woman with gray hair piled into a bun and glasses balancing on the tip of her nose.

"Uh, yes. I'm looking for someone who works here, Rosemary?"

The woman crossed her arms and set her jaw. "I told her I didn't want any...suitors stopping by the store anymore. It was getting out of hand last fall, and she told me she'd solved the problem—"

"I'm not a suitor," Owen cut in. "Just need to ask her a question."

"Oh. Let me get her."

Owen looked at the pre-arranged vases full of bright flowers. He remembered his mom telling him there was an entire language of flowers when he was a little kid. Maybe he would do a little research and make Laurel a unique bouquet.

"Hey, Owen."

He turned around. Rosemary was standing with her hands on her hips, and her nose scrunched up.

"You need some flowers?"

"No, not yet at least. I was wondering if I could have Amée, I mean Laurel," he exhaled. "Could you give me Laurel's phone number?"

Rosemary burst out laughing. He knitted his brows together, unappreciative of her reaction.

"I'm not laughing at you; I'm laughing at the absurdity of it all. She freaked out and fell over a bush, and you still want her phone number."

"Of course, I want her number," he countered. "She said she needed space, so I'm giving her physical space."

"Are you going to text her incessantly? Call her in the middle of the night?"

"Absolutely not. I will text her once and wait for her answer. I will not call her until I think she would want a call from me." It wasn't the course of action Owen wanted to take, but he would keep to this path until Laurel was ready for more.

"Too bad." Rosemary sighed. "Laurel could use an obsessive admirer." She paused. "I'm not in great with her at the moment, so why don't you give me your number, and I'll give it to her? I think if I give out her number, even to you, she'll probably curse me." She cracked herself up.

It wasn't ideal, but Owen would take it. He punched his number into Rosemary's phone and headed back to his cabin.

He needed a long swim in the ocean to clear his head.

Chapter Ten

S lavic names were hard for Laurel to pronounce in her brain. Currently, she was looking into Vladislava Kobliśka. She lived in Detroit, Michigan, was thirty-two years old, and had a picture of a red, boxy symbol as her profile picture on her private Facebook page. It wasn't the same symbol Laurel had been branded with, but there were some remarkable similarities. She was not a member of The Black Hat Haberdashery, unless she used a fake name, which a lot of witches did. Laurel's username was LaurelBHedgy. It wasn't exactly a social security number.

After going through Facebook, Instagram, Twitter, and Linkedin, Laurel decided to go old-fashioned and found a group in Detroit for Slovakian immigrants. There were three Vladislavas in their ranks, and she stumbled upon Vladislava Kobliśka's bilingual dental practice. She was not the witch Laurel had seen and had a nice picture of her working on a ten-year-old's smile.

Laurel huffed and leaned away from her laptop. Another dead end. And from the looks of the Slovakian social group, Vladislava didn't have any other family nearby. There was a chance the ice-haired witch was living outside of North America, but in general, witches tended to stay in their own continent.

Laurel walked out of her room and into the kitchen to get a bowl of raspberries. She needed sustenance to keep up this level of reading. She hadn't read this much since her senior year of high school, which was pretty far into the past at this point.

Her phone was on the counter, taunting her with its ability to reach Owen. Last night, Rosemary had come home bearing Owen's phone number. She'd hemmed and hawed for a long time about whether to call and make plans with him. Finally, at eleven at night, she decided it was too late for anything and went to bed.

The more she thought about it, it didn't feel right getting involved with Owen until she figured out what the brand meant. She could be cursed, for all she knew. While she didn't know Owen yet, she did know he was her soulmate, and the responsible thing was to keep him away from any weird witch stuff she might have going on. She wished Lavender or Verbena could come up with something already. There were much more powerful witches than Laurel, and, if she was being honest, had a much higher chance of solving this.

Laurel sighed. It was better to keep Owen at a distance for now and keep him safe. She could wait until one of her sisters figured this out and *then* she could figure out what life with Owen was going to be like.

Laurel grabbed her raspberries and took them into the backyard. Some greenery and good old-fashioned sunlight could do wonders for her attitude. Because right now, she was feeling down about everything. The brand, the mystery surrounding Amée and Onfroi, and even Owen.

Laurel wished she had some experience past high school with men. She had no idea how she was supposed to behave towards him, especially since he was her soulmate. She didn't know how to flirt or seduce a man or even curb her oddness until he got to know her. Laurel spent years comfortable in her own skin, as witchy as it was, and now she had no idea if being herself was a good idea.

Was she supposed to tell him she was a witch? She would need to eventually, but when? What would stop him from panicking and jumping on the next ferry off the island and far away from her? She knew marriages between magical and non-magical people happened all the time; her parents were a perfect example. But Owen was already aware of their connection. When her parents met, her mom knew they were soulmates while her dad simply thought he was dating someone amazing. Laurel wished she could call her mom and ask her what to do. She'd never even thought to ask her mom how she told her dad she was a witch. It wasn't something her teenage self ever thought she would need to know.

"Hey, neighbor."

Laurel whipped her head around and saw Luke walking through the woods between their two properties towards her.

"Hey," she answered without attempting to hide her surprise. "What brings you to this side of the property line?"

"The dogs. Sage said she'd check in on them tonight. I'm going to Boston for the night." Luke held up a key.

"Big plans?" she teased.

"Celtics game. I got playoff tickets from Joe Jacobs, he's one of the summer bums...and you don't care." Luke smiled and shook his head.

"I honestly couldn't remember what sport the Celtics were. Baseball, right?"

"For Christ's sake, Laurel." He rubbed his forehead. "Basketball. I know you didn't grow up here, but you've been here longer than I have."

"Sports are not my thing. Tarot cards. Pretty crystals. The fashion choices of Stevie Nicks. Weird books."

"I know, I know. You prefer the woo-woo to organized sports." Luke handed her the key. "Can you make sure Sage gets that?"

"Yes. On one condition."

Luke exhaled and raised an eyebrow. "Is this going to be weird?"

"Hell yes."

Laurel shuffled the cards three times, then set the deck in front of Luke. "Anything in particular you want to find out? Do you have a question in mind?"

"I didn't know I was getting my tarot cards read until four minutes ago. Do I need a question?"

"Not necessarily. I can give you a general one if you'd like. Or you can think about career, spirituality, or even love."

"I'll take a general one."

"Cut the deck and try to let your mind be blank then."

Luke cut the deck, then leaned back and rubbed his forehead with his hand. "I can't believe I'm allowing this but," he let out a long sigh, "give it to me straight."

"All right," Laurel laid out a simple pull, a card for past, present, and future as well as one for the client. "Let's begin by saying this isn't a medical diagnosis. If you're looking for one of those, go see Dr. Roberts. Next, try not to look so grim. Unless you've murdered someone and hid the body, I don't think this reading is going to be as horrible as you think."

Laurel flipped over the first card, Three of Swords. "Hell," she muttered.

"What? Is it bad?" Luke panicked. He sat forward now, his forearms resting on either side of the cards.

"No, it's not bad, especially looking forward. This is your past. Three of Swords usually means sorrow or emotional pain. You've definitely had some trials you've had to overcome." Laurel was surprised. She had never seen Luke as anything other than her perpetually cheery neighbor. He was always smiling and teasing, never a grumpy look on his face. But by his reaction, a slow crumple of his brow that spread to his chin, she knew it was right on target. He wasn't a lifelong resident of Star Island and Laurel had never thought to ask him where he was from. It didn't seem the right time to do so now, though.

She flipped the next one: Sun.

"Hm." She tapped her finger on her jaw, working something out in her brain. Luke's energy was all over the place. It was making it difficult for her to settle on an interpretation.

"You're going to have to stop reacting to every card in such an ominous way."

"I'm not being ominous. I'm giving my brain and my spirit a moment to read what this particular card in this particular position means in this particular reading."

"That's a lot of particulars."

"Well, reading cards is very particular." She paused. Normally, the sun was a positive card, but she wasn't getting any sort of happiness off Luke as she sat across from him. She took a deep breath. "All right. Your present is usually fun and warm and successful, which makes sense because I know your bar does well, and you appear to be genuinely happy. But at this precise moment, you're feeling a little down. You're a bit lost and looking for your path. You want your sunny days back."

Luke gave her the smallest of nods. She'd take it.

Laurel pulled the next card: Ten of Cups.

"That's what I'm talking about!" she shrieked. "Your future, my good neighbor, is lovely. Ten of Cups is celebrations and parties and happy homes —you have a great future ahead of you. No need to let yourself be muddled by the past or confused by the present, the future is bright."

Luke raised an eyebrow, as if he didn't believe her, but eventually nodded.

"Thank you." He set the key on the table and started to stand up.

"We're not done yet. The last card is your card, the card that represents you." For a moment, Laurel thought back on her own reading, how she'd gotten a spread completely unlike her usual ones, and what exactly that meant for her future. She shook her head to clear it. She needed to stay focused on Luke's energy and reading.

"Luke Karnes, you are," she turned over the last card, "The Knight of Cups! Hey, not bad! You're a charmer, which I already knew, have a wild imagination, and can be very romantic. I'll leave those last descriptors to your own conclusions. But overall, the Knight of Cups is a great card. You'll definitely be someone's knight in shining armor one day." Laurel leaned back in her seat, quite pleased with the reading. She'd been so busy with researching symbols and potential enemies that she hadn't done a good old-fashioned reading since the girls' weekend party. "Do you want to take a picture of your spread?"

"Why would I take a picture of it?"

"Seventy-five percent of the people I do readings for take pictures for social media or so they can reflect on it at a later date."

"Seventy-five percent of the people you do readings for are attendees at bachelorette parties who then come throw up in my bathroom. I'd like it if, occasionally, you told them to lay off the tequila in their readings. Tell them you see a terrible hangover in their future."

"Next time I have a bachelorette party, I'll look really hard for that kind of thing in the spread." She laughed.

"Speaking of people coming into my bar, I met Owen."

"What?" Laurel felt her cheeks redden immediately. She busied herself stacking the cards and folding up her velvet cloth.

"Whoa, there. I only met him. Seems like a nice guy and enamored with you."

"He talked about me?"

"Mentioned you," Luke corrected.

"What did he say?" Laurel pressed.

"Not telling." Luke smirked. "Why don't you give yourself a reading, see what the cards say?"

Laurel pursed her lips. "As if I haven't already."

"I'm going to head back. Nice to see you, Laurel. Make sure Sage gets that key and thanks for the complimentary tarot reading. Next time you're in the bar, first drink is on the house."

"I'll remember that and order the most expensive thing on the menu," Laurel teased.

"Say hi to your sisters." Luke called over his shoulder.

"I will. Enjoy the rest of your afternoon, Sir Cups."

⁂

"I am so tired of researching most likely innocent women. My eyes hurt. And my head hurts. Laurel, give me a neck massage," Rosemary commanded. All five Bay sisters were sitting in the attic, nearly empty cups of tea placed perilously along the bookcases, the desks, and even in the middle of the floor. On the main table, a plate with two cupcakes left from the dozen that Lavender had put out this morning tempted the sisters.

"Has anyone looked in the Stoch family yet?" Lavender still had her nose in the *Compendium of North American Magical Families*.

No one answered.

"Currently living, there's a woman named Morana, thirty-years-old, and she has two brothers, Ivan and Miloslav, both of whom are full-fledged warlocks."

"Both of them?" Laurel repeated. It was very odd for men to inherit magic from their mother, but full-fledged warlocks were even rarer. To have two in one family was downright peculiar.

"They live in Montana, or at least they did during the last census, which was five years ago."

"What sort of witch is Morana?" Rosemary asked, walking over to stand beside Lavender.

"That's the weird thing. Morana is listed as 'multi-disciplinary.' What does that even mean?"

"Don't look at me. You're the best resource on that book," Laurel answered, peering over her shoulder. Her brother, Ivan, was listed as a metal warlock and Miloslav had no specialization listed. The entry was incomplete compared to the rest of the families.

"Um, Laurel? Come look at a picture of Morana Stoch," Sage called from her place on the chair with her laptop perched on her lap.

Laurel crossed the room and glanced at the computer screen. Right there, sitting on the grass at an outdoor concert with a beer in hand, was the witch from the Hedge World. Her hair was still ice blonde, her eyes nearly piercing blue. She was wearing regular clothes—a t-shirt and jeans—rather than the garnet cloak. Laurel was positive that it was her though.

"We've got a name. Morana Stoch."

Within the next hour, they had combed every corner of the Haberdashery. They found out a lot about Morana Stoch, and none of it was helping to ease Laurel's anxiety.

"So, we've got a hedge witch who dabbles in curses, is very active on the blood magic boards, and has asked several questions about how witches can live forever, how to break unbreakable spells, and possession curses," Laurel rattled off. She was pacing the room, wringing her hands together. "Cool, no big deal. She's basically a souped-up sorceress who branded me in the Hedge World, connected us, and might be after me for some reason. Great. Perfect. I can handle this."

"Are you having a nervous breakdown?" Verbena asked. She looked at Laurel like she was a cornered animal about to either fight or run.

"I don't think so. But maybe a panic attack?" she admitted. Laurel sat down on the floor and put her head between her knees. "I think I might faint."

"Okay, lie down," Lavender commanded. "I'm going to go get you something to help you calm down." She turned to her other sisters. "Make sure she doesn't pass out and hit her head."

Laurel tried to still her mind. On top of all the added anxiety Morana had brought along, she was very nervous that if she fainted, she'd end up in the Hedge World or in a strange dream.

"How's Owen?" Sage asked, sliding down to sit beside her.

"What?" Laurel felt her breath catch in her throat. She tried to steady it. Oh, she was going to throw up.

"Let's take your mind off Morana. How's Owen?"

"I don't know. I haven't talked to him again."

"What?" Verbena interjected. "Laurel, he's your soulmate. You need to talk to him."

If Laurel wasn't on the verge of tumbling into unconsciousness, she would have snapped at Verbena to go talk to Luke.

"I've been telling her that over and over again," Rosemary chided.

"I will. There's a lot going on now. Even more now than thirty minutes ago."

"Doesn't matter," Rosemary said and brushed her hair off her forehead. She danced her fingertips over Laurel's forehead, and it did wonders to soothe her. "Talk to him. He might make you feel a lot better."

"Shouldn't I wait until we figure this out?"

"And what if we never do?" Rosemary countered. "Don't waste time. You're supposed to be with him, so be with him."

Laurel let her eyes drift close as she nodded slightly.

She would talk to Owen.

Ten minutes later, Laurel was tucked into her bed after a very strong dose of skullcap guaranteed to calm her down, knock her out, and prevent any dreams of other lives or other worlds.

Chapter Eleven

Winter winds howled like packs of wolves in the darkness. Onfroi sat next to the dimming fire deciding whether to put another log on. He should go to bed, but his mind was racing.

He'd seen a man die today in the most gruesome of ways. It had taken hours for him to finally let go, and Onfroi could still hear his wife's wails as she sat beside him. He'd bring her some firewood in the morning.

He put another log on and settled into his seat. Sleep wouldn't come for hours; he might as well be warm.

It was nearing midnight when a knock disturbed his contemplation. He furrowed his brow and got to his feet, eyeing his knife on the table. He didn't usually have midnight visitors, but it was beyond freezing outside. He could at least see who the poor soul was before deciding to turn them out to the elements.

He opened the door slowly, letting the light of his fire spill into the darkness.

"Bon nuit," a small voice murmured.

It was Amée. Onfroi grabbed her by the shoulder and dragged her inside out of the cold. Her cheeks were reddened from the wind and her cloak nearly threadbare.

"Venez-ici, warm yourself by the fire." he offered, pulling her towards the fire. Once she was seated, he quickly pulled the blanket off his bed and laid it over her legs. "Amée, what are you doing here? It's the middle of the night. You didn't say you'd be coming."

She didn't say anything for a few moments, only stuck her hands out to warm them by the flames.

"I wanted to be with you tonight." Her eyes lifted to his, full of hope and wonder.

"You're still so cold," he commented, drawing her into his arms. "You could have come in daylight. I would welcome you in any hour of any day."

"I could have," she answered, snuggling against his chest, "but you know how others talk. I don't want you to be associated with me."

He cupped her chin and tilted her face up to his. "I love you, mon petit oiseau. I don't care what anyone else says. You are the sweetest soul I've ever met. Every moment with you is a blessing." He couldn't wait another moment and pressed his lips against hers. There'd been no one else before Amée, and there would be no one else for him.

She melted against him, and her hands snuck around his neck. She was so tiny in his arms, so fragile. He felt like she could break at any moment and needed to be taken with the utmost care.

They moved slowly together, relishing every touch or glimpse of skin. It was perfect in all its imperfections. They fumbled together, giggling between kisses, still learning what each other liked as they went along. Onfroi memorized every inch of her usually covered skin, a freckled thigh, the cinch of her waist, the bright purple bruises on her elbows that she insisted were part of the trade. And she in turn explored the thick scar on his abdomen, a reminder of when a plank of wood nearly halved him, the muscles of his thighs, and the calluses on his hands.

When they finally came together, Onfroi thought he might die of sheer joy. She was his, and he was hers and life was perfect.

And then she was gone. He was alone in the cold, shivering in his isolation. Amée, the house, the fire—they were all gone. Onfroi sat in nothingness and ached for her.

Owen woke from his dream or memory or whatever that was while he slept with an overwhelming feeling of helplessness. Something happened to Amée. It didn't feel like they were apart, or she had left him. She felt missing. He couldn't shake the feeling that something terrible had happened to her in that life, and he'd been unable to protect her.

Owen got out of bed and found his phone on the dresser. It was four in the morning. His chest felt tight, and his brain couldn't relax. He tried taking some deep breaths, but it didn't help. He needed to see Laurel. He needed to make sure she was okay. He wished he had her phone number. Even a text from her would do something to calm his nerves.

After ten minutes of pacing the cabin and a five-minute shower, his anxiety had done nothing but grow. The rational part of his brain told him he was only troubled by the memory, but his emotional side won out. He started to feel like Laurel was in imminent danger. Maybe this was the magical thing he needed to help with? He was sent here by a pretty powerful seer.

He needed to get to her.

Before he knew what he was truly doing, Owen was taping a flashlight to the handlebars of his bike and riding through the dark night of Star Island.

The eastern sky was beginning to take on the deep blueberry that came when dawn was near. There was no one on the road, other than Owen and his homemade headlight. He waited for a wave of 'what am I doing' to crash over him and send him back home, but it didn't. With every passing minute, he knew he had to get to Laurel. He had to see her, to touch her, to make sure she was safe. There was something seriously wrong. He had to help.

"I'll save her this time," he whispered.

He nearly skidded to a stop. He had no idea where that came from. This time? Owen pedaled faster.

Something was going on, and it was beginning to feel magical.

Owen pulled up to the cottage, which was dark, and parked his bike beside the porch. He took the steps two at a time and thumped loudly on the door ten times before remembering Laurel lived with several sisters. Within moments, multiple lights flicked on in the house, and there was a clamoring inside.

A woman Owen recognized from the bakery opened the door slowly.

"May I help you?"

"Yeah. I'm so sorry, I know it's the middle of the night. Is Laurel here?"

"Laurel?" she repeated.

"Holy crap is that Owen?" another voice called from inside. Within moments, the first woman had been pushed aside and a new, unrecognizable face peeked around her. "Are you Owen?"

"I'm Owen."

"Why the hell is Owen here?" That voice he recognized. It was Rosemary.

"Can someone tell me if Laurel is all right?"

"All right?" The first sister's eyes snapped up at him. "Why wouldn't she be all right?"

"I had a dream—" he began, but before he could say anything else, all three of the women rushed away from the door and pounded up the stairs. The front door was left open, so Owen took it as an invitation and walked through the threshold, closing it behind him.

He could hear the women all talking upstairs and felt a wave of relief when Laurel's voice joined the conversation. She was okay. It was just a dream.

"Owen?" Laurel walked slowly down the stairs. "What are you doing here?"

"I'm sorry. I had this dream that something bad happened to you, and I needed to make sure you were ok. I know it sounds ridiculous..." He looked over her shoulder and saw three pairs of eyes staring at him from a few steps behind her. "Is there somewhere we can talk?" She was so close to him, close enough to wrap his arms around. His heart thudded against his rib cage, his immediate fears placated, but now excitement took over. Laurel was in front of him, and she was captivating.

Her hair was loose and tangled, hanging over her shoulders. She was wearing a silk nightgown that skimmed her legs right above her knee. She tucked her hair behind her ears and glanced back at her sisters.

Owen took a step back and inhaled deeply. His brain and body couldn't be trusted this close to her, especially when she said she needed time. Because right now, Owen didn't want to take another moment away from Laurel, emotionally or physically. But if she told him to leave, he would. He'd do anything she asked at this moment.

Chapter Twelve

"Let's go to the garden," Laurel suggested, throwing a look over her shoulder at her sisters. Owen was clearly upset, beyond a normal nightmare. Laurel might not know much about men, but she was confident waking an entire household before sunrise wasn't a normal occurrence. They needed to talk, without the prying eyes and ears of three other witches in the room.

She slipped on her flip-flops and led him out of the house to the screened porch, where they each grabbed a lantern and then went into the yard. They carefully made their way past Rosemary's herb garden, careful not to trip over the basil, then to the path.

Laurel was acutely aware of his steps behind her, the soft sort of scrape against the gravel as they walked. She couldn't see his face and wondered what he was thinking. He was deeply fearful of something, but she wasn't sure what that something was.

Now it was her turn to be afraid. She walked into the darkness with her soulmate behind her. She knew she loved him, or rather, she would love him. She *would* feel for him what no other person on this earth could manage to pull from her. But he was a stranger to her. She knew Onfroi, or at least she thought she did, but Owen was a mystery. He may have Onfroi's past, but he wasn't him. Past lives didn't work like that. A person's soul was shaped not only by its intrinsic characteristics, but the life the person led. Laurel doubted very much she and Amée had much in common. There were multitudes she needed to learn about Owen, and he her. She didn't even know his last name.

"It's right here," she said, pointing towards the arched walkway through the stone walls. "There's a bench in here. We can sit down."

Hoping to exude a confidence she didn't feel, Laurel walked briskly towards the bench and took a seat. She risked a glance at Owen's face. Though light and shadows took turns flickering over him, she could see a slight apprehension in his features.

"I'm sorry I came in the middle of the night. I had a dream, and my mom told me never to ignore dreams. She's kind of a hippie."

Laurel smiled. "It's a good sentiment." Laurel felt some of her anxiety quell. "What did you dream of?"

"Of you," he answered quickly. "I mean of Amée and Onfroi."

"You saw something bad?"

"I don't know what I saw…I don't know what it meant, but I woke up with an overwhelming need to protect you from something." He exhaled. "I thought you might be in danger. I know this sounds crazy. We've only just met, I know, but—"

"It's ok. Let's start with this." She stuck her hand out. "Hi. I'm Laurel Bay."

"Nice to meet you, Laurel Bay." His hand enveloped hers. She almost gasped. The calluses were there, the rough skin like Onfroi's. "I'm Owen Davies."

"Hi, Owen Davies. That's a good start. Where are you from?"

"Maine. What about you?"

She laughed and waved her hand toward the house.

"Yeah, but have you always lived here?"

"No. I moved here thirteen years ago. Before that, I lived in Ohio."

"Oh? Where in Ohio?"

"Geneva? It's a small town but close to the Pennsylvania border. Right on the shores of Lake Erie."

"Sounds nice."

"It is. But not as nice as here." She smiled. "Owen Davies from Maine. What else is there to know? What do you do?"

"I'm a carpenter," he replied.

"Oh! That makes sense. When I shook your hand, I noticed that it felt like Onfroi's, and I had deduced he was a laborer of some kind, but if you're a carpenter, maybe Onfroi is, I mean, was too." She stopped and blushed. "Sorry, I'm rambling."

"I don't mind." He inched slightly closer to her so that their knees were touching. He was wearing shorts, and she only had on her black nightdress. She should have changed into something a little more covered. But, as it was, his knee was bare and pressing against her knee, and she couldn't help her heart from racing.

He reached out and ran his thumb across her wrist before snatching it away. She didn't panic this time, only regarded him with wide eyes.

"Sorry, I'm having a hard time keeping my hands off you." He paused, looking like he was mulling something serious over in his mind. "I need to tell you something," he said slowly.

"Ok. Tell me." Laurel saw no reason for him to hold anything back. This was the beginning of a relationship that would hopefully last a long time.

"I'm having a hard time not touching you not because you are a gorgeous woman, you are, but I think you're my soulmate." He looked at her as if waiting for her to burst out in screams or denials. "I know it sounds crazy, but soulmates exist. And I think you're mine. It would explain our dreams when we were Onfroi and Amée. Also why I rode a bike here in the middle of the night to check on you. Oh, and my mom is a witch. Like a real one."

Laurel raised both her eyebrows and was sure her facial expression read pure disbelief.

"I get that it might take a while for you to get used to the idea that magic and soulmates exist, and I don't want to rush you into anything, but—"

"Wait, you're a sonofawitch?" Laurel interrupted.

"Yes." Now, it was Owen's turned to look confused. "Sonofawitch? You know what a sonofawitch is?"

"Um, yes."

Owen's eyes narrowed, and he scrutinized her for a minute. As if something in his brain clicked, his expression relaxed to one of pure astonishment.

"Holy shit, are you a witch?"

"Yes." She nodded while a smile claimed her mouth. This was not what she was expecting. She knew there was always the chance her soulmate would have some magical blood, but she went into this thinking he would be a regular guy. "I am a witch."

"Now I've got a million questions," Owen laughed. He rubbed his hands over his face and exhaled.

"So do I," she admitted.

"What kind of witch are you?"

"A hedge witch. The first time we met, we were in the Hedge World."

"I don't know anything about hedge witches or the Hedge World," he admitted. "What does that mean?"

"I can visit the Hedge World, which is sort of like another realm. I don't know if I brought you there or if Onfroi could go there, but that's where I was when we met. In terms of magic, I specialize in divination. I read tarot cards and occasionally have visions. I can accidentally end up in people's thoughts, but I actively try not to do that."

"Really? I would think that would be very tempting."

"Absolutely not. People's thoughts are weird. And very jumbled. The few times I stumbled in, it wasn't a fun place to be. I'd rather stick to the cards. And then, of course, if I get bored, I can always jump the hedge."

"Crazy."

"What kind of witch is your mom?"

"She's a water witch, sort of a mix between storm and sea. She's also a seer," Owen said.

Laurel's mouth dropped open. "You're a Davies of the Davies water witches?" she nearly exclaimed. "They're one of the most powerful magical families on the continent."

Owen smiled and shrugged. "I never knew anything different growing up. Only that my aunts and cousins can get a little crazy and it wasn't a normal kind of crazy."

"Oh my goddess, do you have any sisters?"

"Just my brother and I."

"Your parents didn't keep going for a girl?"

"Nah, I think my mom was relieved to get two relatively non-magical boys. My cousins are...a handful. Morgan—she's a sea witch—she had a vision that I should go to Solaris. Guess she was right." He shook his head and laughed. "Water witches are hard to keep in public company until they learn how to control their powers. I think life was easier for my parents with only my brother and I."

"Wow. Wait, you said relatively non-magical. Are you a registered warlock?"

"Oh, no. My powers are not impressive. I can tell when a storm is coming, like I can tell you that the closest storm system to us right now is about fifty miles south of here and won't hit us on its path. Sometimes I can dissipate an extremely weak storm. Like a gentle rain. Maybe some slight rumbly thunder. No hurricanes though."

"Neat."

"So, you're a witch."

"I am," Laurel confirmed again.

"I guess you can tell me, for certain, then. Are we soulmates?"

Laurel felt heat rise to her face and her heart reminded her of their proximity. It was a simple question; it had a simple answer. But speaking it, telling Owen that they were destined to be together felt like crossing a threshold she could never jump back over. Once it was spoken fact, their future love would become like a pact between them, one neither of them could escape.

Laurel took a deep breath. Was it fair? She had a threat hanging over her, a threat she didn't yet understand. Maybe she should keep Owen in the dark. Lie to him; tell him she didn't know.

She looked into his eyes, full of hope and curiosity and a glimmer of something infinite and perfect.

"Yes," she whispered.

Owen broke into a grin. "I knew it. I knew it had to be you. It's strange, isn't it? Feeling like this?"

"Yes! I mean, I don't know you, but my brain and my body keep sending me messages like, 'trust this guy, he's the one.' It's a very weird landscape in my mind right now."

"Your brain and your body?" he said slowly, letting his eyes wander down for a minute. "Hell, sorry. I'm really trying to not be creepy. I can't stop looking at you. You look so good. When you were Amée, you looked beautiful, but starving."

"Trust me, you were pretty thin as Onfroi. Probably a side effect of the

Middle Ages. And between the visions and dreams, I've been able to put together that neither of us were noble, so we were most likely both half-starving most days."

"You've seen other things? What have you seen?" Now he looked at her urgently.

"Nothing much. I saw us talking by the river, you leaving a lantern out for me when I was coming home late from a patient."

"A patient?"

"Oh, I think I may have been a healer, but a terrible one. That vision was a little dark. My patient died, and I mentioned her entire family would probably die too." She paused. "I'm glad we're meeting now where things like hospitals and antibiotics exist."

"I had a big scar on my abdomen." He furrowed his brows for a moment. "A huge piece of wood nearly split me in two. Man, if that happened now, I'd be at the hospital so fast." He shook his head. "It's a miracle we lived long enough in that life to meet." Owen leaned back in his seat but kept his eyes on Laurel. "So, what happens now?"

"What do you mean?"

"Do you want to date? Do you want to get to know each other first? Do you want to go jump into bed? Should we go to Vegas and get married? What's next?"

Laurel felt her cheeks redden. She wished she had some experience with men. Ugh, why didn't she take Rosemary's advice and at least date a few people in her twenties? She wasted an entire decade waiting for her soulmate, and now that he was here, she was insufficiently prepared.

"Um," she stalled. "Not Vegas. I've never been, but I can't imagine that's the sort of wedding I'd want."

"No, that was a joke." He looked at her deeply for a moment. "Something outside I would think, lots of flowers, maybe at night."

"Something like that," she mused.

"How about this: you set the pace, and I'll follow. Tell me what you want to do next."

Laurel licked her lips and nodded. She would set the pace. She could live with that. Unless she wanted him to throw her over his shoulder and take her up to her room right now. She'd been without any real physical connection with another human for twenty-nine years and was finally in the presence of her soulmate. What was the point of waiting at this moment?

"Laurel?"

"Sorry. Yes. I will do that. Set the pace, I mean," she garbled.

"All right, then. What's the plan?"

"Hm?" she could barely keep her mind in one place. Suddenly, the only thing she could concentrate on was the swell of Owen's bicep beneath his t-shirt. She wanted to know what it felt like to run her teeth against his shoulder.

"When can I see you again? Unless you'd like me to stay, though I don't know what your sisters would think of it."

Laurel shook her head. She needed to focus.

"Why don't we have dinner tonight? I have some readings today."

"Readings?"

"Yes, a few of the locals who I read for regularly have scheduled appointments."

"Oh, yeah. Tarot. Funny, when Luke, the bartender, told me you were the resident tarot card reader, it made me think you were even more perfect for me."

"Yes, he told me you talked."

"I did. I needed a couple of strong drinks after we met and you..."

"Panicked," she finished.

"It was a lot to take in," he said between chuckles. "It was definitely a memorable first meeting."

"I don't usually trip over basil plants," she began, then thought better of it. "Or I don't do it often." By the beginning of September, Rosemary's herb garden was so out of control that Laurel always tripped over a collection of plants at least once before the autumnal freezes sent them all dormant.

"I promise I'll be there to lend a hand whenever a shrub takes you down."

"My hero," Laurel laughed, clasping her hands over her heart.

She let her hands fall and accidentally brushed her fingers over his knee. She froze, then quickly moved her hand to her own knee.

"Can I ask you something?" Owen began. She nodded. "Are you afraid of me? I'd never do anything to hurt you. I'm pretty sure it would go against my DNA make-up to do anything other than protect you."

Warmth blossomed in her chest at his endearing confession and Laurel believed him. Even now, he sat next to her, but leaned away, his hands were folded on his own lap, and he looked at her with concern, rather than hunger.

"Afraid of you? No. I'm a little afraid though," she admitted.

"That we've met? That life is changing as both of us know it?"

"When you put it that way, more than a little," she laughed nervously. "Mostly, I'm afraid of disappointing you."

"Disappointing me? How so?"

"I don't know how to date. I haven't had a boyfriend since I was sixteen. I sort of skipped the entire dating scene in my twenties since I was living on this tiny island. I don't know how to be, like, a girlfriend."

"I'm not looking for a girlfriend," Owen said slowly. He leaned forward and took her hand between both of his. His thumb ran over her knuckles, tracing circles over her skin. "I've been looking for you. Just you. I don't want to have a handful of dinners and drinks with you before we can start being honest with each other about who we are. I want to know you, all of you, as soon as I can so we can start being together." He took a deep breath. "I've been looking for you forever. I knew I had a soulmate at about twelve and by sixteen, I was actively searching. I used to stare at any girl I saw in public, hoping to catch a glimpse of my soulmate." He smiled. "I'm so relieved I found you." He brought her hand up to his lips and pressed a quick kiss against her palm. A jolt of longing surged through her body. If he could drive her wild with a kiss to her hand, Laurel was both terrified and excited to see what else he could do.

"I'm glad you found me too," she whispered. "I wasn't doing my share of looking by staying on Star Island for so long. I've never even been to Maine."

"Doesn't matter. We've found each other now." He came to his feet and pulled her to stand next to him. Before she could say a word, he wrapped his arms around her waist and pulled her body against his. Her hands flew up to his chest, palms pressed against him. "I'd like to kiss you good night now, Laurel Bay." He hovered his mouth close to hers until she closed the distance. It was a gentle kiss, a quiet hello. There were no hints of insistence or pleading, simply a first meeting of their lips, but Laurel was on fire. She melted against him and couldn't contain a sweet sigh.

"Ok," Owen mumbled and peeled his body off hers and took a step away from her. "I'll be back for dinner tonight. Do you want me to walk you back to the house?"

Laurel's eyes were still closed, and she wasn't sure she ever wanted to open them again. She reached out for Owen but found he had moved completely out of reach.

"Hm?" She slowly opened her eyes, still dazed.

"Should I walk you back to the house?"

"No. I'm going to sit here for a while," she said as she slid back into her spot.

"I'll be back tonight. How about six? I know it's a little early for dinner, but honestly, seven is waiting too long." He let a smile slowly break across his face.

"Pick me up at four forty-five. We'll beat the dinner rush."

"Early bird special it is."

Chapter Thirteen

Owen was behaving slightly irrationally. Usually, when he was anxious or overwhelmed or had too many feelings swirling around his chest cavity, he did one of two things.

The first was very specific to the job he was on and didn't work unless the timing was exactly right: demolition.

Owen liked to demo. If he was in the middle of demoing a house, he would get to work early (or even in the middle of the night) and go nuts on whatever needed to be knocked down. Walls, countertops, old toilets, and bathtubs, nothing stood a chance when placed in front of a stressed Owen. Four years earlier, when twenty-two-year-old Morgan had called him because she was stranded in upstate New York after meeting a warlock who wasn't who he seemed online, Owen had driven the five hours, threatened the warlock with powers he didn't have, driven her home, kept it all to himself, and then absolutely destroyed a bathroom.

But there weren't always rooms to be demolished. If Owen found himself needing to calm down without a kitchen that needed to be dismantled, he would make a piece of furniture. His usual plan of action was to do the big work, carving down the wood and the construction of the piece when he was upset, then save the intricate work for times when he was more relaxed.

Now that Owen had met Laurel, his honest-to-god-and-goddess soulmate, he wanted to make her something. His hands were itching to start a huge project, and his heightened emotion over their dinner tonight could use some release. Maybe a set of outdoor furniture. Or a bookcase! Witches liked books. The only problem was he found himself without his tools, raw materials, or the space to construct something. He also needed to ask his mom what sort of symbols a hedge witch would want carved on the side of a bookcase.

He sighed and got out his sketchbook. If he couldn't make her something, he could at least plan for it.

He took a quick glance at his plans for the actual house he would build someday (which now felt sooner) and felt a wave of clarity. Now he knew what that extra room was for and exactly what he'd build to put in it.

A few hours later, Owen was dressed in the nicest thing he packed (jeans and a plain blue shirt) and walked into Therese's Flowers. This was not how Owen thought he'd be picking his future wife up for their first date: on a bicycle, wearing jeans, and taking her to a diner because a damn family reunion had reserved the entire Italian restaurant on the island. There was no way he was showing up without flowers.

The door chimed as he walked in, alerting the employees of his presence. Unsurprisingly, Rosemary came to greet him.

"Good to see you again," she laughed. "Especially while the sun is up."

"I'm very sorry. It wasn't until after I banged on the door, I remembered that Laurel lived with all of you."

"Apology accepted. And you didn't even meet all of us," Rosemary mentioned.

"What? How many Bay sisters are there?"

"Five all together. Verbena lives a few buildings down in an apartment. She's a realtor. So, if you find yourself suddenly in the market for permanent accommodations on Star Island..." Rosemary raised her brows and smiled wickedly.

"Thank you for the recommendation, but this afternoon, I need your expertise."

"You do?"

"Yes. I'd like to bring Laurel some flowers, but since I don't know her very well, I'd like your advice."

"My advice! Of course." Rosemary powerwalked deeper into the store and Owen leapt forward to keep up. "She absolutely loves lilac, so that will be the focal point." Rosemary grabbed a bunch of pale purple blooms. "Then, we'll flank it with some coriander and a bit of bay laurel for some green, and well, her name," she chuckled to herself, "top it off with two red roses..." Rosemary tied the bouquet with a piece of twine and wrapped the whole thing in craft paper before presenting it to him.

"That's beautiful," he exclaimed, taking the flowers. "How did you do that so quickly?"

Rosemary looked side to side, as if she were about to spill some huge secret and didn't want any eavesdroppers.

"I'm a garden witch. It's sort of my thing."

"Makes sense."

"Doesn't it?" She tossed her hair over her shoulder and shimmied a bit. She was wearing a bright orange floral dress and a flower to match in her dark hair. "Well, off with you. Don't want to keep Laurel waiting." She winked and shooed him out of the shop.

Owen knocked on the door, this time politely and at a reasonable hour. After a few moments, one of the sisters answered.

"Come in, she'll be down in a second," she said, turning around and walking into the house.

Owen stepped over the threshold, this time taking in the room in the light of day. The house was very well-maintained. Judging by the style of the exterior and the diamond pattern painted over untreated hardwood floors, this house had to be around two hundred years old.

"Sorry, I'm Sage." The woman who answered the door walked back into the living area he stood in. "I have a bad habit of not making small talk." She paused and looked around the room. "I heard you fixed our front step."

"I did."

"Thanks. That was a pain in the ass." She crossed her arms in front of chest, but it didn't seem rude, only that she was nervous. "Do you know how to replace grout in a bathroom?"

"Um, yes."

"Can you fix a ceiling fan?"

"Probably."

"What about a doorknob that sticks?" Owen was beginning to think he would be returning tomorrow with a list of handyman duties. It went without saying that when a carpenter started dating a woman with four sisters living in a two-hundred-year-old house, they might have a few jobs for him.

"Sage, go away."

Owen turned his head to the staircase. Laurel was on her way down and he couldn't help his mouth from falling open.

She was wearing a long, flowy black skirt that fell mid-calf, a black tank that left little to the imagination when it came to the swell of her breasts and the curve of her waist, and black sandals that tied around her ankles. Her hair was down, falling in loose, black waves, and framed her face perfectly.

Owen wanted to kiss her. He wanted to say screw the restaurant and throw her over his shoulder and run back to his cabin. Or ask Sage to go outside for the next two to three hours and ravish his soulmate right there on the living room floor.

"You look gorgeous," he said instead, because a pre-first date ravishing seemed out of sorts. But he looked forward to lots of pre-date ravishing in the future, especially if she continued wearing that outfit and looking at him with those eyes.

"Thank you. You look nice."

"I didn't bring anything nicer than this. I wish I had something nicer."

"Don't. You look good. Trust me." Her voice was seductive but then a moment later she looked like she realized how seductive and blushed furiously.

"These are for you," Owen said, holding out the bouquet.

"You got me flowers? No one has ever gotten me flowers!" she squealed.

"That's insane." He let his eyes memorize her face as she cradled the blooms lovingly. She inspected each flower, then a smirk appeared on her lips.

"Did Rosemary or Therese help you with these?"

"Rosemary," he answered slowly. "Why?"

Laurel giggled and walked into the dining area, opened a large armoire, and took out a vase. She motioned for him to follow her into the kitchen, where she filled the vase with water.

"Have you heard of the language of flowers?"

"My mom knows it. I don't."

"Basically, every flower means something different. And when picked by a garden witch, they can instill certain...feelings. Not really a true spell, more like a gentle nudging."

"What on earth did your sister have me give you?" He hoped he hadn't offended her.

"Let's see, purple lilacs, my favorite, are for the beginnings of love."

"So far, so good, I hope."

She smiled and licked her lips. "Deep red roses are romantic love. I'm sure she stuck bay laurel in there to get a laugh out of me, but they're for wisdom, and lastly, we have coriander."

"The spice?"

"Yes, these tiny white flowers are coriander."

"Is coriander bad?"

"No, coriander is...how to put this delicately...lust?"

"Lust?"

"Yup. One of the first years Rosemary worked at Therese's, she was in a mood and put coriander into all the bridesmaids' bouquets at a wedding for a particularly nasty bride. Let's just say some of the bridesmaids had the best night of their lives."

"Did your sister put a lust spell on us?" Owen asked. Not that he needed it. He didn't need anything other than to look at Laurel to be completely smitten, and turned-on, by her. If he wanted to get really aroused, he had to start thinking about what it would feel like to run his hand up her thigh and see where it led him.

"No! No. She wouldn't be able to. I'd sense that a mile away. Trust me, she's tried and failed at that ruse." Laurel shook her head and smiled. "She was probably trying to nudge you towards romantic and sexy feelings in my direction, that's all."

"I don't need nudging," he said plainly. "I'm already there."

She didn't say anything or meet his eyes for a few beats, just finished arranging the flowers and set them on the dining table. He wasn't sure if he'd overstepped. He felt ready to jump headfirst into this, but he could tell Laurel was hesitant.

But then she looked up at him, big slate eyes sparkling, and held her hand out for him to hold.

"Let's go."

Owen was planning on asking Laurel if she had a car. Or if she minded walking. Or if there was a cab service on this island, which he highly doubted. But, as soon as they descended the front steps, she tied her skirt into an elaborate knot, hopped on her bike, and glanced back at him.

"Ready to go?"

"You can ride in that skirt?"

"I can ride in a ball gown," she retorted.

He climbed onto his bike and pulled up next to her.

"I'll let you in on a secret, since you're my soulmate and all," she continued.

"Go ahead."

"I don't have my driver's license."

"Really? I guess there isn't much use to having a car here if you can bike everywhere," he answered logically.

"Um, you can't bike anywhere here from December until March. All my sisters have their licenses. Lavender, Rosemary, and Sage share a car, and Verbena has her own."

"So, why don't you?"

"Honestly, I can drive. If there was ever an emergency, I could drive a car. But I never saw a point in having a license. I ride my bike in the nice weather, most of my clients come to me, and the ones that don't, I can usually hitch a ride to town in the morning with Lavender or bug Verbena into picking me up. Never had much use for it."

"Understandable. I have a license. And a car—a truck. Which is currently in long-term parking on the mainland."

"You drive a truck?"

"Yeah, I use the flatbed for hauling lots of supplies and materials around. Carpentry comes with some pretty big items."

"Much larger than a deck of cards I can fit in most pockets," she teased.

"Definitely."

They rode back into town, Laurel pointing out small landmarks along the way. He was surprised to find that Luke, who had called himself their next-door neighbor, lived a good two minutes away by bike.

They pulled up to Mable's Diner, parked their bikes on the bike rack across the street, and walked in.

"You're not worried someone is going to steal our bikes?" Owen asked as he held the door open for Laurel.

"Bikes in general? Sure. Our particular bikes? Absolutely not."

"Why not?"

"To begin, yours is a rental from Pat. If a teenager steals your bike, they'd have to hide it in their yard forever because if Pat ever saw someone riding it around town, he would probably push them off the bike as they rode past." They grabbed a booth by the window.

"Good to know. I'll try not to cross Pat."

"And no one would steal my bike."

"Why?"

"Oh my sweet mainlander, no teenager in their right mind would steal the island witch's bike. I could hex them," Laurel answered matter-of-factly.

"Hex? Do you make it a point to hex teenagers?"

"Of course not. I don't make it a point to hex anyone. But I do really, really enjoy riding my bike in autumn while wearing all black with Nyx perched on my basket between the hours of midnight and two in the morning." Laurel's eyes glinted with mischief.

"Two questions. First, who or what is Nyx? Second, are you the only one of your sisters who is such a blatant witch?" Owen handed her a menu and grabbed one for himself from behind the napkin dispenser.

"One, Nyx is my familiar. She's a great horned owl."

"Your familiar is a great horned owl?" Owen nearly shouted.

"Keep your voice down and yes. What's your mom's familiar?"

"A lionfish."

"Okay, well that seems even more flamboyant than mine! At least mine only comes out at night."

"My mom doesn't ride her bike around my hometown with her lionfish. It lives in a fancy fish tank in the living room."

"Different strokes," she sighed. "And I am the most witchy of my sisters. I'm the only one who wears almost all black, I have a witch-centric job, and I don't mind the attention. The Celestials—"

"Celestials?"

"Oh, native Star Island-ers, they see Lavender as the baker, Rosemary as the florist, Verbena as the realtor, and Sage as the farmer."

"And Laurel's the witch."

"You bet your ass I am."

They ordered dinner; Laurel insisted that if Owen liked BLTs this one was out-of-this-world, and she wasn't wrong. They talked about their childhoods and hobbies and families. It felt like a relatively normal date. There was no discussion of soulmates or past lives. Onfroi and Amée stayed in the past tonight. This dinner was all about Owen and Laurel.

After staying at the diner for over four hours, Owen knew it was time to take Laurel home. He didn't particularly want to, but he also had the feeling that if there wasn't a hard end, they might spend the entire night together, which didn't feel like taking things slow. He also wasn't sure how much longer he could stare at her and not assault her with kisses. The other patrons at Mable's didn't need to see that.

They rode back slowly in the dark. Laurel had a permanent light on her bike, which flickered against the trees. Owen's flashlight was still taped precariously to his handlebars and would work fine to illuminate his way home. When they pulled up to the path that led to Laurel's front door, she jumped off her bike and faced him.

"Let's say goodnight here," she started. "There's no way my sisters won't have their faces pressed against the window if we make it to the porch."

He laughed. He could picture an audience waiting for them, and he didn't want an audience right now.

Owen slid his hands around her waist and pulled her body against his. His fingers found the seam of her shirt and tucked beneath it to smooth the skin of her lower back.

Laurel sucked a breath in, her hands moving to his biceps. She mimicked his movement, sliding her fingers beneath his shirtsleeves and grasping at his arms.

"Good night, Owen," she whispered. Her eyes peeked up at him through her lashes, and he stifled a groan.

"Good night, Laurel," he answered and kissed her. It was soft at first, allowing the passion to build. After a few moments, he teased her lips apart, letting his tongue seek hers, taking his time to taste her. He put everything into that kiss, every sweet smile, every soft laugh, every raised eyebrow from the evening. He made it count for everything he wanted to do with her and would once they got to know each other a little better. He kissed her like he hadn't seen her in hundreds of years and never wanted to let her go again.

But he did. He broke their kiss, gently released her body, and took two steps backwards.

"I'll see you tomorrow," he called over his shoulder. He had to move quickly before his body ignored his sense, and he rushed back to her arms. Owen heard Laurel mumble a good night, then jumped on his bike, and began the ride back towards town.

Chapter Fourteen

L aurel stood with her feet glued to the ground.

She couldn't move.

She couldn't think.

She still hadn't opened her eyes, even though she had heard Owen pedal away at least three minutes earlier.

That was a kiss.

It was a kiss that made Laurel wonder what other things he could do with his mouth. And understand how people became obsessed with people. And obsessed with sex.

Laurel was obsessed with Owen.

She'd always accepted the whole soulmate idea because she'd been privy to the knowledge since childhood. When some parent would gently tell their children that at some point, they may or may not find a person to love on a long-term basis, Laurel's parents were much more 'your soulmate is going to show up, but we don't know when.' She was used to waiting around for him to make an appearance, but she had never been overly excited about it.

Now she was excited. She was so excited that when she got inside her house and was met with four pairs of inquiring eyes (Verbena had come over when she heard there was a date), she squealed, and then quickly covered her mouth out of embarrassment.

"Is this what I have to look forward to?" Sage asked, eyeing her sister's outburst. "Yikes."

"You shut your mouth, Sage Juniper. I, for one, cannot wait to feel this giddy after a simple kiss goodnight. It takes a little more than that to get me that excited." Rosemary smirked.

"Details, please. I've got a conference call with a group in California in thirty minutes," Verbena reminded the room.

"It was wonderful. He's wonderful. We didn't even talk about the soulmate-magic-witch stuff, at least not too much. I can't explain it; I feel so connected to him." She shrugged her shoulders. Laurel didn't know how to explain it. Owen lit her on fire, mind, body, and soul. She couldn't wait to spend the rest of her life with him.

"I'm glad things went well. I, for one, have to be up early and will be taking my leave," Lavender said. She turned back towards Laurel, "I'm happy for you, really."

Laurel's eyes followed her oldest sister as she walked into her bedroom and shut the door. She didn't look happy. She didn't look closed off either. Lavender looked decidedly sullen.

There was no way Laurel would be getting any sleep tonight, so after her other sisters left or went to bed, she decided to do a little reading. She didn't want to freak herself out further over Morana Stoch, so instead she picked up *The History of the Bay Witches*. She cuddled up on the couch in the living room with a cup of chamomile and the story of all her ancestors. It was cool to have a tome like this in the house. It was like delving into her ancestry without having to do any actual research work.

When she was younger, she used to read her mom's page over and over.

Holly Bay: House Witch of the Bay Line. Traditional Education. Employed as an interior designer. Married to David Kowalski. Five daughters: Lavender, Rosemary, Laurel, Verbena, and Sage.

The page went on to detail a few spells her mother had created and the details of her death.

Laurel sighed. She was used to this feeling when the grief of losing her parents would hit. It always happened around big events. Her high school graduation, when she started her small tarot card reading business, there would be more to come that would be harder. Laurel would have to face the fact that her parents would never meet Owen or hold their grandchildren in their arms. She knew these waves of grief would never lessen, but she welcomed them; it kept her connected to her parents. The last thing she wanted was to get over their deaths. At some point, the grief over losing them had blossomed into something new. It wasn't raw or stinging anymore. It was dull, but so full of love.

Laurel flipped back to the eighteenth century, one of the portions of the book she hadn't read over in depth. It was a little dreary. They were coming off the witch trails, but the Bay witches were still careful when using any witchcraft. At this point, very few witches actually practiced their magic. It was too risky.

A strange-looking page caught Laurel's eye. It wasn't an entry, but a scribbled down collection of notes. She shifted closer to the light and got reading.

12 January 1714 – Bristol

> *We write this as a warning for future Bay Witches. The Fortworths have taken action against us. Though Katherine has the power, we know it is Jonas who wields it. Eliza's refusal of him has cost us dearly.*
> *A curse was laid upon our line – if a witch were to collect the blood of all living Bay witches, they would add the power of the Bays to their own.*
> *We fear Jonas will come for us. We hope that our relatives in the colonies are keeping our line safe. Beware Jonas Fortworth.*

What. The. Hell?

Laurel nearly knocked over her teacup flipping the pages forward and backward trying to find information on any of these women. She moved to the dining table and turned all the lights on. She glanced at the clock: eleven.

"Rosemary?" she hissed. "Are you still awake?" Laurel heard a shuffle upstairs.

"Did you call me?" Rosemary stood at the top of the stairs, her eye mask on her forehead, in her nightgown.

"Get down here."

"Do you want me to drive you to Owen's? Let me throw some clothes on." She started to turn around.

"No! This is about our family. Come here," Laurel hissed.

Rosemary sauntered down the stairs.

"Read this," Laurel said, thrusting the book in her direction. Rosemary sat down at the table, rubbed her eyes, and looked at the entry.

"Whoa," she breathed. "Can you find anything else about them? She says we and one of them is named Eliza."

"I was starting to look when I called you." Laurel flipped the book a few pages forward and found *Eliza Bay*. "Here we go. Eliza Bay: Undetermined specialty. Born 1690, Bristol. Childless. Died in a house fire, 1718. That's it."

"That's it? No specialty, no kids, died in a fire?" Rosemary furrowed her brow. "Let's try to find her mom. Then we can see how many sisters she had."

Laurel flipped back a few pages; there were several entries of other branches of the Bay family in America and other parts of England at the time.

"Here!" Rosemary pointed. "Anne Bay: Healer. Born 1663, Bristol. Three daughters (Mary, Eliza, Alice), Two sons (William, John). Died in a house fire, 1718."

"Wait, 1718? Did the whole family die in this fire?" Laurel flipped through a few pages, finding that Mary and Alice also died in a house fire that year. Pages for men weren't included until the early twentieth century and then only if they showed some magical promise.

"So, this line of Bay witches was completely snuffed out in 1718, but they talk about relatives in the colonies. We must be descendents of them." Laurel leaned back in her chair and rubbed the bridge of her nose. "There's a curse on our family. And a most likely evil Morana was searching for Bay witches. I'm going to go ahead and leap to conclusions and guess she's after our blood."

"Maybe," Rosemary said slowly, "but didn't she say you were the witch she was looking for? If she was going after all of us, she'd probably be content with any Bay witch to get the blood-collecting ball rolling."

"Good point." Laurel laid her head on the table. "So, I have an evil witch after me, but all of us have this curse hanging over our heads?"

"Sounds about right." Rosemary patted her back. "Let's go to bed. We can put together some sort of plan tomorrow. There has to be an anti-curse somewhere that we can put to good use, right? It'll be easier to figure it all out once we've gotten some sleep."

"Here's hoping."

The next morning, Laurel was up at five to catch Lavender and Sage before they left the house.

"Rosemary and I found something last night," Laurel blurted while Lavender brushed her teeth.

"Shit!" she screamed, dropping her toothbrush into the sink. "What the hell, Laurel? You scared me to death!"

"Sorry, but not really. There's a curse on our family and—"

"Shh," Lavender interrupted, putting her hand up. "I'll be downstairs in a few minutes. Tell me then. And make me a cup of Wake Up Shake Up."

Five minutes later, Lavender and Sage were both in the kitchen, leaning against the counter, drinking a cup of Wake Up Shake Up and listening to Laurel.

"It's a weird page in the book, sort of stuck between entries. It looks like a warning. Basically, this branch of the family tree was cursed, probably because Eliza didn't want to marry this Jonas clown, and then they all died four years later in a house fire."

"If they died in a fire, their blood would have been, you know, burned up." Sage took a long drink of tea.

"Yes, obviously, but we have powers. So, they didn't get their blood. Or maybe Jonas killed them, took their blood, burned the house down to cover the murders, and never managed to get to the colonies, or rather here, to get the blood from the rest of the family. He was probably kicking himself that the Bays had cousins in North America instead of, like, Ireland."

"What happened to the other Bays in England?" Sage asked.

"Their line died out over the next one hundred years. They didn't practice magic, so Jonas might not have known they even existed. No one was forthcoming about magical identities back then, even to other witches and warlocks."

Lavender was quiet, stirring her tea and occasionally taking a sip. She was clearly mulling something over in her mind.

"Do you think you could find out what actually happened to them?" she finally asked.

"What do you mean?"

"You're a hedge witch. I know you tend to stick to predicting the future for bachelorettes and bored housewives, but you're supposed to be able to divine all sorts of things, heal, summon spirits—"

"Don't undermine my clients," Laurel said sharply. "And I was pretty certain summoning spirits was off the table for all Bay Witches after Rosemary accidentally called Ralph Waldo Emerson's ghost to our attic, and we couldn't get him to leave for three weeks."

"Oh, Goddess. That was so annoying," Sage huffed. "He wanted to proofread all my lit assignments and was extremely critical."

"This is different," Lavender said. "We need more information on the curse—if it's breakable, who else knows about it. A visit from Mary, Eliza, and Alice might be what we need."

Laurel was in the Hedge World.

She hadn't jumped the hedge. She knew she hadn't. She was sleeping, but somehow, she was there.

She wasn't in the woods or on the path or even by the river, but in an old house. It felt like something from a different time, a time when floors were dirt and slit windows were covered with animal skins. Laurel sat in one corner, her back pressed against the uneven, raw wood of the structure.

She took a moment to look around the room and decide her course of action. There was an empty straw mattress on the wall next to her with a threadbare blanket pulled over it, a table with a pitcher and what looked like bones strewn across it sat against the other wall. Her eyes traveled and landed on a figure tending the fire. Laurel felt her shoulders start to jump but stilled them. The figure was hooded and sang quietly in a language she didn't understand and couldn't place.

Laurel didn't move. She wasn't far from the door, barely a few feet, but she didn't know if she could make it there without disturbing the fire tender. She also had no idea where she was in the Hedge World and how to get out. She'd never been there in her dreams before.

"Fire burns and metal bleeds, minds are lost and witches need," the figure mumbled, hands twisting into painful shapes over the hearth. "Lost in worlds of ice they shiver and now that power, do deliver."

Laurel cowered further against the wall, wishing she could burrow straight through. The fire blazed high, sparks flying towards the figure who cackled now.

"Oh, Bay Witch?" she sang and came to her feet.

"Shit," Laurel breathed. It was Morana Stoch, that ice-haired sorceress who was probably trying to kill her.

"Don't be afraid," Morana hummed, crooking her finger in her direction. "Flavie just wants to talk."

Laurel furrowed her brow but stopped moving. Flavie? Wasn't her name Morana? Did she have a twin? This had to be the same witch she'd seen in the picture.

"You don't remember me?" the witch questioned, then threw her head back laughing. "Oh, poor little Bay Witch. Hasn't even begun to look into her memories."

Laurel scrambled to her feet now, trying to sprint past her, but she caught Laurel's arm and pulled her against her body.

"Don't you dare run away from me. I've looked for you for centuries, you suka. You'll pay. You will pay." She dug her fingers into Laurel's arm. Laurel tried to pull away, but she held fast, squeezing her so hard Laurel worried the bone would break.

"I bind you to me. Wherever you go, I see. Wherever you hide, I am. You can never outrun me, Amée of the Bay Witches. I will find you." She pushed Laurel hard and sent her body through the wall.

She crashed through wood and shrubs and snow until she was flying through the air of the Hedge World, completely unbound. Her arms reached out, trying to grab anything she could, but were met with nothing but night air.

This was how she would die; Laurel became convinced of it. She'd never stop flying or falling or whatever she was doing. She wished she could pass out, but her mind stayed active.

She tried to still her thoughts, to concentrate on something calm.

Owen.

She saw his face, both now and when he was Onfroi. She focused on his smile, his eyes, the calluses on his hands. She remembered the feel of him against her, holding her like she was a precious thing, something to be cherished.

Suddenly, she stopped. She didn't crash to the ground or hit a tree; she simply stopped. Laurel slowly opened her eyes.

She was sitting in a chair with her head lying on the dining table. She slowly sat up, careful not to make any jarring movements. Her head was still spinning like she'd just gotten off a roller coaster.

"Is anyone home?" she said quietly, afraid anything louder would break her head into a million pieces. There was no answer. She took a deep breath and backed away from the table.

Her arm stung where Morana or Flavie or whatever the hell that woman's name was had grabbed her. She brought her right hand up to rub her forearm and touched raw skin.

On her left forearm, burned into the skin, was a maze with a circle in the center. Laurel ran her fingers over it carefully, her breath coming in pants. It hurt, stung, and showed no signs of disappearing.

"Help," she whispered.

Chapter Fifteen

Owen woke up completely relaxed. Life seemed easier now, or at least like it was laid out in front of him. He had found Laurel, and she was the center of it. They had time to get to know each, to figure out how their lives would fit together. Thankfully, Laurel had a very transient job. It wouldn't be a big deal for her to move to Maine when it came to it. All that mattered was that they were together; the other pieces of the puzzle would fall into place.

He got up and brushed his teeth, threw on a shirt, and grabbed his phone.

> Owen: Good morning, mon petit oiseau.

After he sent it, he smacked his hand against his forehead. It was probably too early for pet names. But he'd called her that before when they were Onfroi and Amée. He wondered if she remembered.

When she didn't answer after two minutes, he started to panic.

> Owen: Onfroi called Amée mon petit oiseau. It means little bird. I don't know if you remember that.

Owen: If it bugs you, I won't call you that. We can leave the past in the past.

Owen: I'll think of a new nickname for you.

Owen: If you even like nicknames.

Owen threw his phone across the room before he could text her again. He'd sent five texts with no answer at nine in the morning. She might think he was a hoverer. She was probably still sleeping. She was going to think he was obsessed with her. Well, he was obsessed with her, but not in a creepy way. He was obsessed with her in a soulmate way. Big difference. He hoped.

His phone dinged, and he dove across the room to retrieve it from where it landed under the dresser.

Laurel: Can you come over? Something happened.

Owen: I'll be there in ten minutes. Are you ok?

Laurel: I'm ok. But come now.

Owen didn't like this feeling. He didn't like the lurch his heart did when she sent that something had happened. He didn't like that his pulse had yet to slow since that text. Mostly, he didn't like that he wasn't already there.

It was a strange thing to become accustomed to. A few days ago, he wouldn't have known Laurel Bay from a stranger on the street, and now he couldn't imagine being away from her for more than a few moments. He needed to be with her, or at least near her. Especially since she was a witch.

His mom was a relatively subtle witch. She didn't get involved in too many scuffles between witches, but he knew it happened. His cousins were a bunch of slightly mad water witches. That wasn't fair. A few of his cousins were slightly mad water witches, the rest (Morgan included) were simply extremely powerful water witches. He was familiar with the tempers of powerful witches and how feuds were easily stirred up.

Owen rode his bike as quickly as possible to the Bay cottage, the entire time wishing he had his truck. At this point, he wondered whether it would be worth it to take the ferry back and pick it up for use on the island. He wasn't heading back to Maine any time soon; he might as well have a car. Especially since he found himself racing to Laurel for the second time in as many days.

He jumped up the front steps and knocked.

"Hey," Laurel said as she opened the door slowly. She looked exhausted.

"Are you ok?" he asked again, no longer satisfied with the text answer.

She exhaled and mustered a weak smile. "Come in. It's a long story."

Owen followed her through the living room and up the stairs. She led him into her bedroom, which he hadn't been expecting. Laurel collapsed onto the bed, stuffing multiple pillows behind her head, then rolled onto her side to face him.

Owen stood on the other side of the room, leaning against her dresser with his arms folded across his chest. He didn't think this was the right time to curl up next to her in that mess of blankets.

"Sorry," she sat up quickly, "I didn't even think. Would you be more comfortable in the living room? I didn't want my sisters walking in on this conversation."

"This is fine. Lay back down. I'll stay over here for now. Unless you want me to sit?"

"Whichever you want. I can barely keep my head up." She laid back down, tucking her knees into the fetal position.

"What happened to you?" It had to be something bad. She looked like she'd fallen down a flight of stairs from the way she winced with every move.

"A lot. Let me start at the beginning. One night last week, I was in the Hedge World looking for you. Or for Onfroi. I was looking for whoever I kissed by the river."

"It was me." He may have looked like Onfroi, but that was definitely him.

"You, then. I was looking for you. The world was all off, though. Dark and dangerous feeling instead of its normal otherworldliness. Anyway, I got to the river, and someone was there. It was a witch who ended our meeting by pressing our foreheads together and doing some sort of spell. She also seemed to know me from another time. Somewhat related to that, I recently found out that there is a curse on the Bay Witch line. Back to the original story—"

"A curse?" he interrupted. "What kind of curse?"

"Eh, if a witch collects the blood of all living Bay witches, she can steal our power. And maybe kill us? That part wasn't clear."

"Ok." Owen had a million questions, and he wasn't certain his brow could furrow any deeper than it currently had, but he decided to let her finish before bombarding her.

"I haven't gone into the Hedge World since the whole thing with Morana."

"Morana?"

"We figured out who the witch with the forehead move is. Her name is Morana Stoch. She has two warlock brothers and lives in Montana. So, yesterday, I fell asleep at the dining room table. I haven't been sleeping well. But I ended up in the Hedge World. I've never gone there without specifically willing myself there, at least not since the first time I landed there, and I wasn't sleeping that time. Basically, I was in a shack and Morana was there. She put a spell on me, burned my forearm, and sent me hurtling through time and space until I finally woke up. It was awful. I took two Dramamine as soon as I could lift my head."

Owen stood completely still letting the story wash over him. There was an evil witch putting spells on his soulmate, there was a curse on his soulmate's family, and she'd been tossed through the air last night.

It was a lot to take in.

Owen took a shaky deep breath, trying to keep his mind from jumping to every worst-case scenario.

"The biggest difference is the first time she marked me, the symbol on my forehead disappeared pretty quickly." Laurel delicately pushed up the sleeve of her black t-shirt. "This one isn't going anywhere, and it hurts like hell."

Owen crossed the room. On her arm was a maze that looked like a cattle brand. Owen sucked a breath in.

"Holy shit," he breathed and reached out to touch it.

"Don't!" she shrieked. "Sorry, don't touch it. It stings. Rosemary and Lavender made me some ointments, but for now, they're only taking the edge off. And I don't want to go to the hospital—"

"Because you'd have to come up with a reason for having a brand on your arm."

"Exactly." She swung her legs over the bed and sat up, her knees against his legs.

Owen looked down at her huge gray eyes, full of uncertainty. She looked so helpless at that moment and, for the first time in his life, he wished he was a full-fledged warlock. He wanted to hunt down this Morana Stoch; he wanted to unmake the curse. But unless she was a storm over the Atlantic, he didn't even know how to find her.

He felt useless. He was no help in a battle like this. His plan of action would be to call the police if someone terrorized the person he loved, but that wouldn't work here.

"What do you need?" He settled on, unsure what he could possibly do. He crouched in front of her, taking her hands in his, careful not to bump the burn on her arm.

"Honestly? I'm exhausted. I'm afraid to fall asleep. Can you stay by me? Wake me up if I seem like I'm having a bad dream?"

"Of course." He stood and started to go back to his post against the dresser, but she didn't release his hands.

"Will you lay by me? Just until I fall asleep. You can move then if you want. I don't know if I can fall asleep with you staring at me." She mustered a smile.

"Sure." Owen slowly walked to the other side of the bed and laid beside her. It was a full-size mattress and immediately apparent to him. His feet knocked against the footboard, and he had to lay on his side to keep from falling to the ground.

"Thank you," she whispered, rolling on her side to face him. She took his hand in hers and pulled it against her neck under her chin. "I only need an hour or so."

Four hours later, Owen was lying on his back with a sound asleep Laurel curled up against his chest. His arms were wrapped firmly around her, his chin tucked over her hair. She had slowly gotten into this position over the past few hours and had recently added her leg over his.

She felt so good, perfectly tucked against him. She also smelled amazing. Owen was used to all the herbal smells witches tended to surround themselves with, but this was different. It was deeper. He was certain pheromones and the fact that she was his soulmate had something to do with it, but she smelled like all his favorite things, leaves burning in autumn, vanilla, and...maybe jasmine? He couldn't place it.

He glanced around her room. It suited her well, all dark and starry. Her walls were a deep navy with mirrors of different shapes and sizes hanging on all the walls. She had a collection of crystals on her dresser next to a deck of cards he assumed were tarot. There was a single picture frame on the dresser, and he couldn't quite make out who was in it, but it looked like a family shot, including parents.

Owen felt a twinge of regret he didn't know more about Laurel. He knew he was going to love her forever, but he didn't really know her yet. He didn't know her parents' names or what it had been like to lose them so young. He didn't know her favorite book or color or what she liked for breakfast.

He sighed and cuddled deeper against her, risking a quick peck to the top of her head. They'd figure all those things out. Once the situation with this Morana character calmed down, they'd take a weekend or a week or a month and get to know each other. All of each other. Because he'd be lying if he didn't say that knowing her body was as enticing as knowing her mind.

He was quite impressed with himself at the moment. He had managed to keep all his thoughts towards her of the chaste and protecting kind, rather than allowing his imagination to run wild while he had her in his arms.

He exhaled. There went his good streak. Now his mind was turning to all sorts of dirty thoughts. No, not dirty. Nothing dirty about showing his soulmate how he felt about her.

He reached his hand up and carefully brushed her hair away from her face.

Laurel popped up out of his arms with a start, fully awake and sitting up. She looked at him, then around the room, then back him.

"Hi," he said.

"Hi. Yes, I did ask you to stay with me so I could sleep." Her cheeks flushed a little. "Thank you. I slept really well." She rubbed her eyes quickly.

"No dream visitors?"

"Not exactly. No Morana, no Hedge World, no new burns. So definitely a successful sleep. What time is it?"

"Close to two."

"What? I thought I was going to nap for an hour."

"You looked so peaceful; I didn't want to wake you. Do you have any clients today?"

"No, I canceled my only one this morning after the burn. I'll take a couple days off to heal. Usually my clients are very understanding if I have to reschedule. Unless it's a bachelorette party, and I don't cancel those."

"Wait, you said not exactly. Did someone visit you in your dreams? Was it Onfroi?"

She smiled and took his hand slowly, slipping her fingers between his.

"I didn't see Onfroi. I don't know if I will anymore now that I know you and we're together. I feel like it was our souls trying to find their way back to each other, and now that we're together, I don't think I'll be seeing you in my dreams. Other than just random, normal, non-magical ones." She took a deep breath and smiled. "I saw three ancestors I have been considering summoning, and I think seeing them was a push in that direction. So, once the sun sets and my sisters can all get here, there's a very good chance we'll be raising a trio of ghosts tonight. At least."

Owen ran his thumb over her knuckles a few times trying to process the information she had offered. She was going to summon not one, not two, but three ghosts tonight.

"Have you summoned a ghost before?"

"Me? No. Rosemary has summoned a couple. And I think Verbena summoned one accidentally, but she's more about sending them away. But hedge witches are supposed to be good at summoning spirits. I've never been very...into developing my abilities, but summoning is in my wheelhouse. It'll be fine. Our ancestors have no reason to come after us. And they're probably bored sitting around in the afterlife waiting to be reincarnated, or maybe they're not being reincarnated so this will be like a fun field trip."

"It will be safe?" Owen asked.

"Of course."

Chapter Sixteen

Laurel had no idea whether summoning the spirits of three witches who had been murdered was safe, ancestors or not. She hazarded that the ghosts wouldn't be particularly angry at the current Bay Witches, but she wasn't the foremost expert on pissed off ghosts. They might have a "burn it all to hell" policy when it came to any humans.

Either way, all the living Bay Witches needed to know more about this family curse, and the three dead Bay Witches from 1718 would have the answers. They were calling some ghosts forward tonight, no matter the consequences.

Of course, it took some scheduling. Lavender had a cake tasting for a couple getting married next fall that she couldn't move because they were out-of-towners. Verbena had a closing that was supposed to be over around six, but then she needed to run home and change in case things got messy. Laurel wasn't sure how raising a few non-corporeal beings could get messy, but nevertheless, she understood that Verbena didn't want to risk her work clothes.

By nine, all five Bay sisters were in the attic prepared to raise a few spirits.

The floor was decorated with pine branches freshly cut from the woods on their property and positioned into a large circle that all five sisters sat within. They each held a bundle of bay leaves, not only their moniker but also a fantastic herb to use when trying to contact ancestors. They each had three unlit candles in front of their persons, one for each of the witches they were trying to reach, a single burning taper, and a small bowl of water.

Normally, Lavender or Rosemary took the leadership role, but Laurel would be leading tonight. She was the hedge witch, after all, the one most likely to be able to commune with those long dead and lost to time. It helped, also, that she had seen the three women in her dreams. It meant they were already connected and reaching them beyond the veil wouldn't be difficult.

While Owen had watched over her sleep, taking care that she wasn't finding anything but rest, three witches with fire for hair had come to Laurel. They hadn't said a word, only beckoned her with their hands. In hindsight, it was creepy, but Laurel *was* a witch. She wouldn't let a few aflame dead witches scare her. She took it as a sign to call those witches from whatever rest they currently found and find answers.

"The Bay Witches of Star Island call upon our bloodline," Laurel began, each sister lighting the candles in front of them. "We seek the three sisters: Mary, Eliza, Alice. We seek answers to questions only you can answer. We seek justice for your deaths. Come, join in our circle. Join your descendants in magic. Join in the power of the Bay line."

The five sisters lit their bundles of bay with the candle in front of them. As soon as each bundle began to smoke, they quickly passed the smoldering herbs in a circle in the way of the sun, starting slow, then moving their hands so quickly, the entire circle filled with the pungent smoke of the bay leaves. The smoke gathering in the center of their circle crackled and sparked with lightning, the air no longer empty but building and swirling with the power each sister contributed.

The smoke dissipated, and the bay bundles fell to the ground.

They were no longer the only witches in the room.

Three ghosts, gray shades of women, floated a few inches above the attic floor in the center of the circle.

"Holy shit," Sage breathed.

Not unlike Laurel's dream, the three women had fire for hair, dancing flames licking their shoulders in constant movement. They wore black dresses, singed in places, and no shoes. The tips of their fingers and toes were burned black, ash slowly falling from them.

"The Hedge Witch," one of the sisters said, staring at Laurel. "You called us forth for questioning and vengeance."

"We would like vengeance," another sister cut in.

"We'll get to vengeance," Laurel answered. "We need to know about the curse. And who is who? Which one of you is Mary?"

"I am Mary," one said.

"I am Alice," said the other, "And that is Eliza."

The third sister didn't speak, only nodded her head in Laurel's direction.

"Who were Katherine and Jonas? The Fortworths? What exactly does the curse entail?" Laurel's questions spilled forth.

Eliza Bay flinched at the question, her eyebrows twitching and her mouth becoming a hard line.

"Katherine Fortworth was a powerful witch. She was one of few in our time who was strong enough to practice openly without fear of burning. Their family was far too important." Mary glanced at Eliza. "Her brother was a second-rate warlock, but a master of manipulation. He used her power to his own ends."

"He was a cruel person and did not believe any should challenge him. He wanted to marry Eliza. He knew that he needed magical children to control. Katherine wouldn't live under his thumb forever. Our family was an established bloodline and the merging of our two lines was sure to produce an even stronger group of witches."

"She refused," Alice cut in. "She couldn't marry a monster. It didn't matter to him that she hated him, he wanted her, and he wouldn't stand for a refusal."

"He convinced Katherine to curse us. If blood from the entire magical Bay line is collected by a witch or warlock, that person will accumulate all the power of the Bay line. He threatened Eliza with this: if she didn't marry him, he would kill every one of her relatives, end our line, and take the power for his own."

"She still refused. So, he cut out her tongue and slit her throat. Then, he waited for us and our mother to return, slit our throats, took our blood, and burned our house down."

"But you had relatives in the colonies. He couldn't finish his work," Laurel said.

"Correct," Mary answered. "He did come here but died before he found them. The curse hangs over our line, though, and with so many generations of few children, you are the only magical Bay witches left. And you live on the same small island. You are an easy target."

"We found out about this curse like two minutes ago," Verbena said under her breath. "Sorry we didn't have time to spread out and get knocked up."

"Can we reverse the curse?" Lavender interrupted, ignoring her sister's snark.

"I do not know. I was not a powerful witch, none of us were. We collected herbs in secret and whispered spells after nightfall. We knew nothing of curses."

"Does Jonas cutting out her tongue keep her from speaking?" Rosemary asked, nodding at Eliza.

"She can speak, but the living cannot understand her." Mary's eyes flashed. "Now, as to our vengeance."

"I don't know how much we can do for you. The Fortworth line died out over fifty years ago."

"I care little for punishing the descendants of that terrible man," Mary continued. "His bones are in Baltimore." She whipped her gaze to the bookcase, where a book fell off the shelf and flipped open. "In that field. Bind him to that place so his soul may never reincarnate. Keep him stuck in the cold ground with nothing but his own mind to drive himself insane."

Laurel didn't answer. That was a terrible fate for anyone to endure, and she wasn't sure she could promise to follow through with something so dark.

"I'll do it," Sage said.

"Sage!" Laurel hissed. "It's a horrid spell."

"He murdered at least four women because one of them wouldn't bear him children. Fuck him," Sage retorted, crossing her arms. She turned back to the ghosts. "I'll take care of it."

"Thank you, Bay Witch." All three women turned to Laurel. "Look into your past for the rest of the answers you need. We don't have them."

With that ominous line, they disappeared.

Lavender quickly stood and collected the still smoldering bay bundles, , and dunked them into the water they had waiting. Then she unlatched the window and let the smoke clear from the room.

"Put out your candles," she said. "I'll be back with tea for all of us. And I'll give it a kick. Goddess knows we all need it tonight."

"Basically, there's an unbreakable curse on our family and we all should have been popping out babies and living in different corners of the world for at least the last decade." Rosemary added a little more whiskey to her tea. "Fantastic."

"We don't know that it's unbreakable," Laurel pointed out. "Mary admitted they were barely practicing witches. We are strong witches. And there are five of us. We could figure out how to break it."

"Maybe the answer is in the past," Lavender said quietly, swirling her tea around her cup.

"Excuse me?" Laurel's eyes went wide. Her oldest sister had never said anything positive about the past.

"What? They said to look into the past. Maybe that's where we'll find the answer."

"Whose past, mine?" Laurel asked. "Or one of yours?"

"Let's start with yours," Lavender said. "You've been wanting to see it, might as well look there first." She paused and inhaled sharply. "It won't be good. Witches don't have happy pasts. Even now, look at the witches in our family. Mom died in a car crash before seeing her daughters grown. Grandma outlived her husband by nearly twenty years after watching him waste away from cancer. Great Aunt June lived alone, and no one found her body for a month. Witches don't have happy endings."

The five of them sat in silence letting Lavender's assessment wash over them. It was a pessimistic outlook, but well supported by their family's past. Maybe they weren't going to get happy endings. Maybe Laurel and Owen would only have a few years of happiness before being met with unmeasurable sadness. Or worse, maybe they'd only have a few weeks. The thought made her heart hurt and her soul lurch. If they were only going to have limited time together, she wanted to spend as much of it together as possible. She wanted to know Owen, really be with him. Hell, she wanted to sleep with him. Intimacy was something foreign to her, be it physical or emotional. Her heart had been closed off for twenty-nine years waiting.

Sure, she had just met him, but he was made for her and when he had promised to protect her and adore her, she believed him. If their time was destined to be limited, she wanted to make the most of it.

"We'll break it," Rosemary spoke up, nearly slamming her teacup on the table and shaking Laurel out of her thoughts. "The five of us will break the curse. I refuse to believe happily ever after isn't in the cards for all of us. And you know what? Mom had a great life. She died young, yes, but I doubt she would have traded the five of us for a non-magical life. And Grandma and June? Every person sees sadness if they live long enough. Such is life. Not everyone is going to die holding the hand of their soulmate surrounded by their children at age one hundred. Keep some perspective." She turned her gaze to Lavender. "Quit it with the gloomy outlook. We've got a terrible curse over our heads and an evil witch on her way to...drink our blood or at least bleed us out. Either way, I assume we've got a fight on the horizon. We don't need to be wallowing in self-pity or resigning ourselves to terrible ends. Buck up, Lav. You're a fucking Bay witch." With that, Rosemary pushed her chair away from the table and stood. "Laurel, you've got a past to visit. Let's get that spell ready."

Chapter Seventeen

"We can do the thyme one if you really want to," Rosemary began, eyeing her gorgeous thyme bushes in the yard the next morning, "but it will definitely set us back in terms of teas, tinctures, and cough syrups."

"I don't think the blood magic one is a good idea," Laurel said, "and I did get the spell from that other witch, but it's extremely complicated. I don't know if we'd be able to handle it." Paige, a crystal witch and new age shop owner in Mountain View, California, had sent along a ten-page spell in both Latin and Gaelic that Laurel had no idea how to even begin to do. It was like asking a regular third grader to try her hand at calculus. It'd take about ten years of work to get there.

Rosemary ran her hands over the full thyme bushes wistfully and crouched down to smell them. "It'll be worth it."

"Stop mooning over your plants," Lavender's voice broke through. "We can do the spell I know." Lavender turned around without another word, the screen door slamming behind her.

Laurel turned to Rosemary. "Do you know what on earth happened when she looked into her past life?"

Rosemary shook her head and gave her thyme bushes a loving pat. "No. But I know she looked right before Mom and Dad died, when she was at school. Who knows, maybe Mom warned her away from it, but she did it anyways and feels guilty?"

"She told me she bled to death in her past life."

"Well, shit." Rosemary blew her breath out. "Here's hoping you slipped away at the ripe old age of ninety. In medieval France." Rosemary couldn't contain a smile. "Yeah, that's not likely."

Laurel left Rosemary to tend to her herbs and went to find Lavender. It wasn't as if Lavender had ever been forthcoming about the past life spell, which Laurel had asked for more than once, but she had been the sister to insist Laurel be the first to look to the past for answers.

She found her in the kitchen surrounded by baking supplies. There were three types of flour, white and brown sugars, a mountain of dried herbs, milk, oil, and three lemons.

"Lavender, what are you doing?" Laurel asked slowly. She expected her to be poring over spell books in the attic.

Lavender blew a few stray pieces of hair out of her face and paused. "I'm preparing the past life spell."

Laurel knitted her eyebrows together and looked around the kitchen. "By making muffins?"

"It's a bread and yes. You and Owen will each have a slice, and you'll faint and spend the better part of a day reliving your most important past life and then wake up very hungry and with a slight hangover and hopefully some knowledge as to either how to break this curse or why Morana Stoch is stalking your subconscious."

"Most important past life?"

"We each have more than one past life. I don't know how many. But a lot of them are regular lives, where nothing of note takes place. This will send you to one where stuff actually happened." Lavender leveled off the whole wheat flour.

"Your past life spell is a bread?" Laurel peered over the ingredients more closely. "Are you in a kitchen witch group online? Or did you know one before we moved?"

"No." Lavender measured out the sugars by eyeing them. "I made it up."

"You made this spell up? How?"

"I did it in college. It took probably six months to come up with. Honestly, there were some bumps when I did it, but I've tweaked it. A few other witches have used it with success. But there is, of course, the catch."

"What's the catch?"

"Your soulmate. Even if Owen didn't have a slice of bread with you, he'd still faint and be incoherent for a while and wake up with the knowledge of his past life. So I don't recommend using it to anyone whose soulmate isn't on board. Or to anyone who hasn't met their soulmate. That could be potentially damaging and dangerous. Imagine being thrust into another world abruptly without any warning." Lavender's face hardened, and she turned back to her ingredients.

"You are literally describing my first trip to the Hedge World. And it was sort of awful. But at least I knew I was a witch." She paused. "So, this is going to involve Owen?"

"Didn't it already? I mean, thank every goddess you met him because the four of us were getting tired of pronouncing 'Onfroi' correctly. You couldn't have been banging a guy named François?"

"I was not banging Onfroi—"

"Oh, yes you were." Lavender laughed and added a splash of vanilla. She picked up a lemon and cut it in half.

"We were probably sleeping together, but it was way more than that! He wasn't some one-night stand and honestly," she scrunched up her nose, "I've never had a memory of us actually sleeping together."

"Trust me, you were. We Bay Witches put out when it comes to soulmates. Even in the worst of circumstances."

Laurel left Lavender to finish the bread. She said it would take about six hours for it to finish and that Laurel should probably broach the subject with Owen. The recipe made a whole loaf, and Lavender was planning on freezing the rest. There was no reason to waste it, and if Laurel's venture proved unsuccessful, a few of the other sisters might be jumping into the past as well, once they could notify their soulmates.

She fished her cell phone out from her purse and opened her messages.

Laurel: Can I come over?

Owen: Of course. Are you ok? Are the ghosts back?

Laurel laughed. She had texted Owen after the other Bay sisters had dispersed to let him know the spell had been a success.

> Laurel: The only Bay Witches in the cottage right now are me and my sisters. I need to talk to you about something, and I'd like to do it face to face.

> Owen: Ok. I can come there if that's better for you.

Laurel bit her lip. If he came here, Lavender was home and Sage was in the fields. Rosemary would be leaving soon for work, but there would still be two other people here. If she went to his house, they'd be alone. Truly alone. In a house. And she assumed that house had a door that locked and a bed. And, obviously, Owen was there, in all his enticing glory.

> Laurel: No, I want to come to you. Text me your address. I'll be there soon.

Laurel changed out of the black t-shirt and yoga pants she had been wearing. Sure, she and Owen were in it for the long run, and he would eventually see her in everything—maybe even colors! Perish the thought—but for now, she wanted to look nice, witchy, and maybe even a little sexy.

She settled on a black tank with lace around the plunging neckline and a black knee length gauzy skirt and added her silver owl necklace. She slipped on a pair of black wedges, left her hair down and wild, and hopped on her bike.

"You look absolutely beautiful."

Laurel's eyes widened. That was a greeting. Owen stood framed by the doorway, his forearms resting on each side of the threshold.

"Hi. Thank you. You look," she began. Laurel let her eyes sweep over his form in its entirety. He had on a gray t-shirt that stretched taut across his chest and arms, once again giving her clues as to how delightfully his body had been formed. He had on jeans, no shoes or socks. His short hair somehow managed to be tousled, and she thought if he left it to grow, it would probably be a mop of curls.

"You look like you could throw me over your shoulder and carry me for ten miles," Laurel said before she could think better of it.

Owen's face broke into a silly grin. His hands fell from the doorway, and he reached for her hand. "Come in. You want some coffee?"

"I'm a tea drinker."

"Of course," he shook his head. "I should know that. My mom only drinks tea."

"Oh no, Lavender drinks coffee in addition to tea. And Verbena drinks Coke like they're going to stop making it. I'm not into the taste of coffee though. Unless it's basically a milkshake with all the add-ons."

"I'll keep that in mind. Next time I run to the market, I'll grab some tea. What's your favorite kind?"

"Earl Grey in the morning, chamomile at night. You don't have to buy any; Lavender and Rosemary make tons of teas. I can bring some over next time I'm here." Her heart did a little flip in her chest at the thought of coming back. And having a cup of nighttime tea. Followed by a cup of morning tea. The fluttering sensation traveled lower when she thought of what might happen in between those evening and morning cups of tea.

"Do you want anything else to drink? I can only offer water, milk, and orange juice." He wandered into the kitchen area.

"I'm ok, thank you."

"Do you want something to eat?"

"I already ate." Laurel couldn't keep a big smile from escaping. "You don't have to give me anything."

"Sorry." He shook his head a little. "I'm still thinking about when we were Onfroi and Amée. You looked starving. You were starving. I can't help wanting to feed you now. I don't think I did a good job of keeping you well fed in that life."

"It was the Middle Ages; most people weren't going to bed full. You were pretty undernourished yourself."

"I'm glad we're both healthy this time around." He took a breath. "You want to sit down?"

"Yes. I need to talk to you about something." She followed him to the couch. She started to glance at the chair beside the couch, but he pulled her down to sit beside him, her knees touching his.

"You said you were ok, but are you really?"

"I am," she reassured. "I need to look into my past, that's what the ghosts told us. I don't know what answers I'll find there, but there's something in that life, when we were Onfroi and Amée, that'll help."

"Is it dangerous?"

"No, not at all. It's basically like watching a movie. Except you feel things. Lavender has done it." She scrunched up her nose. She couldn't let him go into this blindly. "The only downside is whoever does this spell sort of relives their entire life, including their death."

"What does that mean?"

"According to Lavender, I'll know what it feels like to die in the manner that I died."

"That sounds awful."

"There's more. The spell Lavender used, and the one I'm planning on using, it's for both of us. Since we're connected, as soulmates we'll both experience our old lives again. I can't do it by myself. Or rather, I probably could, but the spells that I would need to do instead are either super hard, involve pledging myself and my children to Hecate, or burning my sister's entire supply of thyme. She wasn't happy with that idea."

"Please don't pledge our children to the servitude of Hecate," Owen said quickly. "We can do the spell together. That makes the most sense, and I don't want you to have to go through that alone. And I'm kind of curious. I've only seen pieces of our past life together. It'd be nice to see all of it laid out."

"Did you say our children?" Laurel asked quietly.

"I guess I did," he said, scratching the nape of his neck and grinning sheepishly. "You're my soulmate. Oh. Do you not want kids?"

"No, I want kids. Honestly, I've always wanted a mountain of kids."

"A mountain?"

"Well, at least a hefty handful. I'm twenty-nine so more than five is probably out of the question biologically."

"Five kids, huh?" Owen was still smiling.

"Sorry, we've known each other for a few days, and I'm already talking about kids. And way more than most people want. Why don't we start with two or three and then we can discuss further babies? Who knows if I'll even like being a mom? Or childbirth. I'll probably hate that," Laurel blurted out. "Sorry. I'll stop. We can talk about it later. And come up with a compromise."

"You don't have to stop. The idea of having kids with you doesn't scare me. It makes me, I don't know, excited? I've been looking for you for years. Having a lot of kids sounds nice. But I like the idea of starting with a couple and seeing how it goes."

Laurel's heart felt full and achy in the most delightful way. She timidly tucked her hand in his. The meeting of their skin, even in such a small way, felt like exhaling a breath held too long. She glanced up at his face.

"The spell won't be ready for a few hours. We have some time to pass."

"Mhm," he hummed, circling his thumb over her wrist methodically. "Do you want to go for a walk?" His hand traveled further up her arm, stroking the soft skin of her inner arm. "Or we could go out to eat?" He moved closer to her.

"I want to climb on your lap and kiss you."

"Please do that," he said quickly, his hands coming to her waist and lifting her to straddle him.

She pressed her mouth against his, immediately insistent. She had thought kissing him might quell the fire building within her, but it only fed the flames. She wanted to devour him and be devoured in return. She needed more beyond physical touch. Laurel wanted to crawl inside his soul and know every inch of him.

She stopped, overwhelmed by her own feelings, pulled back and looked at him.

"Are you alright?" he asked, releasing her waist, and instead moving his hands to hold her cheeks.

"I was thinking about this, us, how insane it really is. How can I feel so attracted to you? Like I need you so much? I don't know how to navigate this." She ran her hand through his hair and pressed her forehead against his.

"I don't either. We'll figure it out together." He shifted her off his lap to sit next to him, but kept his hands on her, one on her thigh the other over her belly. "We don't have to rush the physical. I don't want you to feel like we need to jump into bed immediately. We've only known each other for a week."

She couldn't stifle a giggle and put her forehead against his shoulder.

"It's not that. Not that at all. I seriously cannot believe how attracted I am to you."

"You're attracted to me?"

"Of course, I'm attracted to you, look at you! You're like the perfect man. You make me feel..." she trailed off.

"I make you feel what?" he prompted.

She took a deep breath. "I don't have a lot of experience with men. I've never felt attracted to someone the way I'm attracted to you. Also, I've never had sex. With a person." She added the last part quickly, then squeezed her eyes shut.

Laurel didn't know how Owen would react. If media told her anything, Owen would either be thrilled she'd saved herself or bummed she wasn't experienced. There wasn't a lot of middle ground on that.

"I didn't tell you that to pressure you into, I don't know, making my first time mind-blowing," she continued. "I wanted to tell you so you'd be prepared for me to be, well, not amazing in bed the first time." Laurel risked a glance at Owen. He had a single eyebrow raised and his mouth pressed into a firm line.

"Laurel." He took her hands in his and quickly kissed both of them. "I... ah." He closed his eyes for a moment before popping them open. "I don't have a lot of experience with women. I'm not a virgin," he added, "but I haven't had sex in close to a decade. It didn't feel right to me to lead women on who I knew weren't my soulmate. And one-offs aren't really my style. So, as a guy, I'm as good as a virgin." He kissed her quickly. "We'll figure it out together."

That night, Laurel and Owen rode back to the Bay cottage together, not knowing what exactly lay in front of them. But they knew no matter what, they would be together through it.

Chapter Eighteen

"We just eat the bread?" Laurel asked, eyeing her plate suspiciously. Lavender had covered a portion of the attic in pillows where she and Owen sat, slices of past life bread in hand. "Yup. Eat the bread. You'll pass out in a few minutes. I recommend laying down as soon as you finish chewing." Lavender sighed. "It's like falling asleep. I'll come back and check on you periodically," she added and walked downstairs.

Laurel and Owen exchanged a glance. This was big. Once they both took that first bite, there was no going back. They were in this together—good or bad.

They each took a bite, then hurried to finish their slices, and laid down on the pile of pillows Lavender had prepared.

"I'm scared," Laurel whispered and rolled towards Owen.

"Me too." He snuck his arm beneath her and pulled her to his chest. He wrapped her hand under his and laid it over his heart. "We'll be ok. It'll be ok. We'll be back before we know it." He kissed her forehead quickly and held her tightly. Whatever happened, they were together.

The world is dark and harsh. Winters last forever and summers are for toiling beneath the sun, pulling any sustenance from the earth that can be gained. It is terrible and grueling, and it is life.

Amée had been alone for years already, though she was only seventeen. Her mother died four years earlier, and with no family, she simply continued her life. She planted her vegetables, relied on the charity of neighbors in the winter to survive, and found work helping tend to animals. It was a solitary existence.

But now, at seventeen, Amée used her other skills. She worked herbs into tinctures, whispered spells beneath full moons, and delivered children into the world. Her healing powers were great, and townsfolk came to her with hope and fear when they were sick or laboring or nursing a broken heart. And Amée gave them what she could.

Onfroi did not remember his mother. She lived until he was a toddler, but any memory of her had long since faded. It was only him and his father now. His younger sister joined the church two years ago as a postulate and was raised to novice a few months earlier. He did not see her any longer. Onfroi thought a calling from God was a curious and confusing thing, but at least now Helene wouldn't starve to death or die in childbed.

His father was a carpenter, just as his grandfather had been, as well as a long line of fathers before that. Onfroi was apprenticed to his father as soon as he could hold a hammer and was glad for it. Carpenters were skilled and paid well when the work could be found. They could afford chickens that provided eggs and meat when the foxes didn't get to them and managed to keep hunger away most days.

The days were long, and life was full of hardship, but it was the only way they have ever lived.

"Mon Père, please let me send for someone. Helene, at the very least," Onfroi begged at his father's side. The man had been coughing for nearly a week, sometimes with blood staining his spittle. It was late spring, no one else in the village was sick, and Onfroi was overwhelmed with worry.

"Do not bother Helene. I doubt the Abbess would allow her a visit.

Fetch that young white witch, tell her we can give her eggs as payment. She's so skinny she would probably come for a crumble of cheese." His father tried to laugh but only hacked into his bedsheets.

Onfroi raced through the village to the place where the forest met the edge of town. The witch lived there, not quite part of the village, but not truly removed, her hovel surrounded by trees and wild herbs. Onfroi had never spoken to the girl before, but he had seen her at the market once or twice. She looked wild, nearly feral, to him. Her hair hung in knots, her face was always dirty, and many people crossed themselves when she passed. Onfroi did not know if the devil resided in her, but his father had asked for her, so he would bring her.

"Witch! Are you there?" he called, carefully stepping over the greenery in front of her home. He wasn't certain what most of the things growing there were, but he had no doubt she would curse him for trampling some important herb.

"Amée!" a voice shouted from behind the hovel. "My name is Amée, not witch. What do you want?" She stepped into his sight, hands on her hips. Her arms were dirty up to the elbows, as if she'd been rooting around in the earth like an animal, and her hair was tied away from her face in a scarf. For the first time, Onfroi noticed she was young, and maybe even a little pretty. Her cheekbones were high, her eyes bright beneath her accusing brows, and though she was thin, there was no question she was a woman.

Onfroi shook his head clear, remembering why he was there. "My father is ill and asked for you. Would you come? Amée?"

She nodded in agreement immediately, not bothering to argue with him over whether or not he deserved her attendance.

"Let me get my bag." She wiped her hands on her dress and scurried inside. "What ails him?" she called out.

"A terrible cough. Sometimes blood."

She pushed back outside, her head nodding, knife in hand. Onfroi took a few steps back, unsure what she planned to do. She rummaged through the plants between them before cutting bunches of several and adding them to her bag.

"Do you have ale?"

"We do."

"And a fire going?"

"Of course," he answered.

"What's your name?"

"Onfroi."

"Show me the way to your father, Onfroi."

The man was dying. Amée could tell as soon as she walked into the house. Death hung over that home like a cloak pulled tight in winter. She could ease his symptoms, but the grave already had its claws in his soul.

She rummaged through her bag, finding the thyme cuttings. They would do little this far along, but she could not face his son, the boy with his eyes on her at that very moment, without trying to help. She found that even when there was truly nothing she could do, she had to do something, if only for the loved ones.

"This will relieve the worst of it, make it easier for him these next few hours," she mumbled. The man was sleeping fitfully, unaware of the world around him. "But it will not save him. He will die soon. I am sorry." Amée watched as the young man's eyes closed. His breath released in a large puff that sounded like defeat.

"Is there anyone you would like me to fetch? Someone to sit with you while you wait, someone who will want to say goodbye?"

"I only have my sister, but she is a novice. They won't let her leave."

"I will get her for you." Amée quickly added the thyme to a cup of ale. "When he stirs, bid him to drink this. I don't have any honey, but if you know anyone who might, that would be helpful as well."

"The nuns keep bees."

"I will ask them."

"Are you sure the nuns will receive you?" he asked quickly, his eyes falling over her suspiciously.

"Because the townspeople call me witch? The nuns have no hate for me. We are on different paths to the same destination. We serve the people for the glory of God."

. . .

Amée walked the path to the abbey, a path she had nearly taken herself four years earlier. When her mother died, she wondered if joining the nuns was her only option left. But she knew her heart. She knew that her body would never be content to sit inside stone walls covered with layers of heavy fabric, sequestered away from the suffering and toil of mankind. She needed the earth and the bounty it brought. She needed to help people in a tangible way, not simply pray their troubles away.

She lifted her hand and knocked, then took a moment to tuck errant hairs back beneath her scarf. Soon it would be warm enough to bathe in the river and untangle some of the knots, but for now, she pushed the snarls away.

"Amée?"

She lifted her eyes and smiled. Sister Marie was exactly who she was hoping to find.

"Good morning, Sister Marie. I trust you are well?"

"Every day in the eyes of our Lord. What brings you to the Abbey?"

"A man is dying. He would like to see his daughter one last time. And her brother could use the support of a sister at the deathbed. Sister Helene."

A shadow crossed Sister Marie's face. "She is in prayer. She will be until sunrise two days from now."

"She will be in prayer for the next two days?"

"Yes."

"Can she end her prayers early? Her father may die before then."

"No. She's not to be disturbed. If she is meant to see her father before he dies, God will see to it." Sister Marie nodded simply, smiling in the way the religious did when they put all trust in the divine.

Amée fought the urge to yell at the woman. She took a deep breath and reminded herself that this was the exact reason she did not join the Abbey. She had faith in God, of course, but perhaps God had sent Amée to fetch Helene and interrupt her prayers? But the nuns never saw it that way.

"Please send her home as soon as you are able. And prepare her that she may be returning to a visitation and not a farewell." She inhaled sharply. "May I have some honey for the patient?"

Sister Marie hesitated. "The bees have not been producing much yet and as you said, he's unlikely to survive this illness. I would prefer to save it for a child..."

Amée put her hand up to stop her and turned on her heels. She would get no help from the nuns today.

Amée came back with words of disgust for the church and without Helene or honey. Onfroi's father had taken some of the brew she made but then had fallen back into a fitful sleep.

"I will stay with you until your sister comes," she said. She didn't look at him but set to tidying the house. They didn't live in squalor, but the last week had been difficult. There was washing to be done and bones and eggshells that needed to be cleaned out. Onfroi wanted to tell her not to bother, that he would do it later, but he couldn't find the words. He felt that if he spoke, he might cry. He didn't want her to think he was weak. So, he let her busy herself in his house, ducking in and out to fetch water or hang cleaned clothes.

"Why don't I see you?" Onfroi asked late into the night. She had finally stopped tinkering around and sat beside him, fiddling with an herb. The fire had dimmed, and he pushed the remnants around, milking every last spark they could muster.

"No one sees me unless they need me." She was painstakingly pulling leaves off stems and arranging them into a pile. "I have little need for the markets and less to trade, I don't like to barter my services, and I make several people nervous, so I stay away."

"You don't make me nervous," he answered but was met with a barking laugh. "What? You don't!"

"I might not now, but this morning, or rather yesterday morning, you came to my home and called me a witch. In my experience, those that call me witch fear me, whereas those that call me healer revere me."

"I'm sorry. I'll only ever call you healer again."

"I would prefer you simply call me Amée. I do not need a special title."

"Amée. You must have been well-loved by your parents to be named as such."

"Ah yes. My parents were married for many years before I came, and I was a well-loved and much prayed for gift from God."

Onfroi leaned away from the fire and looked at her. She was beautiful, he decided. Her beauty was untamed and raw, like the beauty of a field on fire or the flooding river or a fierce snowstorm. It was powerful and terrible and real. She was frightening, but so enticing. He couldn't stop staring at her.

"I thought about joining the church," she continued, "when my mother died. I even spoke to Sister Marie of my intention. But she and I both knew I was never meant to be cloistered behind stone walls. I need the forest and the open sky to feel alive. So, I do my work here, and they do theirs in there."

"And you are free to marry," he interjected. He closed his eyes in embarrassment.

"I suppose I am free to marry, though I do not know if I would be a good wife."

"Why not?"

"I like my independence. I like helping people. Look at us now. If I had a husband, he wouldn't want me staying the night with a handsome young man. He'd probably call me a whore and kick me out of the house."

Onfroi thought on it. There was truth in the statement. If she was his wife, he would not want her spending the night with another man, grieving or not.

"Handsome?" he repeated, a grin on his mouth.

"I see no reason to lie. You must know you are handsome. You will make some woman a good husband one day with your strong hands and fine face." She set her work down and looked at him. The flames flickered over her face and Onfroi swore he saw her eyes sparkle.

"And you will make half the village mad with your marriage refusals."

She clapped her hand over her mouth to muffle her laughter. He liked the sound of her laugh. He wished she wouldn't try to smother it. He liked the way her shoulders shook and her nose wrinkled up. She was good company. In the worst time of his life, he was glad she was there.

In the end, Helene did return in time, and Amée left the siblings with the father. She made plans to return the next morning. By then, he would have passed, and Amée could bring them some comfort before the burial.

She was relieved Helene came in time. Amée knew what it was to lose an important parent, and she knew what it was to sit alone throughout the entire affair. She'd never forget when Michel, the blacksmith, had happened upon her digging a grave. She hadn't known what to do when her mother died, but she knew enough to bury her. It had been back-breaking work for a young girl. Michel had sent her inside, finished the grave, then sent his wife with food and company. They both died a year ago.

When Amée returned home, she found Flavie waiting for her. She didn't care much for the woman, three years her senior and already widowed once. She was wealthy, never had to work for her food or her life. Her father was youngest brother to some lord, and they lived in a big house in the center of town. Amée didn't care much for the nobility, but they didn't affect her life in any way. She was too poor for them to tax and no use as a soldier due to her sex. She had the added benefit of being somewhat frightening to both men and women so none of the Lord's men hassled her.

"I've been here for nearly an hour," Flavie said immediately, her arms crossed.

Amée regarded the woman with suspicion.

"What do you need, Flavie?" Amée had no patience for her today.

"I'll take a bundle of sage, rosemary, and a few roses." She glanced down at her nails. Amée put her hands on her hips.

"Flavie, why don't you grow these things yourself? I can't be keeping you and I stocked in herbs. And get roses from your own garden. I'm certain you've got a mountain more than I do."

"My father doesn't like me spending too much time in the garden. And I'm currently being courted. I must stay as clean as possible," she added, looking down her nose at Amée.

"I'll give you a bundle of sage. It's too early for rosemary, mine is just beginning to take root. And my roses are mine. Use your own." She unceremoniously slashed a bundle with her knife and thrust it in her direction. "Take it and leave, Flavie. There's work to be done."

"Tsk, tsk," Flavie clucked her tongue as she took the bundle. "It will do you well to remember who should respect whom."

Amée pushed past her into her hovel and collapsed to the ground. She had enough to do without Flavie coming to take her supplies. She hadn't slept in two nights and needed rest. But first, she would eat one of the three eggs Onfroi had gifted her and be glad of a full stomach.

Spring and summer passed in a blur of grief and recovery and suddenly, autumn was upon them. Onfroi had work, good steady work. The church had decided to expand. It would not be anything as grand as a cathedral, which Onfroi had never seen but had heard stories of, but it would be twice the size it was now. The final product would use stone, not wood, but Onfroi was commissioned to lay the framework. He was one of three carpenters, and the work would take them at least a year.

He had not talked to Helene since their father's passing. She was present for the burial, and he occasionally caught a glimpse of her in church on Sundays, but they never spoke, and she never visited. On the other hand, he had seen Amée every week. On Saturday evenings, after he finished his work for the day, he would bring her something. Usually eggs, but he once brought her a chicken and sometimes a loaf of bread he'd gotten from the market. He'd even gifted her a few wild roses he found in the woods. They would sit outside in her garden while she harvested herbs or berries or vegetables. Onfroi had never tasted berries as sweet as those found in her garden. They were ripe and so purple they were nearly black.

On this particular Saturday, Onfroi had come a few hours earlier. They'd finished their work for the day, and it looked like rain. He came to Amée's home with a slight hope that he would be stuck in a storm there.

She wasn't in her garden or her home, so he set off into the forest. Within a few steps, he could hear her singing.

She sat beside the river, her feet dangling in, singing a song about a warrior come home from battle and the woman he'd left behind. Onfroi stopped for a moment, content to simply look at her and listen.

She stopped singing and quickly turned to see him. The look of apprehension melted away from her face and was replaced with a smile.

"I thought I heard someone." She motioned for him to join her. "Not too many days left warm enough for this." She pointed to her submerged feet.

"Are you injured?" he asked, noticing the remains of blood and grime on her hands. He fell to his knees beside her.

"No, but you are." She reached for his hand, finding a splinter wedged into his palm. She bent her face to inspect it, then pinched the wood out and tossed it into the water.

Onfroi's heart swelled. He couldn't help himself any longer and quickly kissed her mouth.

"Amée," Onfroi began, his forehead pressed to hers and his heart thudding against his chest, "will you come to me tonight? To my house? To my bed?"

She said nothing but smiled and turned her face back to the river.

"I must go check on Cateline. Her baby will arrive soon."

Onfroi nodded and stood. He wouldn't press it with her. She had told him she never wanted to marry. Perhaps she felt nothing for him. Perhaps he was the only one consumed with desire.

Amée decided to go. She wanted Onfroi all the time. Her body hurt with wanting him. Her sleep was interrupted with wanting him.

She waited until nightfall, unsure if he wanted anyone to know she would be spending the night with him. Or if she should allow the village to know her as a woman who spent the night with a man. She didn't hold fast to the idea of her virginity, but she also was in no hurry to be labeled a whore.

With her hood held tight, she knocked quietly.

Onfroi answered, his face a picture of hope. She stepped through the threshold quickly, stripping off her cloak as she did. Her body was on fire.

"You came."

"I had to," she said as she glanced around the house. It looked the same since the last time she had been here, but so much had changed. And now, they were truly alone.

She set her cloak on the table, and immediately brought her hands up to cup her shoulders. She wasn't sure what to do.

"I love you, Amée."

She whipped her head around to look at Onfroi. "You do?"

"Of course. For months now. I would have asked you to marry me last spring if I thought you'd have me."

"I love you," she answered. A few moments earlier, she had no plans of admitting such a thing, but when she gazed at Onfroi, she saw nothing but happiness and joy. He was kind and handsome and looked at her as if she was the most precious thing.

Amée took a step forward and placed her hand on his chest. His hand quickly covered hers, and he moved closer to her so there was no space between them. His other arm wrapped around her waist, firmly grasping her dress.

"I'm going to take my dress off," Amée said slowly, then backed away.

Onfroi didn't respond but stood very still, his gaze burning on her. She took a deep breath, then pulled her dress over her head. She had nothing on beneath it and was suddenly very concerned with her nakedness. She quickly raised her hands to her head and began to unwrap the scarf that tied her hair back and shook her hair free. It was not lovely or shiny or anything other than hers, but so few had seen her without it tied back, and she wanted Onfroi to know her as none other did.

"Amée," he whispered and reached for her. His hands were moving on her skin. His thumbs found her hips. "You are beautiful." He buried his face against her neck. "I love you, I love you, I love you," he whispered over and over. His hands traveled the length of her body, finding her breasts, her neck, her bottom. They roamed and rubbed and caressed and rolled, bringing jolts of pleasure wherever they went.

"Take your clothes off." Amée tried to pull his tunic over his head, but it got caught on his shoulders. He laughed and took a step away from her, freeing himself of it. "Leggings too," she added.

He complied, and they stood across from each other, neither moving nor saying a thing. Amée could feel her chest rising and falling with her breath. A shiver ran through her, and she wrapped her arms around her waist for warmth.

"Here," he offered his hand. "Come to bed. Get under the bedsheets with me."

She took his hand and climbed into the bed. Their bodies pressed together. Amée shivered again, but this time with anticipation.

Onfroi pushed her hair away from her face and kissed her mouth. The kiss was urgent, pleading, and full of want. Amée returned it with just as much fervor. She was impatient.

She rolled him to his back and climbed over his body, her need pushing any nerves or fear far out of her mind. She straddled him with her hands pressed against his chest.

And then, they were together. It was jarring and stunted and at times they laughed at their inexperience, but it was no less wonderful. Amée felt adored and loved and taken care of in Onfroi's grasp. She was happy within his arms.

Onfroi stirred awake. He could feel Amée moving beside him, and he reached out to pull her to him.

"I need to leave," she whispered, trying to squirm out of his grasp.

"Leave?" He opened his eyes. It was still dark, and the night felt decidedly cold. "No, you'll stay until it is light, and I will walk you back to your home. After I've made love to you again." He flung a leg over hers to keep her pinned beside him.

"Onfroi," she protested but giggled when he nuzzled her neck. "Onfroi," she began again. "No one can see me leave here."

"And why not?"

"Because I'm already a witch. I don't want to be labeled a whore as well."

Onfroi stopped his nuzzling and looked at her.

"I love you and you love me. I'm not paying you."

"Yes, but no one will understand why—"

"Why I would want a beautiful woman in my bed?" He palmed her bottom and tipped her hips towards him. "Other than loving her." He kissed the line of her jaw. "I've changed my mind. We don't need to wait until the morning." He rolled over her, shifted between her legs, and found her mouth with his.

She returned his kiss and sighed. Amée wrapped her arms around his neck.

"I have a question." Onfroi trailed his mouth down her neck. "What happens if I get you with child?"

"What do you mean?"

"You don't want to be married, and I understand that, but if there is a child? What then?"

Amée loosened her grip on him, her mouth pressed into a thin line. "We'll decide what to do if that happens."

Onfroi nodded and laid his head against her belly. "I'm yours if you'll have me."

Winter passed. There were births and deaths and fevers that swept through the town. Amée was thinner than the summer months, but she wasn't starving. She had delivered three healthy babies into the world during the winter and gotten good payment in return: a jar of wine from an exuberant first-time father, some pork from the butcher's wife, and a piece of silver from the blacksmith's daughter, which she immediately used to buy food.

She and Onfroi were together most nights. She still had her hovel, a place to keep her garden and work with herbs. But, in the evening, Onfroi would collect her and bring her to his house.

Amée couldn't believe the comfort of sleeping in a bed with a warm man next to her. Winter was nothing at all when she could climb beside him and snuggle against his chest and be warm in moments. He also did wondrous things like chop any wood they needed, carry the water from the river to the house, and occasionally catch rabbits in the woods when he didn't have work to do. It was wonderful to have a partner.

"You come here later and later," Flavie complained as Amée returned to her hovel.

"What do you need, Flavie? I've got two women that need looking in on." The winter had been cold, and many of the women in the village were expanding. But not Amée. While she and Onfroi enjoyed each other frequently, her monthly bleeding still came at every half-moon. And it was fine. They were happy with each other, content to spend every spare moment with one another.

"I'm to be married on Sunday. I need something for fertility."

"Flavie, you are young still. Come back to me in half a year if you're still not with child," Amée answered. Flavie was a woman Amée knew never went hungry. If she was barren, there'd be little Amée's herbs could do for her.

"Give me something, witch. A bundle to put under the marriage bed perhaps. I need a baby immediately."

Amée let her gaze drift over Flavie's form. True, she was always well-fed, but now Amée noticed her waist was thicker than usual. She looked back up at the woman's face. It was a bit fuller than normal, and her cheeks shone with life and vitality.

"Do you need something for fertility or virility?" she asked with her hands on her hips. If Flavie was already with child and intended to pass it off as her new husband's, she didn't need a fertility spell. She needed a husband who would bed her seven times in the first two days of marriage. "I can make something for your husband to drink, if that's what you need."

"If you tell anyone," she began, her voice low and threatening.

"Come back tomorrow closer to noon. I'll have it ready by then." Amée wasn't stupid, nor was it any of her business. She cared not who Flavie had lain with. She felt no loyalty to the woman's betrothed. If he could not see the signs of a baby, well, it was his own fault.

Flavie nodded her head once, then stomped away.

Amée went about her day. She visited two expectant women and guessed they would probably deliver near the end of summer. She worked in her garden. Now that the wet spring had ended and summer had begun, she could dry some of her herbs. She cut large bundles of thyme, basil, and sage and hung them within her hovel. The lavender and rosemary could wait a little longer.

She collected some carrots, peas, and greens to add to a stew for her and Onfroi tonight. That with a bit of chicken would make for a nice meal this evening.

"Good afternoon, mon petit oiseau," Onfroi called.

"I thought you would be late tonight?" Amée answered. She walked to meet him and quickly kissed his cheek.

"I will. I came to walk you home."

"Onfroi, I am capable of walking myself home," she chided.

"I know, but..." his voice trailed off as his brow furrowed. "The Lord's men have been loitering around the village today. I'd rather see you home myself than wonder if they bothered you."

Amée scoffed. "They are more afraid of me than I am of them, I promise you." She wiped her hands on her apron. "But thank you all the same. Let me fetch the vegetables."

They walked home, hand-in-hand, on the warm summer evening. Amée wished that Onfroi wouldn't be going back to work. She wanted to strip out of her clothes and feel the cool air of night against her skin while he worshipped her.

There were several unfamiliar men walking the streets of the village that night. Onfroi took Amée inside with instructions to bolt the door and a promise to hurry home as soon as he could.

Onfroi didn't like the Lord's men in town. They were rude, rough, and he'd seen a handful of them grab women as they walked by. One even whistled at a nun.

He was busy with his work at the church and didn't like leaving Amée for so long with them about. She was all alone in her hovel, tending to her herbs. When his mind turned to them happening upon her, he didn't like what could happen.

He shook his head out of those thoughts and tried to concentrate on the work in front of him. He was working on a bit of scaffolding for the stonemason to use on the archway he was constructing.

Onfroi saw Helene. She was with a group of sisters, mostly the higher up ones. He wondered if they had come to see the church.

Onfroi quickly descended his ladder and rushed to her side.

"Good morning, brother," she said.

He wanted to embrace her, but he wasn't sure if it was allowed.

"How are you? Are they treating you well?" He didn't know how long they had to talk before she would be whisked away behind stone walls once again.

"Of course! Truly, I am very well. And your work here looks exemplary. I am glad you have a purpose since losing father. You are using your craft to give glory to our Lord." She smiled. "Tell me, how are you?"

"I'm very well. Actually, I am better than that. I am in love. I've found the woman I want to spend the rest of my life with."

"You have! Who?"

"Amée. You remember, she sat with me and Father until you arrived." As soon as he spoke her name, the color drained from Helene's face.

"Onfroi, you can't. She's a heathen."

Onfroi laughed. "A heathen? Hardly. She's a healer and a midwife. Sister Marie loves her."

"She doesn't come to mass."

"She does. Just not every Sunday. I'd like to see you at mass after being awake for three straight days with a sick child."

"Onfroi, I beg you. You are a stalwart young man; any woman would be lucky to have you. Don't settle for a woman who's taken you to bed. Think of how many men have lain with her before you." He started to protest, but she waved her hand at him. "I'm a nun, not an idiot. Think on what I've said."

Onfroi did think on it, and it did nothing but made him angry. He loved Amée; his sister should have understood. He tried to explain away that the nuns probably filled her head with ideas of chastity and the sanctity of the marriage bed, but he didn't care. Helene was his sister. She should understand him.

Onfroi went home that night, happy to smell a meal well on its way to being ready. He walked through the door, ducking beneath the threshold.

He smiled. He would never tire of coming home to find Amée.

Tonight, she dozed at the foot of the bed while a stew cooked over the fire. He ran a finger over the sole of her foot, stirring her awake.

"There's food," she mumbled, smiling.

"Smells amazing." He let his hand wander to her calf and knelt next to the bed. "Did you eat yet, mon petit oiseau?"

She shook her head. "Waiting for you."

He bent his head and kissed her knees, skimming the hem of her skirt a little higher. His fingers trailed a path up her thigh now.

"Are you planning to seduce me before eating?" she laughed.

"Could you be seduced?" His hand was on her bottom now, pulling her towards him. He nudged her legs apart with his chin and kissed her right above her knee.

"I think you've already accomplished it," she laughed, squirming towards him.

Onfroi couldn't believe how lucky he was. Amée was a piece of him. And he would treasure her.

The village was changing. With the near completion of the church, the Lord's men were spending more and more time in town. There were murmurings that the church would bring in money and rumors that there would soon be a relic of Saint Anthony to draw in pilgrims.

Amée did not like the changes. There were more priests now, with judgmental gazes upon her. She gave up going to mass all together, though Onfroi still attended.

Amée had thought she was with child once. Her monthly bleeding didn't come for close to four moons, and she had bled heavily when it finally did come. Whether or not she had lost a baby, she didn't know. There had never been a quickening.

Flavie hadn't stopped hassling Amée. She had given birth, and as far as Amée knew, the husband believed himself the father, but the child had been born sickly and died soon after. She had another child not long after, a girl. Now, Flavie came constantly begging for a myriad of spells.

"I need something to keep my husband's eyes on me and no one else," she snapped.

Amée put her hands on her hips and stood to face Flavie.

"Flavie, you're a witch, do it yourself."

Flavie's lips pressed into a thin line and her eyes went wide. "How dare you speak of me in such a way!" she growled.

"You know it to be true. Do your own spells. I have no interest in calling on such favors for someone else."

Flavie's eyes narrowed at Amée. For a moment, she worried the wealthy woman might hit her. But instead, she reached for her basket, filled it with herbs that Amée had taken the time to cut and dry, and turned to leave.

"You will regret this," she threatened.

Amée sighed and looked over her table. Flavie had taken nearly all her sage and half of the lavender. She grumbled and collected her sack. She would forage in the woods today to try and replenish what had been taken.

The next morning when Amée left their house, for it was hers as much as Onfroi's now, two of the Lord's men followed her to her hovel. She tried to ignore them as best she could, but once they reached the edge of the village, her nerves got the better of her.

"Are you looking for something?" she asked. "Perhaps a salve for those bites?"

"Bites?" he barked back at her.

"Those are flea bites on your face. I could put something together for you—"

"Are you calling me unclean?" he challenged and took three large steps in her direction.

"No," she replied slowly. "I am asking if you want help."

"We don't want help from you," the other cut in, putting a hand on his partner's shoulder. "Witch," he added. They both crossed themselves, then walked back into town.

Amée exhaled. She would like to see them treat her as such and call her witch with a dagger in their bellies. More likely, she'd be burning their wounds shut as they cried for their mothers.

A week later, the Lord's men followed her again, but this time there were four. They also did not stop but surrounded her once she began to tend the garden.

She was afraid, but there was little she could do. They were four, and she was one, and even if she screamed and someone came, no one in town would go against the Lord. He clearly had sanctioned whatever they were about to do.

Amée brushed her hands on her apron and got back on her feet, determined to meet them at eye level.

"Why are you here?" she finally asked after moments of silence.

"We've come to collect the witch," one of them answered.

"Healer. Collect me for what?" She crossed her arms and set her jaw. Her heart was beating rapidly against her breastbone, and she couldn't still it.

"Judgement," a different guard answered. He had his hand on the hilt of his sword and malice in his eyes.

"I'm not a witch, and I've not done anything ill to anyone. I deliver babies and heal sick people. I don't have a malicious bone in my body."

"Don't lie to us, we know about the curse," the first one spat out and grabbed her arm.

"Curse? I've never cast a curse." Amée wasn't stupid. She didn't cast curses. She had no reason to believe she couldn't, but she'd never done one. There was no one in the town she hated enough to risk being accused of witchcraft.

She started to panic. Onfroi was repairing the roof at the Abbey today. It had begun leaking a few days earlier during a terrible storm. She needed him. She needed him to explain that she wasn't evil. She didn't cast curses. She made tonics and salves and delivered babies into the world. She was good.

Another man grabbed her other arm, and they proceeded to drag her into town. Amée knew this wouldn't end well. When she was seven, the people had burned Old Emilée for putting a spell on her neighbor's cow. It wasn't true, Amée knew it wasn't true, but that didn't stop the people from cheering as that poor woman writhed in pain and died screaming.

"Please," she begged. "Fetch Onfroi. You know him, the carpenter. He will tell you I am good, I am not a witch. I am a healer," she babbled.

"The man you've put a spell on? The man you refuse to marry in the house of God?" They laughed. "No one will get him for you."

"Then Margot. I took care of her children when they caught the fever last winter. Or Rosalie, I helped her deliver all five of her children, even when I was only a child myself. Or fetch Yseult, I sat with her while she raved after the death of her husband. Any of them will tell you I am good."

"We're not fetching anyone for you, witch. I'd just as soon fetch the devil for my own soul."

Onfroi wiped his brow. The roof repair was proving more work than he initially prepared for, but now he'd be able to get a little more compensation for his efforts. The nuns had noticed some water coming in during the last storm and wanted it fixed before they were hit with a deluge. He wasn't a thatcher by trade, but he knew enough of the skill to do the work as well.

Onfroi didn't see Helene. As if he were a leper, the higher-ranking nuns shooed all the young ones away from him. Onfroi smiled to himself. It wasn't like he would attempt to woo any of them to break their vows. He was beyond happy with Amée and hadn't looked at another woman with interest in the years he'd known her.

They were happy together. He accepted that they may never have children and was content with it. It would have been dangerous also. Amée was the best midwife in their village. If she delivered a baby, she would have to rely on Old Didiane to help her through the process. The woman was kind, but her grandchildren had children old enough to work in the fields. Onfroi didn't imagine her eyesight, hearing, and strength were the same as Amée's.

He set back to work, weaving the thatches tightly, hoping that he wouldn't be back in another few weeks. They should replace it with slate for a building this large, but the church saved expensive materials for grand churches, not small nunneries.

He heard a rumbling in the center of the village and strained his eyes in that direction. A large group of people were gathering in the market square. He could hear shouts and screams but was too far to discern what they were saying.

Onfroi looked down at the thatch work he had done so far. It was nearly complete. He could take a moment to see what the fuss was before returning to work.

"Please, please!" Amée shouted to the masses of people gathering around her. The faces of her townspeople flashed before her. Margot was there, clutching her youngest daughter, Clothilde, to her breast. Her eyes were full of tears, and she shook her head in disbelief, but made no move to help her.

Amée reached for something to grab onto while the men dragged her, but she was met with shrugs off and pushes.

Where were the people she had saved? The ones she comforted over the loss of loved ones, nursed through fevers and injuries? Where were the mothers she caught babies for, the ones she held through their screams when the babies did not survive? Where were the fathers that celebrated with her when their child was healthy? Had they all abandoned her?

"Amée!" Onfroi yelled over the roar of the crowd.

"Onfroi!" she yelled back, whipping her head from side to side trying to see him. He was pushing his way towards her, his eyes wild.

"Take care of that one," one of her captors spat out, nodding in Onfroi's direction. One of the men behind them disappeared into the crowd towards Onfroi.

"Leave him!" Amée begged. "I'll stop fighting if you leave him! Please!" She went limp to prove her point.

One of the Lord's men grabbed her around her waist and flung her over his shoulder.

"Hold him back," he called over his shoulder.

"Amée, no! Fight back! Get off me!" The crowd became eerily quiet and only Onfroi's voice could be heard.

From her position, Amée could see the guard who held her begin to ascend wooden stairs, and her stomach dropped. He set her on her feet and quickly backed her against a pole, tying her hands behind it.

"No, no, no," Amée whimpered. Her feet crunched on the kindling beneath her.

"If you fight this, we'll kill him," the guard muttered, securing her hands tightly.

Amée looked over the crowd and found Onfroi in the middle of it. He was still struggling against the three men that held him.

"Amée, witch of the woods, you have been accused of witchcraft and will be burned to death. Your dealings with magic bring evil upon our village and the good people of our Lord who dwell here." It was a man she didn't know, but his clothing was clean and expensive looking. He must have worked for the Lord.

"Who accuses me of witchcraft?" she called back, trying to keep her voice calm.

"Lady Flavie. You cursed her first husband to die and threatened to do the same with her current husband."

"Flavie?" Amée spat out. Her eyes burned through the crowd and found the hateful woman near the front. She wore a crisp red dress and white veil over her hair, her face the picture of vengeance.

Amée turned to Onfroi. "Stop fighting, my heart," she commanded. "I love you and pour all my blessings onto you. May we meet again if it pleases our Lord." She took a deep breath. Someone lit the kindling and she only felt heat at first. She quickly turned her gaze to Flavie.

"I curse you, Flavie! With this dying body and soul, I throw all my power at you. You will never bear another child. The one you have will wither and die before the next winter. Your womb will be like a dried apple, your husband impotent," she could feel the first flames licking her dress. It wouldn't be long now. "I curse you to wander this earth, never finding happiness or love or comfort in anything. Food will taste like ashes in your mouth, you will never slake your thirst. Those that give you shelter will have evil befall them. Those that turn you away will be exalted into good fortune. As long as you walk this earth, the curse will hang over you. No one can undo this curse because I cast it as such!" Amée's words turned into screams as the flames reached her legs. The heat was nearly unbearable. She flew her head to the sky. "I serve you! I have always served you! Punish only Flavie!"

"Let me go!" Onfroi shouted, using all his strength to try to get to Amée. He needed to save her; his life was nothing without her. He could hear her speaking, yelling at someone else in the crowd, but he no longer registered what she was saying.

But then he heard her scream, a horrific, painful, pleading scream. Onfroi threw the guards off him and pushed the people in front of him. He had to get to her.

"Get back here," one of the guards shouted, then grabbed his collar and threw him to the ground. In a flurry of movement, six boots were on him, stomping his chest and face. He tried to roll to the side and find a way through them, but he was stopped. Now, there were hands on him. Strong fists pummeled his ears and nose. The blood rushing down his face choked him. His hands attempted to block them, but they were held down.

He couldn't breathe. His throat filled with blood, and he struggled to turn his head to the side to let it pour out but couldn't. He couldn't move. He couldn't break free.

He couldn't save her. His body went limp with the realization. He failed her. He was meant to protect and love her forever. He failed.

She wasn't screaming anymore.

He wasn't fighting anymore. There was nothing left to fight for.

He turned his mind to the first time he really saw her when she sat with him as his father slipped away. The wild witch from the woods. He remembered the way she crinkled her nose when she smiled, the way she hummed when she chopped her herbs. He thought of the first time he held her and then about this morning when he'd kissed her shoulder while she ate. He filled his head with every blessed image he could conjure of Amée. Beautiful, lovely Amée.

He couldn't feel anything. His body was heavy in its broken state. He couldn't think of anything but her.

Mon petit oiseau.

They would be together.

Chapter Nineteen

She was whimpering.

Owen's eyes flew open, his breath coming in heavy spurts.

He sucked in oxygen like he hadn't taken a breath in...eight hundred years. He opened his eyes. They were sticky, like they'd been closed for longer than ever before.

He had to get to her.

"Amée!" he yelled. His voice was raw against his throat.

"I'm here."

Owen whipped his head to the side. She was there, tucked right beside him, where she should be.

Her eyes were closed, tears streaming down her cheeks. She reached her hand towards him, and he enveloped it with his own.

"Amée," he began, his brain still fuzzy in terms of reality. She wasn't Amée anymore. Amée was gone, turned to ashes before his eyes. She was different.

"Laurel," he corrected himself. "Laurel." Laurel Bay, the hedge witch with black hair and stars in her eyes. Still his little bird, though. She would always be his little bird.

Owen grabbed her with both hands and pulled her to him. He pressed his body against hers, his hands scratching at her back. She was here. They were together.

"Onfroi. Owen," she sobbed. "You're here." Her hands went to his face, pulling him away so she could look at him. "You're here," she repeated and leaned her forehead against his. "That was..." she shook her head and squeezed her eyes shut. "Did they," she continued, "did they kill you?" Her chin was shaking, and she had her bottom lip trapped between her teeth.

"Yes," he answered. She let out a small cry. "I couldn't save you, Laurel. I tried, but I couldn't get to you. I'm so sorry. I should have...I should have protected you." His chest panged, and he held onto her. He wasn't sure he'd ever be able to let go of her again. "The sight of you up there...your screams. I should have saved you. I wasn't strong enough."

"No one could save me. Owen, look at me." She grabbed onto his shoulders. "I was a witch in the Middle Ages. I was going to die, there was no way around it. It was not your fault. You didn't accuse me of witchcraft. You weren't one of the guards. Lavender warned me that it would probably be terrible." She exhaled. "The fire...I don't know if I'll be able to light a candle for weeks." She shivered. "I remember the pain, the heat, the terror. Do you?"

"I do. The blood and the sounds...but then the memories stop." Owen searched his brain back to their last moments as Onfroi and Amée. It was a muddle mess of anguish and agony, but there was something he didn't understand still. "You were talking to someone after you said goodbye to me. When I was trying to get to you, there was someone else."

Laurel's eyes went wide, and her hand flew up to cover a gasp.

"What? Are you ok?"

She nodded. "Flavie. The woman who accused me. That was Morana. Holy shit. Flavie was Morana. That's why she's been looking for me. Oh, hell." Laurel put her head in her hands. "This is my fault. This is all my fault. How could I be so stupid? Damn it!"

"What's your fault?" Owen didn't remember anyone called Flavie, but he didn't talk to any women in the town besides a few of the merchants and Laurel. There weren't many opportunities to chat in medieval life.

"I cursed her. Oh my goddess, I cursed her, and it must have worked. Of course it worked. I was being burned alive and cursed someone. That has to be one of the most powerful ways to lay down a curse. And now she's after me. Fuck! Why did I do that?" Laurel babbled.

"What was the curse? Can you reverse it?" Owen asked. He didn't have much experience with curses, but most spells could be undone.

"I cursed her to be barren, food to taste like ashes, to be forever thirsty, to wander the earth alone, never find love, some other stuff and for the curse to follow her into other lives. Oh my goddess, I cursed her child to die! I'm a monster. I'm literally the worst person I've ever met. And I declared it unbreakable." Laurel rubbed her hand over her forehead. "This woman is going to torture and murder me. And I don't blame her. What if she's had multiple lives between this one and our last one? She might have decades of magical experience! And lifetimes worth of pain to avenge. I'm screwed. Oh, fuck. I'm going to die."

"You are not going to die," Owen said through clenched teeth. "That is not going to happen. And Morana or Flavie or whoever the hell this evil incarnate is will not kill you. I will rip her throat out first." Owen couldn't believe the words escaped his mouth, but he knew they were true. That woman had sentenced Amée to die. There was no way in hell he was going to watch Laurel die again. Already, he was piecing together a plan to keep her safe. He would protect her with his life, and this time, he would not fail.

Eventually, Lavender walked up to check on them and found them awake and clutching each other.

"You both need to eat," she pointed out. "You've been out for about twenty hours."

"Twenty hours?" Owen exclaimed.

"Yup. Think about it: you basically watched a movie of however many years on fast forward. And your brain downloaded the memories of another being. Your bodies and minds are fried. I'll bring up trays. Don't try to stand up yet. When I did this, I fell over and hit my head and needed stitches." Lavender disappeared down the stairs.

"Your sister did this?" he asked.

"Yeah, she doesn't talk about it. She did it in college. We didn't live together then. I don't remember her getting stitches." Laurel laid back against the pillows and let her arms fall overhead. Owen immediately joined her. He couldn't stand to be away from her yet. The memories were too fresh. Every time he blinked, he saw those men dragging her to the pyre.

His stomach turned, and he inhaled sharply.

"What is it?"

"I can't get it out of my mind," he admitted.

"Dying?"

"Watching you executed for no reason. Those people...you were so good to them. You took care of everyone. How many of them owed you their life? They did nothing to help you."

"They were afraid," she began. "Afraid that if they helped, they would be tied up beside me. The people I helped...they were women and children and elders. They were giving birth or dying. I wasn't tending to injured soldiers and earning their loyalty. The Lord's private guard owed me nothing. As evil as they were, they were following orders. Orders that came from Flavie." She sighed and pressed her cheek against his chest. "Lavender warned me that I probably met a violent end. She warned me I would know what it felt like to die. I'll be honest, I wasn't planning on being burned at the stake."

Owen chuckled. "What did you have in mind? Dying in your sleep at eighty?"

"That'd be nice, but no. After reading about the time period, I figured I died either giving birth, of an infection after giving birth, the plague, or general poor health. Before antibiotics, a run of strep throat could knock out a town."

"What was that herb you made me eat throughout the winters?" Owen asked, suddenly remembering chewing on dried herbs every night before bed.

"Thyme! It's a good one to eat to prevent bacterial infections. That was good advice. Thyme probably kept us a lot healthier than the rest of the town." Laurel smiled for a moment, but then it disappeared. "You had a sister."

"I did. Helene. I wonder what happened to her." His heart thudded singularly. A weird sense of mourning washed over him. The chances of her being alive again, at this particular moment in history, had to be miniscule. He had been so angry at her in the end. Looking back with his modern lens, he wasn't surprised she warned him away from Amée. Helene probably thought she was saving his soul.

"She was as safe as she could be, living with the nuns. She probably lived a long, solitary life. She most likely knew how to read, think of that! No one knew how to read, but your sister could probably read Latin. I definitely wasn't writing or reading anything. That's pretty cool."

Lavender returned, bearing a tray that looked like it contained well over five thousand calories. There were muffins, piles of eggs and bacon, a whole cake with pale green frosting, two bowls of oatmeal, a loaf of French bread, a brick of cheddar cheese, a pot of tea, a pitcher of water, and a carton of orange juice. Sage was close behind with plates, cutlery, napkins, and cups.

"Eat slow but try to eat as much as possible. Your stomachs are empty, but if you eat too quickly, you might get sick."

"Was it terrible?" Sage asked, peeking over Lavender's shoulder.

"Sage! Don't ask them about it," Lavender hissed.

"No, it's ok. It was wonderful and terrible. And informative." Laurel snatched a muffin off the top.

Owen grabbed a plate and piled it high with eggs and grabbed one of the bowls of oatmeal. Lavender wasn't kidding; he was ravenous.

"I know why Morana is coming after me," Laurel said, her mouth full of muffin. She poured herself a cup of tea.

"Why?"

"Because I cursed her pretty severely in the midst of my death in my past life."

Lavender's eyes looked like they were about to pop out of her head.

"You should probably call Rosemary and Verbena. I can tell everyone together then. And I want Owen to stay here tonight. And maybe longer. I don't know yet. But I feel like I can't close my eyes without him right next to me." She risked a glance in his direction.

"I'm not going anywhere," he promised. He set his oatmeal down and squeezed her forearm.

"Well, at least you got some information. I'll let Rosemary and Verbena know we need to meet tonight. You two, eat, drink, and then maybe stretch for a good thirty minutes before you stand up."

The next three hours were spent slowly eating and stretching. After doing three successful laps around the attic, they decided to try their luck on the stairs and made it to Laurel's room.

"This is very weird. And hopefully temporary. Why do I feel like I haven't used my legs in months?" Laurel carefully sat on her bed and motioned for Owen to join her.

"I don't know, but I feel the same way. I wish I could get into the ocean."

"Why?"

"I guess I recharge there. Probably something to do with my mom being a water witch and my weak storm powers, but wild water is extremely healing for me. Baths don't have quite the same effect, but they'll do in a pinch." He eased himself next to her. Laurel immediately snuggled against his chest and wrapped her arms around his waist.

"I feel the same way about the ocean." She sighed.

He exhaled and set his hand tentatively on her back.

"Do you want me to move?" she asked, resting her chin on his collarbone so she could see his face.

"No."

"I know we aren't Amée and Onfroi, but we sort of are. And I feel insanely connected to you and comfortable around you. Tell me if I'm being too forward." She pushed her hair behind her shoulder.

Owen snaked his hand up to brush his thumb over her cheekbone. She was so beautiful.

He loved her. He still had a lot to learn about her, but he loved her. He'd loved her for hundreds of years, and he didn't think he could ever stop.

"You're not being too forward. Honestly, the idea of letting go of you right now gives me a pit in my stomach."

"What about when I peed thirty minutes ago?"

"I was miserable," he admitted with a crooked smile.

"Me too! Oh, thank every single goddess." She laughed. "What are we going to do? I don't think I can go the rest of my life missing you when I need to pee."

"And I'll eventually need to work again." He let his thumb wander to her bottom lip and rested it there for a moment. Right now, he didn't want to think about going back to work. "It'll fade. But for now, I don't mind needing this. Needing to touch you."

"I don't mind it either," she whispered. She caught his thumb between her teeth and ran her tongue over the rough pad.

That was the only invitation he needed.

Owen pulled her on top of him and guided her mouth to his. They kissed frantically, a wild meeting of lips and teeth and tongues. She moaned against him, and he was undone.

Owen grabbed her legs behind her knees, spreading them wider and giving her room to straddle him. She shifted and let her body melt against his.

"Laurel," he breathed against her neck, his teeth scraping against the tender skin there. "I want to touch you."

"Touch me," she responded quickly.

Owen suppressed a chuckle.

"I want to really touch you."

"Owen," she stopped kissing him and took his face in her hands. "I remember sleeping with you. It was fantastic. Touch me. Please. Touch me everywhere." Laurel sat up and slowly pulled her black t-shirt over her head.

Owen didn't move. He laid completely still, his hands resting on her thighs. He wanted to remember this perfectly.

He wanted to remember how her hair was falling out of the ponytail she'd tied it back in and was now resting on her left shoulder. He wanted to remember the spray of freckles on her left shoulder that looked like an expanse of stars in the sky. He wanted to remember how her expression was soft and serious, how so full of hope and trust she looked. He wanted to remember it all.

"Owen?" she asked timidly. "Is everything ok?"

"I don't want to forget this," he answered truthfully and moved his hands to the skin of her belly before traveling to her shoulders. He gently pulled on the straps of her black bra, sliding them down her upper arms enough to expose the taut tips of her breasts. He moved one hand to test out a caress and was rewarded with a view of Laurel throwing her head back.

Owen sat up, shifting Laurel lower onto his lap, and replaced his hand with his mouth.

"Oh, goddess," she moaned, digging her fingers against his back.

He attended to one nipple, taking turns sucking and nibbling, loving Laurel's reactions. Her skin pebbled beneath his lips, driving him mad. His hands slid down her waist and around to cup her bottom. He pulled her closer to him, wishing there was nothing between them, but knowing they would go slow. They would take their time. This moment was important. Laurel pressed harder against him, her hand gripping his neck, guiding him to do more. By her squirming and incoherent noises, he guessed she liked it.

And he liked it—no—he loved it. He loved the feeling of Laurel's body, hot with need, pressed against his own. He loved listening to the small moans that caught in her throat and the feeling of her responses to him. He loved the way she clawed at his back like a wild, feral creature.

"More," she demanded.

He loved that most of all.

Owen flipped her onto her back and spread his body over hers. He kissed her mouth, neck, collarbone, the tops of her breasts, until she forcibly guided his mouth back to her pebbled nipples.

"You like this?" he teased.

"Very much," she answered between pants.

Owen returned his attention there, his hands wandering lower, finding the waistband of her pants, looking for a button or zipper or anything that could get him closer to all her skin. Her hands moved under his, pushing them away for a moment and slinking out of her pants.

"Thank you," he mumbled and pressed a kiss against her belly.

"Take your shirt off," she commanded.

Owen came to his knees and pulled his shirt off, immediately tossing it to the side and diving back onto her. He wanted to touch her, feel her, pleasure her. At this moment, Owen wanted nothing more than to make Laurel feel amazing.

He ran his hands over her breasts, her belly, her hips, and caught the waistband of her panties in one hand.

A loud knock at the door had him jumping nearly halfway across the room.

"Laurel!" Lavender called from the other side. "I don't know what you are doing in there, but all four of us have been waiting at the table for twenty minutes. So...maybe wrap it up?"

"Oh, fuck you, Lavender!" Laurel shouted and rubbed her hands over her face a few times. Even now, with the magic of the moment clearly ruined, Laurel looked gorgeous. Owen couldn't help staring at her, naked, other than a disheveled pair of panties.

"I didn't mean that. Be down in a second," she called back to Lavender. She turned to Owen, who was standing in the middle of the room, willing his hard-on to go down. "That's not how I wanted this to end."

"Me neither." He exhaled. He retrieved his shirt from the floor and slipped it over his head. "We have time. We have lots of time. I'm going to need a second, though, before I go downstairs and have a very serious meeting with your entire family."

"Shit, I want a cold shower, but I doubt they'd wait." She giggled.

"I'd like a cold shower too. Or a hot shower. With you. But then they'd have to wait a very, very long time," Owen teased. He found Laurel's shirt and tossed it to her. "If you put that on, it might help me become more presentable."

"You look perfect to me." She let her eyes wander to the front of his shorts, clearly tented.

"If you keep looking at me like that, I'm never leaving this room," he pointed out.

"Sorry! Okay. Let's see. Do you know that before Amée met Onfroi, she treated several cases of boils? They were absolutely disgusting. And she never used soap afterwards. She basically gave her hands a good rinse in river water, which was probably teeming with bacteria, and then onto the next patient. My last life was disgusting."

Owen burst out laughing and doubled over. This woman was perfect. Hilarious, sexy, beautiful, and enchanting.

This life was going to be wonderful.

Chapter Twenty

"Why is Owen in the kitchen?" Sage asked, peering through the doorway.

"He isn't joining the meeting unless he's invited, and he can't be too far away from Laurel," Lavender explained. "It's a whole thing, and hopefully it will clear up soon."

"It's not an ear infection. This isn't something a round of antibiotics is going to do away with," Laurel replied. "We'd rather not be apart right now, but he respects the fact that I need to talk to the four of you alone."

"And you're not the only one," Verbena cut in, "but you go first."

Laurel eyed her younger sister but carried on.

"So, real fast, Owen and I were in love in medieval France. We've had a hard time nailing down a specific date. We think it was in the thirteenth century, but probably on the tail of it. Anyway, I was a healer slash midwife, Owen was a carpenter. Morana was there. She was a rich woman and accused me of witchcraft, and I was burnt alive."

"Oh my goddess!" Rosemary exclaimed. She grabbed Laurel's hand. "Are you ok?"

"I mean, I died. Obviously. But I'm fine now. Also, I used my dying breath to curse Morana over all her lifetimes to never find love, lose her children, never taste food, be turned away from shelter, and I rained blessings on her enemies."

"You did what?" Rosemary shouted.

"Did it work?" Verbena exclaimed.

"I think we can safely assume that it did." Laurel gulped her tea.

"Why don't you just break the curse?" Rosemary asked. "That will at least appease Morana for a little while. She'll probably go nuts for a few months eating. I know I would. Oh! We can give her a stack of Lavender's baked goods as a peace offering. Maybe a couple of good bottles of wine too. If she's drunk and full, she'll leave us alone for months."

"That would be a great plan if I hadn't deemed the curse unbreakable."

"Why would you do that?" Rosemary asked.

"Well, I was very upset. My feet were on fire, no one was helping me, Owen, or Onfroi, was being beaten to death in the crowd and Flavie, that's Morana, was looking at me with a smug little 'I won' look on her face, and I snapped."

"Oh, come on," Sage mumbled. "You know she deserved it. I'm sure we've all done shit in our past lives that we wouldn't do now. And vice versa."

"Thank you, Sage. I appreciate your support."

"It doesn't put us any closer to getting Morana away from Laurel or breaking our family's curse. So, what next? Any ideas?" Lavender asked.

"I went to see Mable yesterday," Verbena began, her hands folded in front of her on the table.

"You were in Boston yesterday?" All the sisters knew about Mable. They'd met about ten years earlier when Verbena was going through a hard time and didn't want to talk to any of her sisters about it. Laurel wasn't exactly sure how they met, but Mable had been friends with Aunt June.

"I was. I had to go to the mainland for a closing and we had dinner." Verbena took a deep breath. "I showed her the mark on your arm. I know we haven't wanted to include outsiders in determining what it might be, but I trust Mable with my life. And she knows what it is."

"She does? What is it?" Laurel leaned forward.

"It's a beacon. Basically, it's a GPS location for Morana to find you. You're like a little flashing light to her right now. She's on her way here, most likely."

"Here? She's coming to Star Island?" Laurel suddenly felt like she was going to have a panic attack. Morana was terrifying in the Hedge World. Laurel couldn't imagine what she would be like in real life.

"Hey, we'll figure it out," Verbena continued. "I've got a new spell I've been perfecting to basically turn our house into a fortress. She wouldn't be able to come in no matter what she threw at it. And I doubt she has any background in house and property magic. Hedge witches don't usually dabble in that stuff."

"Our house will be a fortress," Laurel repeated. "Wait! She might remember Owen!"

At the sound of his name, Owen walked in from the kitchen. He immediately stood beside Laurel and set his hand on her shoulder.

"I can do the spell at Owen's rental too. It's not difficult, but I do need a day or so to collect some supplies. Some of the things are really weird."

"What do we do until then?" Owen asked.

"Be careful? Don't walk around at night? None of us know how powerful Morana is, but I have a feeling she'd have a hard time standing up to multiple witches and a sonofawitch."

"Unless she's afraid of knowing the exact location of the nearest storm, I don't think I'm much of a threat," Owen admitted.

"Not magically," Verbena continued, "but she looks small in her picture. And you look like you could throw someone across the room. We'll keep you around."

"I'm sorry," Laurel whispered. "This is a huge mess."

"It's ok. We'll fix it. We're a good team," Rosemary soothed. "Don't worry. Your sisters will protect you."

Laurel nodded, but it felt like an empty gesture. This was her fault, completely. She made a huge mistake in her past life, and now it was coming back to her. She was a witch, Amée was a witch. She knew the rules. When you cast a terrible spell, terrible things will come back to haunt you.

Laurel wished she was more powerful. She wished she could lay wards like Verbena or make up spells like Lavender. She felt utterly useless.

After a dinner of chicken, peas, radishes, and feta cheese, Verbena headed out to collect her supplies. The other sisters, plus Owen, sat on the screened porch in relative silence until Rosemary announced she and Sage were going to bed and would both be wearing earplugs. Loudly.

"Lavender, you come too."

"I'm not tired yet, Rosemary."

"Yes, you are. Look, it's nine-thirty. You should have been in bed ages ago."

"What time do your sisters go to bed?" Owen leaned in and murmured to Laurel.

"Around ten usually. I'm the only night owl. Lavender has to be at the bakery before five to open by six-thirty. Rosemary likes to tinker in her garden before going to work, and Sage keeps farmer hours."

"Farmer hours?"

"When the sun's up, she's up. When it's not, she's not. She's a real party in December and January, getting into her pajamas at four in the afternoon."

Owen smiled.

"Oh, fine." Lavender turned to Laurel and Owen. "Don't do anything rash. You've both been through a trauma. Keep that in mind. You can't take back something because you did it within a day of living your past life again."

For a moment, a shadow passed over Lavender's eyes, and Laurel thought she might tear up. Instead, she shook her head, picked up her tea, and headed inside.

"Have fun!" Rosemary called. "Laurel, there are supplies in the front hall table just in case." Rosemary winked and left. Laurel was ninety-nine percent positive there was a box of condoms in the front hall table right now. Which made her wonder when exactly had Rosemary stashed condoms in the front hall table.

"Do you want to go to sleep?" Laurel asked.

"Not yet." Owen kissed her temple quickly.

"I think Rosemary wants us to go upstairs and have sex."

Owen choked on his tea.

"Sorry," she giggled. "Rosemary is always trying to get everyone laid. I don't know if it's part of her power or if she's a crazy meddler. Either way, if

Lavender wasn't here, she would have made all my sisters leave for three days."

"I'm not sure how to react to that," Owen laughed.

"I want to go upstairs and go to sleep, honestly." Laurel risked a glance at Owen. "I don't like the idea of being with you for the first time while my sisters are literally surrounding us. This is an old house. The walls are in no way soundproof."

"I definitely agree." He pulled her closer and wrapped an arm around her shoulders, pressing a kiss against her hair.

"Are you sure?"

"I'm exhausted. I must still be on medieval France time."

She laughed and snuggled closer.

"Also, when we are together..." he paused to collect his thoughts. "I don't want it to be stifled or silenced or careful because there are people nearby. I want it to be just us, only about us. I definitely don't want to worry that Lavender is going to knock, or Rosemary is going to cheer."

"That sounds like something Rosemary would do," Laurel admitted. "Ok. It's settled then. Let's go upstairs and go to bed. To sleep. Let's get into bed and close our eyes and fall asleep."

"Deal."

"But feel free to sneak a few goodnight kisses," she added.

"I will."

"Oh shit, not again."

Laurel was in the Hedge World. She was alone, at least, and not trapped in some cabin. She glanced around. She was in the woods. They looked familiar but felt more menacing than the Hedge World had before all of this began. Laurel hoped there would be a time when the Hedge World returned to its former self, but she wasn't optimistic. Morana had poisoned this place to her. She wasn't sure if she would ever get it back.

Instead of sitting and wondering what would happen, Laurel started looking for a way out. She did a quick circle, looking for any paths through the dense trees, but there were none. Instead, she looked up at the night sky and picked the brightest star. She kept her eyes focused on it. She walked towards the star, hoping it would lead her out of this crazy forest at some point. She wasn't too hopeful, though. She had no idea what the parameters of the Hedge World were. This forest could go on for hundreds of miles. But it could go on for a quarter mile and then hit the town.

Laurel flickered her eyes from the sky to the ground in front of her. She didn't want to become too distracted staring at the sky and trip on something. When her eyes did a sweep of the ground, she noticed something, someone.

A red cloak and swirl of ice blonde hair put a pit in her stomach.

"Fuck," she mumbled. Morana had brought her here. Either that or her homing mark on Laurel's arm was really powerful.

Instead of trying to outrun her, Laurel stood her ground. She had no escape plan, but if she was able to curse Morana so deeply in her past life, perhaps she had dormant powers she could awaken.

"Morana," Laurel greeted. "Any reason you've brought me to the Hedge World and the middle of the woods?"

"You know, I learned your name this time around. Laurel Bay. Laurel Bay, tarot card reader and psychic. Available for parties on Star Island. Click here to view packages." Morana was reciting Laurel's web page information for her business.

"Morana Stoch of Circle, Montana. Youngest of three. Now, we both know each other."

"Maybe, but you're not coming for me. And I will find you. Star Island is such a small place, difficult to reach, but I'm nearly there now. I hope you are as excited to see me as I am to see you."

"I don't know, Flavie," Laurel began. She saw a flicker pass over Morana's eyes. "You were never my favorite person. Come on, a witch accusing another witch and letting her burn for it? That has to be against some sort of code."

Morana's voice dropped low. "What I did to you was nothing compared to what you did to me. And I will punish you for it. Tell you what, reverse the curse, and I'll spare Onfroi. He's close to you again, I can feel it."

"Stay the hell away from him," Laurel spat.

"Break the curse, Laurel Bay. I'll still come for you, regardless, but I'll leave your man alone if you break it."

Laurel shook her head. "You deserve it."

"Then I suppose I'll see you soon." Morana stepped closer, her face only inches away from Laurel's. "Ferries twice daily to Star Island from the mainland," Morana mimicked the Star Island tourism website.

Morana shoved Laurel so hard, she flew past the trees. She continued flying, the world becoming a blur of green and black around her. Her flying turned to falling, and she fought the urge to panic. She was going home. This was the way she got out of the Hedge World when she didn't use the door.

Laurel took a deep breath and waited. She would wake up at home. Any minute now.

"Oof. I will never get used to that." Laurel shook out her arms and legs. Next to her, Owen shot awake.

"What happened?"

Laurel grimaced. "Morana pulled me into the Hedge World again, told me she knows where I live and that she knows we're together, and said if I broke the curse, she would spare you but still torture and kill me. So, not the best sleep of my life."

"I should have woken you up. I must have fallen asleep. I'm so sorry."

"I can't expect you to stay up twenty-four hours a day. And I'm fine. She is still very angry with me."

"She didn't try to hurt you in the Hedge World?" Owen did a quick sweep of her for injuries.

"No, I'm not sure she can. I'm not positive, but I've never seen any fighting, or anyone injured when I've been there." Laurel flopped back onto the pillow. It was light out, but from the lack of noise in the house, she guessed the sun had just come up.

"What should we do? Do you want me to call my mom? Or my cousins?"

"No, I don't think that's a good idea. I've never met any of them, and..." Laurel trailed off. It wasn't that she didn't trust Owen's family, per se, but there were a lot of rumors about the Davies water witches. They definitely toed the line when it came to good and evil, and she didn't want to bring a bunch of witches into this that might not end up on her side. "I want to get the protection spells up around this house and your house as soon as possible. And I want to take a shower. And have a cup of tea."

"Why don't you get in the shower, and I'll make you some tea?"

"Perfect." Laurel pressed a quick kiss against Owen's cheek and scooted off the bed and down the hall carefully. She wasn't as dizzy as the last time she had exited the Hedge World unconventionally, but she didn't want to press her luck.

Day time couldn't come soon enough. She needed Verbena to work her magic as soon as possible. Once the wards were up, she would feel better.

Chapter Twenty-One

"What exactly do you need to do here? I don't want to freak out the neighbors." Owen eyed Verbena as she packed up her bag. She had completed the protection spell around the Bay property and the three of them were getting ready to head to his rental house.

"No one will notice. I'm a realtor, so I can always fall back on the explanation that I'm looking at the property for a client. I'll keep all the herbs and talismans in my purse when I'm outside. I'll do separate stuff inside that's a little more intense, but nothing loud. I promise, none of your neighbors will be calling the witch police."

"Are there witch police?" Owen asked. He was certain his mom would have threatened him with that as a teenager if there were, and that they would have gotten involved with Millie by now.

"No, but wouldn't that be something? Then, we could report Morana to the witch police and be done with it. Oh, never mind. Laurel would probably serve a life sentence for cursing someone over multiple lifetimes."

"Oh, shut up. She had me burned alive," Laurel interjected.

"True. The witch police might wash their hands of you two and let you duke it out." She sighed. "All right, let's go."

Verbena had a car, and that small convenience convinced Owen that he needed to pick up his truck soon. He'd grab it as soon as the business with Morana was settled. He wasn't quite sure how it would be settled, but it would be. It had to be. He couldn't face the idea of this ending any way other than happily.

Owen's mom stayed out of witch drama, but his aunts and cousins certainly did not. Owen had spent a large amount of his childhood surrounded by twelve water witches: his mom, her three sisters, and his eight cousins. Owen and Aidan were the only boys on that side of the family, and not only that but they were also the only two without significant power over water in some way.

The more Owen thought about it, the more he wanted to call his family. His mom, at least, could help. Right now, he felt like he should surround Laurel with powerful witches. And some of his cousins...well, there were very dark facets to water witchery. It'd be good to have a couple of them on their side.

Verbena pulled in front of Owen's rental and got out of the car quickly. "This is where you're staying?" She immediately walked up the front steps, then turned around to look at the water. "These places are amazing," she raved. "And a great investment. Your friend made a good choice buying one of these. Value is only going to go up. And once the market takes off, people will be looking for rentals beyond the summer months. I'm guessing we'll have an explosion of spring and autumn visitors in two years. So, what do you think?"

"I'm enjoying it so far." Owen stole a quick glance at Laurel.

"She really loves houses. Obviously. It's in her soul." She smiled and shook her head at Verbena who was doing a lap around the exterior now. She didn't appear to be doing anything other than checking out the building.

"So, inside or outside first?" Owen asked.

"Inside."

Owen unlocked the door and led Laurel and Verbena inside. Verbena set her bag down and started wandering through the house, opening closet doors, looking inside the cupboards, checking out the bathroom, running her hands over every window.

"Is this part of the spell or a realtor thing?" Owen whispered to Laurel.

"I think it's part of the spell," Laurel giggled.

"It is," Verbena cut in. "Go sit in the bedroom while I do these areas. Then I'll have you switch. It will be easier for me to concentrate." She shooed them away and started emptying the contents of her purse on the kitchen counter. Before Laurel pushed him through the door, Owen caught sight of two large bundles of herbs, three candles, and a very large knife. He took a deep breath. He hoped nothing was going to get sliced. He had to put his credit card down for damages incurred.

He turned his focus into the room. Laurel was lying on the bed, sprawled on the left side.

Perfect, he thought. Owen always slept on the right side of the bed.

"Get cozy. This could take anywhere from five minutes to three hours."

"Three hours? Do spells often take that long?" He sat on the edge of the bed.

"Some of them. They also take longer the first time you do one."

"Do you do a lot of spells?" Owen reclined next to Laurel, weaving his hands behind his head.

"Eh, I used to. When I was a teenager and even into my early twenties, I did spells for every little thing. A spell for good luck before I left the house, a spell for clarity before I did a reading, a spell to get a good night's sleep. It was too much. So now, I limit myself to one a month. I'm not that good at spells."

"What do you mean? Don't they just come to you?" Owen had spent a portion of his childhood trying to do spells and failing, thereby placing him in the sonofawitch category and not the warlock lane.

"They don't come to me. I guess some witches are born good at it, but most of them have to work for it. You know, study and stuff."

"And you didn't want to study?"

"I wasn't great at school. Studying isn't my strong suit. Plus, what was the point? Most of my witchcraft is in my readings. And I can just do that. I look at the cards and they speak to me. My visions simply come to me, I don't have to work for it. If I wanted to jump into people's thoughts, I can do it without a spell or anything. But I don't because I hate it." She sighed. "I guess I also had the Hedge World, but not anymore."

"She won't hound you forever," Owen said, wrapping his hand around hers. "We'll figure it out. And by we, I mean you and your sisters with limited support from me." He paused. "There's a big storm about twenty-two miles east of here and another smaller one forty-five miles southwest."

"Are you telling me it's going to rain tonight?" Laurel giggled.

"It's moving pretty fast. I would say we're going to get a howler this afternoon."

"This is going to be extremely helpful when we have a kid who has soccer practice, and we aren't sure if they're going to cancel it."

"Two psychic parents. Poor kids. At least mine is hyper specific."

"All right, that wasn't as difficult as I imagined," Verbena came in only about thirty minutes after she had made them leave the living room. "This room should only take a few minutes, then I'll do a perimeter outside and be on my way!"

Owen and Laurel stayed put on the bed while Verbena brushed all the surfaces with a bundle of herbs, lit a candle in front of every exit, and said some very menacing things in Latin while brandishing the knife and threatening the windows. Nothing was sliced or stabbed, though, so Owen wouldn't need to explain knife wounds to the walls.

"Are you going to have the knife out outside?" he asked.

"No, it will be in my purse. Owen, you're acting like I've never had to banish evil away from a property before. I'm in real estate. And, spoiler, this island is very haunted." She pointed towards the waterfront. "Lots of ships went down around here, lots of sailors crawled to sanctuary on this island, and lots of them were murdered by the early settlers who didn't take kindly to outsiders."

"You should put that in your glossy pamphlets prospective buyers go nuts over," Laurel chimed in.

Verbena furrowed her brow and picked up her supplies, placing everything in her purse.

"I'll be done in about twenty-five minutes."

True to her word, Verbena was discreet. She lit the candles on the tables on the porch, fashioned a small wreath out of the herbs and held it up like she was deciding whether wreaths on all windows would work for the Christmas season, and there was no hint of the knife. Owen could see her mumbling, and at one point, she pretended to talk on her cell phone. She really did have this all figured out.

"I've got to run into town for a minute. Do you want a ride back to the house now or can I come grab you in a few hours, say two o'clock?"

"We'll stay here," Laurel responded immediately. "Do you have an umbrella? Looks like a storm might be coming in." She pointed to the sky.

"I'll be fine. It always looks like rain, but then it never does," Verbena called over her shoulder.

Owen and Laurel sat on the porch for a while, staring at the ebb and flow of the water, listening to the gentle crashing of the waves on the beach. The steady flow of walkers along the coast slowly fizzled as the rainclouds began to look more ominous, blowing in from the east, until the beach was empty. While Laurel and Owen began in separate chairs, at some point, Laurel moved to his lap, where he enjoyed her even more.

"I couldn't figure out what you smelled like for a while, but I've got it now," Laurel said with her nose against his neck.

"What do I smell like?"

"A forest in the rain. First, I thought you smelled like rain, but that wasn't quite it. Then I thought it was maybe cedar or oak, but that was wrong too. A deciduous wood in the middle of a downpour. It makes sense, really. You're a storm sensor who works with wood. Earth and water, that's you."

"I don't think anyone has ever called me a storm sensor before," he began, "but I'll take it."

"What do I smell like? To you? I figure you're magical enough to smell something more than shampoo."

Owen wrapped his arms around her waist and buried his face in her chest.

"You smell like my soulmate." His voice was muffled against her skin, causing her to giggle.

"What do I smell like though? Beyond the pheromones clearly addling your senses. You know, some witches can spot their soulmate by smell alone."

"Let me try again." Owen closed his eyes and breathed deeply. He searched for something beyond that initial jump his brain made to 'have sex with this woman right now' and looked for more. "Flowers. Maybe jasmine?

Or gardenia? I'm not great with differentiating floral scents. But wilder and warmer. Wildflowers?" There was something else. He chased the note until he caught it. "A warm fire at the end of a cold day."

He leaned back to look at her face.

"That's a really nice compliment."

"I can't wait for an actual cold day, to come home to you, my roaring fire."

Laurel ran her fingers through his hair.

"Take me to bed, Owen."

Owen was nervous.

He wasn't entirely sure why he was nervous. He shouldn't have been nervous. It wasn't his first time taking a woman to bed, it wasn't even his first time he remembered taking Laurel to bed. Onfroi and Amée had lived together for years.

It still felt new, though. And more than that, it felt important. It felt like this was the first time they were truly committing to each other, understanding that they were meant to be together. Owen had known the moment he saw Laurel in her garden that she was the woman he was going to love for the rest of his life. He knew it would be his life's goal to make her happy, protect her from harm, and find a million ways to brighten her days.

Laurel, on the other hand, did not seem nervous. If Owen had to categorize the emotion she was currently emitting, it was uncontainable excitement.

She pulled Owen by the arm through the kitchen and living room, pushed open the bedroom door, and flipped around to face him.

"Ok. Deflower me," she commanded with a nod.

Owen couldn't help it and burst out laughing.

"What?"

"Deflower you? Just like that?"

"Sure, just like that." She paused and furrowed her brow. "I've been waiting a long time for you to show up. I've been waiting for an unseemly amount of time to have sex. Do you not want to deflower me?"

"I wish you would stop saying deflower because it makes me think I'm stealing your flower. And I know how witches are about their gardens. Can we use a different word?"

"Sexy time?" Laurel offered.

"Sexy time. Sure. There's a lot I'd like to do before we get to that particular point of sexy time."

"Like what?" She put her hands on her hips and wrinkled her nose.

Oh, Owen thought. She thinks I want to take things slow, spread things out over a few days. His mouth drew up into a wicked smile.

"Hm." He sat on the bed and pulled her to stand between his legs. "Well, I want to devour your mouth until you're begging me for more. And then I'll probably lazily take your clothes off, inch by inch, worshipping every new glimpse of bare skin under my fingertips."

Laurel's face was relaxed now, a hint of a smile on her lips.

"Then what?"

Owen ran his hands up the back of her legs and let them rest right above her knees. The fabric of her skirt brushed against his knuckles.

"I'd rather show you." He pulled her forward until she straddled him at the foot of the bed. "Never been good at narration."

Laurel melted against him. It felt so good, so right, to have her in his arms, especially now that they were alone.

He buried his face against her chest, taking a deep breath of the warm fire. His hand hooked behind her neck and drew her mouth to his.

Her lips were soft, but insistent. She licked his mouth apart, bit his bottom lip, and snuck her hands down his back. She reached for the hem of his shirt and pulled it over his head.

"Yes," she said once he had his shirt off, her eyes doing a full sweep of his torso.

"Yes?"

"Yes, please. I mean, look at you! Look at you. Your shoulders, your chest, your arms! You always say I look so much healthier now; you look like a cover of Men's Health." Her hands roamed over his skin, testing out his reactions on different planes of his body. Her brows were slightly knit together as she scrutinized every inch of his bare chest and arms. "Like these," she began, her hands on his shoulders. "I don't have muscles like these. Onfroi didn't have these. What are these called? Deltoids? I like these."

"A plus side of manual labor and a gym membership. And eating enough calories a day," he teased. He tightened his arms around her waist and trailed kisses from her jaw to her collarbone.

"I like that," she mumbled.

"Good."

Laurel leaned back slightly, putting him just out of reach, and pulled her shirt over her head.

"Yes, please," Owen echoed. She was beautiful, sexy, and dear to his heart. And now, she was in his arms, slowly undressing.

This was turning out to be a very good day.

Chapter Twenty-Two

L aurel wasn't sure what had come over her, but she had a feeling it was Owen.

Because she was straddling a half-naked sonofawitch and was reaching behind to unhook her bra with a confidence she didn't know she possessed. And he was covering her breasts with his hands and mouth. This was bliss. Being with Owen was bliss.

"No, don't stop. Please," she gasped as he leaned away from her for a moment, cool air replacing the mouth that had been teasing her nipple to oblivion. She looked down, trying to catch his gaze, but before she could, he stood up, taking her with him, his hands gripping her thighs.

"Where are we going?"

"Right here," he answered and laid her across the center of the bed. He stood above her for a moment, and she felt her cheeks redden as he took in a long, lingering look at her exposed chest.

For a fleeting moment, she thought to cross her arms but then she realized something. She wanted Owen to look at her like that. She wanted to be desired, to be viewed as a sexual being. She hoped that looking at her drove him mad. Laurel wanted Owen's eyes on her, and she wanted them mad with desire.

His hands roamed to her skirt and searched for the zipper.

"It's in the back," she giggled.

"All right," Owen drawled, flipping her onto her stomach.

Her breath caught in her throat as he palmed her ass before finding the zipper and pulling it down. She swore she could feel each one of the teeth coming apart.

Owen took his time inching the fabric over her ass and down her legs. His knuckles brushed against the backs of her thighs at a deliberate pace, taking their time to linger over certain spots. When he replaced his knuckles with his mouth, Laurel thought she might come undone.

He kissed his way up her leg, beginning at her calf and covering nearly every inch of her bare thigh. She shivered, her mind a muddled mess of need and want and desire. She reached her hand towards him, hoping to find him and somehow ground herself through his touch. Owen wrapped his hand around hers but continued to worship her bare skin. His other hand trailed up her back, dancing over her smooth skin with his rough fingertips. He was using his teeth now, slow nibbles with enough of a bite to make her moan.

"Owen," she rasped. "I need to kiss you."

She heard him hum in response, then his hand hooked around her hip and turned her to her back. Laurel reached for his shoulders and drew him down to her so she could seize his mouth with hers.

She devoured him, starving for him, but unsure how she could ever quell the hunger. Her legs wrapped around his waist, pulling him as close as she could.

She wanted him inside her.

She'd never wanted that before. She'd had a few flings in high school, but she never *wanted* any of them. She had enjoyed the fumbling hook-ups, but that was nothing like this. She felt like she was in the desert and Owen was the oasis.

"You're so beautiful," he said, pulling away from her mouth for a moment. "I want to give you everything you could ever want. Do you want a table? A car? A house?"

"I want you, Owen. You are what I want."

He smiled and kissed her hard before leaving her mouth to string kisses down her neck to her breasts. He paused there, teasing her nipples into hard peaks, making her moan his name and scratch at his back.

He continued, allowing the cool air to dance over her nipples while he licked her belly, finding secret spots to nip and tickle.

"I want to kiss you," he mumbled.

"You are."

"No. I want to kiss you here." His hand cupped her sex possessively. She instantly squirmed against his fingers. "I want to make you come. I want to make you come over and over and over." His mouth moved lower, dragging his lips below her navel. He left her for a moment, got to his knees, and peeled her panties off her body. The fabric slid off her achingly slow, the rough edges of his nails skimming the entire lengths of her legs. He tossed her panties aside and gripped her thighs, pulling her closer to him. "Ready?"

Laurel didn't answer. She didn't say anything. She couldn't. Once his mouth was on her, she was lost. She moaned her affirmative and clapped a hand over her own belly to keep her from bucking against him. His tongue glided over her folds, finding new places to taste and dip, bringing her to a height she'd never reached before.

She tried to give him praise and thank him for all the efforts he was making, but she could only moan, "yes," and "Owen," and "right there." She grabbed the comforter, trying to still her body, but it was of no use. She could do nothing but lie there and take the unending pleasure. He was consuming her body, and she loved it.

"Owen," she panted a moment before falling apart. She held onto her climax as long as she could, but he showed no signs of pulling back and she crashed apart. Her entire body wracked with spasms, turning to liquid heat.

He didn't stop. Owen slowed his work, moved his mouth to her thigh for a moment, sucking on the sensitive skin there, but replaced his mouth with his fingers slowly working inside of her. She groaned softly, enjoying the new sensation. She widened her legs, letting them fall open.

Keeping his hand where it was, he crawled up the bed and licked her nipple slowly, letting his tongue dance circles around the bud.

"I want you to come again," he whispered. "I love your body. I love every inch of it. Oh god, I love you, Laurel." His teeth scraped against the skin of her neck and down to her shoulder, leaving a trail of need in their wake.

Owen loved her. Her brain registered that somewhere, just before breaking into a million pieces again.

This time, he stopped. He slowly withdrew from inside her and gathered her in his arms, pulling her against his chest and letting her catch her breath. Laurel's body molded to his, holding on to him for some sense of grounding.

"I love you," she breathed. She held onto him with her weak arms, trying to pull him as close as possible. "I love you, Owen. I love you." She paused and smiled. "Take your pants off."

Owen looked like he might hesitate for a moment but then rolled off the bed and stood. He undid his zipper quickly and stepped out of his jeans. His thumbs hooked the waistband of his boxers and then he stopped.

"Should I go get a condom?" he asked.

Laurel blinked at him. She was completely naked, ripe for plundering, legs wide open, and presented in front of him. And he remembered birth control.

"I'm on the pill," she said quickly. Laurel got to her knees and crawled towards him until her fingers could curl over his abdomen.

"You are? But..."

"I've been on it for years for other reasons. So, if you're overly concerned about barriers, you can go get a condom, but I would prefer it if you didn't. I want to know what it feels like to be with you, to have nothing between us." Laurel slid her hand beneath his boxers and gripped him. She let her fingers play over the surface of his cock, testing out its girth and length, wondering what it would feel like when he—

"Laurel," he started, his breath hissing. "Laurel, I haven't...it's been a very long time. I'm not going to last long. I promise, next time will be longer," he rambled.

Laurel pushed his boxers down his legs until he stepped out of them.

"Lay down," she said, pulling him back to the bed. She crawled over him, positioning herself on top.

Owen grasped her hips, his chest rising and falling dramatically with every breath he took.

"Tell me if I do something wrong," Laurel said.

"Impossible," Owen responded. He pulled her down for a kiss, then guided her over him.

"Holy..." Laurel braced her arms on either side of Owen's shoulders.

"Are you ok?" His hand came up to her face.

"Yes. I like it. It's intense." She slid slowly up and down him, letting herself grow accustomed to the feeling of him inside her.

"You feel so good," he mumbled. His hands caressed her breasts again, teasing and rolling, bringing her back to the wave of blinding pleasure. "You're the most beautiful thing I've ever seen."

Owen leaned forward, his hands moving to her hips, directing her to take him more deeply. She shuddered. She was going to come again. A faraway part of Laurel's mind was giddy with excitement. Is this what sex with Owen would always be like? Because this was amazing. If this is what sex was always like, Laurel wasn't certain she ever wanted to do anything else again.

"Can I come inside you?" he growled, his hands roughly grabbing her hips.

"Yes. Don't stop. I'm so close again." Laurel's hands pressed against Owen's chest for support, and she fell apart. Her body shook with her third orgasm, and her mind went completely blank. She could feel him coming, too, his body racking with spasms and jolts, his hands grasping all over her body until they both collapsed in an exhausted heap on the pillows.

"Fuck," Laurel breathed, running her hands over her face. She rolled on her side and threw her legs over Owen. "Fuck."

"There's something I probably should have told you before we did that."

Laurel could barely open her eyes. Her body was limp with the bliss of pure exhaustion. Her cheek pressed against Owen's chest, her arms encircled his waist, and she didn't think she had the strength to raise her head.

"Hm?" It was all she could muster.

"It's important to me that I marry you before we have a child."

"Do you know something I don't know?" she answered, unable to suppress a grin. A moment later, her smile disappeared.

"Wait," Laurel continued, propping up on her elbows, suddenly very awake. "Do you? You've got some weird sonofawitch stuff; did you just get me pregnant?"

"I don't think so!" Owen responded quickly. "If I do have the ability to immediately know about the existence of my children in utero, you aren't pregnant. If that helps put your mind at ease. I sense nothing but you in this bed with me."

"Ok." Laurel laid her head back on his chest. "I got freaked out for a minute." She took a deep breath. "Wait. I think I have a glimmering memory from sex ed that it takes sperm at least an hour or so to get there. Maybe days? Keep me posted."

Owen chuckled. "You did tell me you wanted five kids. You'll need to get pregnant at some point."

"Yes, but I would prefer to deal with Morana before then. I don't want to be meeting her for the first time and need to excuse myself to go puke in the bushes."

"Good point." Owen tightened his grip around her. "I don't think I've ever felt this violent towards someone I've never met. What do you think she's going to do when she gets here?"

"Probably kill me."

"Laurel, don't say that."

"That is most likely her plan. I cursed her terribly and have no idea how to lift it. I can't imagine she's coming on a social call." Laurel shrugged. "There's a real possibility I won't win this. I'm not a very good witch or particularly strong. I read tarot cards for a living. Tons of non-witches do that, and if they are intuitive enough, they get stuff right." Laurel sighed.

"You're not going to lose. I won't let it happen." Owen could feel anxiety building in his gut. He couldn't lose Laurel. He wouldn't.

"We need to figure out a way to beat her. There has to be some way," he continued. "Do you know any other hedge witches?"

"A handful from the message boards, one on the mainland from a long time ago, but no one I can trust. My great grandma was a hedge witch, but I never met her. What I wouldn't give for twenty minutes of advice from her."

"Could you raise her ghost and ask her questions?" Owen pressed.

"I don't know. Maybe? I don't want to make it a habit of raising all my ancestors from their supposed rest."

"What about spell books? There has to be something in there. You've never read anything helpful?"

"I told you, not much for school." Laurel huffed. "It might simply be hopeless."

"I know you said you didn't want me to call my family before—"

"I still don't," Laurel answered firmly.

"It might not be a bad idea," Owen continued. "A lot of my cousins are powerful. I've never seen Morana in action, but most humans can't take on a hurricane. They'd be great back-up."

"Last resort. But I really don't want to bring in any other witches."

The storm outside wailed. Verbena had texted Laurel that some of the roads were flooding, and she would come get her and Owen as soon as it was safe. Laurel had responded that they would make their way back to the house in the morning. They were perfectly safe at Owen's for now. The protection spells were all up, plus there was no way the ferry was running in this storm. Morana would have to wait until the morning if she was even that close.

Owen moved the couch to face the large picture window in the living room so they could sit together and watch the storm. Laurel had slipped into one of his t-shirts and Owen had on his boxers. It felt so comfortable and regular to be sitting with Owen on the couch without any pants on.

"Do you want me to make you a cup of tea?" Owen asked.

"I'm ok now. I want to sit and watch the storm with my storm warlock." Laurel giggled.

"You make it sound like I can summon a thunderstorm. I can't."

"Have you tried?"

"My whole childhood. Once I started understanding what I was sensing, I spent countless hours trying to draw storms towards me. But they have a mind of their own. Or rather, they have a will stronger than my own."

"Well, I've never met a powerful storm warlock or witch, so it's very impressive to me."

"You will. My cousin, Maeve, is a crazy powerful storm witch. She's only fifteen, but she can call down a hurricane if she wants to. I wasn't exaggerating about that."

"Seriously?"

"Yes. It's a sight to see. She's calmed down a little now, but when she had temper tantrums as a child, it was terrifying. She made a tornado touch down in Vermont."

"Holy shit. Are there tornadoes in Vermont?"

"There were a couple in 2011. Her mom, my aunt Mary, lost her mind. And Aunt Mary is a pretty intense witch. Once the magic started flying, my mom put Aidan and I in the car and we left that family picnic."

"You make water witches sound like a very different breed than cottage witches."

"Is that what you call yourselves?" Owen snuck a kiss on her forehead and Laurel snuggled against him.

"That's what my sisters and I call each other, and my mom said it too. We're all home and garden and hearth-based witches. I'm a little bit of the black sheep, I guess, but on the other hand, people have been going into witches' homes for centuries looking to learn something about their future."

"Was your dad a sonofawitch or a warlock?"

"Nope. But my mom had two non-magical brothers, so she was used to being around non-magical people. And they both married non-witches, so my entire extended family doesn't get any of this." She turned towards Owen. "It's nice that you do. I'd be lying if I said I wouldn't be sad to give up things like Yule and Beltane."

"Don't worry, I'm firmly on board for celebrating all the Sabbats. I will say my mom is super into Imbolc, so we might have to spend that one with my family."

"Sounds good. Imbolc has never been my favorite. Verbena's in charge of our celebrations and it usually involves a lot of cleansing, which is her fancy way of making us clean out our closets," she giggled. "I'd like to see how water witches celebrate. I'm also only seventy-five percent terrified to meet your mom. I never thought my soulmate would be part of the Davies water witch clan."

"I definitely never thought I had the ability to impress anyone with my last name. I grew up in a small farmhouse in rural Maine."

"I'd still be enamored with you even if you weren't a Davies or a sonofawitch or a storm sensor. Just plain Owen is pretty great."

"Thank you." Owen wrapped his arm a little tighter around her waist and spread his hand over her belly.

"You're also really good in bed," she continued. "Is that weird to say? Is it weird to give you a sex compliment? I feel like you deserve it. I've never personally put in the effort for a three-orgasm afternoon, and you really went for it. Honestly, I didn't think that was going to happen." She stopped talking. She was clearly rambling and needed to stop.

"You can give me all the sex compliments you want to, but expect some in return," he teased.

"Oh?" She raised an eyebrow. "Ok, go ahead."

"Hm." Owen's hand ran over her hip and down to her thigh. "I've never seen a woman with a hotter body than you."

"What? That is not true. I'll take the compliment as 'you have a hot body' and say thank you."

"I'm being serious," he answered. His hand moved back up her leg, grasping her thigh now. He kneaded the inside with his fingertips, coaxing her to open her legs a little more. "Right now, I'm thinking about how badly I want to see you naked again."

Laurel flickered her eyes away from his face and to his boxers. He wasn't joking. Feeling emboldened, Laurel whipped her shirt off, then leaned back against the couch as if they were going to have a normal conversation.

"Well, you should have said so. Now, what were we talking about? Water witches? Our extended families? Favorite holidays?"

"Laurel," he drawled, then clucked his tongue. He slid from his spot on the couch and kneeled on the floor in front of her, drawing her legs to either side of him. "You think I want to talk when I'm looking at you?" He brought both his hands up to her chest, palming her breasts for a moment before swirling his fingers over her nipples.

"Mmm we can keep talking if you want," she mumbled as her back involuntarily arched into his hands.

"Fuck that," he said, releasing her chest and hooking his hands behind her knees. He dragged her to the edge of the couch and buried his face against her sex. He pushed her panties to one side and licked her hard and long.

She nearly screamed.

"You're already wet," he noticed, taking a breath. "Laurel. I'm yours. All of me. Body, soul, heart, mind, everything. All I am is yours."

"Owen," she whispered. She leaned forward, cradling his face between her hands. "I am yours and you are mine. I trust you with all of me." Her lips sought his, drawing him to a soul-soaring kiss. Every bit of her was in love with this man. It was insane. They'd met days ago, and yet...they'd met eight hundred years ago. Like most magical things, this love couldn't be explained.

His mouth moved from hers, teasing a line down her neck until he nuzzled the valley between her breasts.

"Tell me what you want."

"Make me come," she answered immediately.

He pushed up to his knees and pulled her panties off. He lost his boxers and flipped her around and her knees hit the ground. Owen bent her forward slightly, then positioned his cock right at her entrance. Laurel felt his hand smooth the length of her spine before sneaking around to cup her breast. She felt like willing clay in his hands.

"Tell me if I'm too rough or you want me to go slower," he said, breeching her inch by inch.

"You can go faster and harder," she answered. She felt him hum a laugh.

"I haven't started yet."

He gripped her hip with one hand, the other leaving her breast and sneaking between her legs. His middle finger found her clit and brushed insistent strokes.

"Owen," she moaned. Her breath caught as he truly started. His movements were hard and pleading, his body drawing pleasure from and for her body.

They were fucking now. She was sure that's what this was. Earlier today had been about making her come as many times as he could, exalting her orgasms to new heights. Right now, this was for both of them. His cock sliding in her over and over at a dizzying pace, his possessive hold on her hip, his determined strumming of her clit, this was fucking.

Laurel loved it.

She came hard, her hands gripping the couch to keep her from falling on her face. Owen's hand left her clit, grabbing her other hip, before thrusting hard and climaxing. He threw his arms around her waist and held her tightly in place, his jaw resting against her back. His breath was hot against her skin, turning it to gooseflesh.

"Four," she mumbled as he withdrew. She slowly turned to face him and draped her arms around his shoulders for support. She wasn't sure she'd be able to stand on her own for a while.

"Hm?"

"Four orgasm afternoon."

He chuckled. "Let's go take a shower."

After they showered, they sat watching the storm rage and the ocean pound into the beach until it became too dark to see. Then, they had spaghetti for dinner and did the dishes together. When they finally got into bed, Laurel curled against Owen's chest, content to sleep like this for the rest of her life.

This was the beginning of a wonderful life.

Laurel opened her eyes. She was frozen in space, unable to lift her arms or move her legs. She tried to steady her mind. This was a dream. She wasn't in the Hedge World. She was having a simple dream.

Morana appeared, her face inches away from Laurel's own. She tried to flinch away, but her body wouldn't comply.

"See you soon," Morana whispered. Laurel glanced past her face. She could see Morana getting off the ferry in the harbor.

She was here.

Chapter Twenty-Three

A soft wail stirred Owen from his sleep. His eyes opened and took a few moments to register where he was and what was different.

He was in bed at his rental, but this time, someone was in the bed with him. He'd gone to bed with Laurel. He rolled to his side, reaching out for her.

She was upset. She was sleeping, but her face was twisted with worry, and her body shuddered.

"Laurel?" he asked, running his hand over her forearm. She didn't wake up, only continued contorting her face.

"Laurel," he said more insistently, shaking her arm a little. She stayed sleeping and now tears streamed from her eyes.

"Oh, shit." Now he got to his knees and leaned over her. "Laurel! Laurel! Wake up! You're sleeping. Listen to me, Laurel. Come back."

Owen searched his mind trying to figure out a way to wake her up. He jumped out of bed and ran to the kitchen, filling a cup with cold water and grabbing a towel. He hurried back to the bedroom and tucked the towel under her feet.

"Sorry, baby. It's going to be the face if this doesn't work." Owen poured the water over her feet and jolted Laurel awake.

"Fuck!" she screamed and sat straight up.

"Sorry!" Owen exclaimed. "I'm so sorry. But you looked like you were in pain, and I was worried you were with Morana; I couldn't leave you asleep."

Laurel rubbed her hands over her face and inhaled sharply.

"No. Thank you. I was with her. And she's here. She's on Star Island. She came in on the ferry this morning. What time is it?"

"Ten."

"Ok. The ferry got in at nine. She's not at the port anymore." Laurel got out of bed. "She's here. Fuck, Owen. She's here."

"It's ok. We're safe here. Remember, Verbena put up the wards."

He took a breath. He needed to stay calm. "What time does the morning ferry leave?"

"Eleven fifteen, why?"

"Laurel, I think we should be on it." Owen grabbed his shirt from off the floor and pulled it over his head, then searched around for his jeans. He found them, put them on, and then handed Laurel her clothes from the night before.

"On the ferry? Why? We'd be totally unprotected there."

"She thinks you're here. We need to get off Star Island. My truck is waiting in long-term parking. All we need to do is get gas and we can be in Maine in four hours. Between my mom, aunts, and cousins that live in town, we can turn my apartment into a fortress. Or we could stay with my parents. I know my mom wouldn't mind. I don't know the Stoch family, but no witch in her right mind would cross the Davies witches."

"Owen, no. Let's get back to my house." Laurel slunk out of his t-shirt she'd worn to sleep the night before and pulled on her bra and shirt.

"Why not? No offense to your family, but cottage witches don't have the same clout as water witches."

"Thanks, I do take offense to that," Laurel shot back. "And I'm not leaving my sisters. Morana can walk into any shop and ask where I live, and people will tell her. So, no, I'm not going to run away and leave my sisters to deal with my mess and get murdered by someone out for me."

"They can come too. We'll have to bring one of their cars because my truck only seats three, but—"

"Owen, stop! Lavender owns a business. Rosemary has a job. Sage literally does not leave our property during the growing season. I'll be safer with them anyways." Laurel picked up her phone. "I'll text one of them to come pick us up. We'll hang out at my house and come up with a plan."

Owen exhaled. He'd be lying if physically carrying Laurel to the ferry hadn't crossed his mind, but he didn't want her mad as hell at him. Why wouldn't she run? This woman was infuriating. All he was trying to do was protect her. If they were going to face Morana, he wanted to do it with the greatest advantage possible. A small army of water witches on their side seemed like a good option.

"Lavender can come get us in forty-five minutes when the morning rush dies down." She grabbed her skirt off the floor and shimmied into it. "Why are you looking at me like you're mad?"

"It's fine. Forty-five minutes?" Owen grabbed his bag and threw a few shirts and pairs of shorts in there. The air was sparked with tension now, but he didn't want to fight with her over who would best protect her from Morana.

"I'm going to wash my face," Laurel called heading to the bathroom.

"I bought you a toothbrush. It's the purple one."

Laurel stopped walking and turned around. "Thanks."

"You're welcome." Owen finished packing and quickly made the bed. He wasn't sure how long they would be gone and wanted the place put together in case it took a while.

"Bathroom's yours," Laurel said and walked past him.

"Thanks," he mumbled. Owen brushed his teeth, grabbed his toiletries, and headed out to pack them. He grabbed his bag and tossed it next to the door, then collapsed onto the couch.

"Owen," Laurel started as she walked out of the bedroom. She sighed and looked at her phone before tossing it on the table. "Lavender will be here in thirty-seven minutes because she is the promptest person I have ever met. I don't want to spend those minutes fighting."

"Me neither."

"I'd rather spend them fucking." Laurel reached under her skirt and pulled off her panties, dropping them to the floor. "You too mad to have sex?"

"What if I am?" Owen challenged, knowing full well he would never follow through with the threat. Even from here, halfway across the room, he could feel her desire coming off in waves. He'd never deny or turn her down for anything, least of all a morning fuck.

"I'll leave you alone and go sit on the porch until Lavender gets here." Laurel started to reach for her panties on the floor.

"Don't put those back on," Owen cautioned.

"Ok." She straightened back to standing and pulled her shirt over her head.

Owen glanced over his shoulder. The beach was only 200 yards away, with lots of people walking by this morning. It wasn't crowded, and someone would have to look directly into his window to see them, but still.

"There's a window right there," Owen mentioned.

"I see it." Laurel walked towards him; her eyes fixed on him. She stood in front of him, her legs between his knees and smirked. Then she got down on her knees. Her eyes flicked to the bulge currently begging for some attention, then back to his face.

"I don't think anyone can see me down here," she said, slowly, slinking out of her bra. She guided his hands to cup her breasts, and Owen immediately slid forward on the couch for better access.

"I can't reach a lot of you down there," he pointed out.

"You don't need to, yet." Laurel found his waistband and snuck her hand beneath to stroke his already hard cock. Owen responded by giving her breasts a squeeze, then rolling her nipples between his fingers.

Laurel drew his cock out, running her hand over the smooth skin. Her gaze dropped to his member and having her eyes on him like that nearly undid Owen.

"Laurel," he breathed.

"Come on. Yesterday, you said it had been too long since you had sex for me to really investigate. We've slept together twice in the last twenty hours. Let me have a little fun and then I promise I'll lay on my back with my legs wide open for you."

Owen nodded and leaned back.

"You know I love you," Owen said, his voice gravelly.

"Stop trying to distract me with your declarations," Laurel mumbled, then ran her tongue over the tip of him.

"Holy..." Everything flew out of his head. She slid her mouth over him, and all worries of Morana and curses melted away. Owen let himself get lost in the sensation. His hands ran up her arms, grasping her shoulders, kneading her back.

"Ok," he breathed, pulling her off him. "As you said, on your back, legs wide open."

Laurel licked her lips before grinning. "Skirt on or off?"

"On for time's sake," he answered.

Laurel leaned back to the floor, threw her arms over her head, and spread her legs for him. Owen hummed a small growl, then crawled over her. He pulled her skirt out of the way and plunged into her.

"Goddess, I love this," Laurel murmured against his jaw. She trailed kisses down his neck to his shoulder.

Owen agreed. He loved the feel of Laurel's breath against his skin, her thighs clinging to his hips, her fingers twisted through his own. He loved it all. Most of all, her.

He would do anything to keep her.

Thirty minutes later, with Lavender escorting them, Owen and Laurel walked back into the Bay cottage. Sage and Rosemary were sitting at the table waiting for their arrival with a big spread of food set out. Owen was ravenous. They'd obviously skipped breakfast in favor of orgasms and the smell of donuts and croissants wafting towards him caused his stomach to audibly rumble.

"Oh my goddess!" Rosemary shrieked and ran over to the two of them. She threw her arms around Laurel, jumping up and down, then turned to Owen and hugged him in return.

Owen shot Laurel a confused look.

"I said that Morana was on the island, not that we'd seen her or anything. I'm fine," Laurel said.

Rosemary shook her head. "That's not why I'm hugging you. You two had sex!"

"Oh for fuck's sake, Rosemary." Laurel put her fingers on her temples and rubbed.

"What? You did. And..." she looked back and forth between them, "it was amazing. Oh, I'm so happy for you! I have heard of soulmates needing a few tries to get it perfect, but it looks like the two of you will be smooth sailing from here on out! What an exciting beginning!"

"Rosemary, please shut up," Laurel interrupted. "Please, please, please stop talking about my sex life. Right now. This instant. Please."

"I do not understand how we were raised by the same parents. Why are you uptight about sex?"

Thankfully, Lavender stepped in, because Owen was worried both he and Laurel might melt into the ground out of sheer embarrassment.

"Rosie, relax. Seriously. When you meet your soulmate, you are welcome to inundate us with details of your sex life. Laurel doesn't want to. Now, let them eat in peace. Clearly, they've worked up an appetite," Lavender added with a straight face.

Owen glanced at Laurel, who closed her eyes and blew out a breath. Rosemary shrugged and sat back down at the table.

"We've got coffee or my 'kick-the-shit-out-of-today' tea blend. What sounds good?"

"Tea," Laurel answered quickly. She turned to Owen. "It tastes sort of like citrus and basil but also like you drank a Red Bull, but in a good way."

"I guess I'll try a small cup of that to start."

Owen sat next to Laurel with Sage on his other side. Their table was huge, definitely meant for twelve people. Laurel had mentioned something about each of the Bay sisters being destined to meet their soulmate in the next six months. Owen was looking forward to those seats filling up, and not being the only outsider at the breakfast table, especially if Rosemary was going to be asking for details about the mind-blowing sex he was having with Laurel.

Owen remembered having sex ten years ago. It was great, fun, and satisfying. But sleeping with Laurel was completely different. It was physically amazing, but beyond that, simply looking at her made his heart feel like it was going to burst. When Laurel gave her body to him, he wanted to worship her.

"If you want me to stop making comments about the two of you, Owen's going to need to tone down the longing looks." Rosemary took a long sip of her tea, her eyes full of mischief.

"We're going to eat on the porch," Laurel announced and picked up her plate. "Come on."

Owen wasn't sure how long he was going to be able to stand living with Laurel's sisters.

Chapter Twenty-Four

It had been twenty-four hours since Morana arrived on Star Island, and yet, nothing. No sightings, no unexpected jumps into the Hedge World, no new curses as far as Laurel could tell. She had expected Morana to hit the ground running when it came to making Laurel miserable and/or straight up murdering her, but apparently that wasn't her jam.

"I don't think it's plausible for me to stay inside until Morana decides to attack me. I could be stuck in the house for weeks." Laurel brought up while she, Rosemary, Sage, and Owen ate lunch.

"Lavender said," Rosemary began.

"I know. Lavender wants me to be locked in my room until, I don't know, I become an expert curse breaker. I have a bachelorette party tomorrow morning."

"You canceled it, right?" Owen prompted.

"Not yet. It's my job. If I don't do it, I won't get paid. And they'll leave me a bad review. It could kill my business."

"Is there someone who can cover for you?" Owen continued.

Laurel raised her eyebrow. She glanced at Rosemary and Sage. "Anyone at the table want to read tarot cards tomorrow for eight twenty-five- to twenty-eight-year-olds?"

"Absolutely not," Sage replied.

"I don't think I can," Rosemary answered. "I don't read tarot cards and there's always that one woman who has actually studied them and could call me on my bullshit. Plus, I would tell everyone happy things. I don't think I can give bad news."

"See," Laurel said. "No one can cover for me."

"Well, you're not going to a bachelorette party. Morana could attack you there. That would be stupid."

"Excuse me?" Laurel pushed away from the table. Rosemary shot a glance at Sage, and they both quickly fled outside.

"Did you say I was stupid?" Laurel reiterated.

"No, I said working a bachelorette party would be stupid. Tell them you're sick."

"I will not. I gave them my word I would do this party, and barring emergency, I will."

"Laurel. This is an emergency. The woman who threatened you is on Star Island." Owen shook his head. He stood up and walked across the room. "Are you being serious right now?"

"Yes, I'm serious. And it's not an emergency. If it was, I could call the police and tell them that a woman I knew in a past life and have seen in the Hedge World is on Star Island to steal my blood and my innate witch powers. But I can't."

"The fact that the police wouldn't believe you doesn't make it not an emergency. C'mon, Laurel. It's not like you're a doctor. It's a bachelorette party. No one will die if you don't go to work."

"Don't demean my work," she spat. "I am an entertainer. I work when I am sick. I give people a good experience during their last hurrah. This woman booked me three months ago. So yes, while I am not a doctor, my work is important. And if I get a bad review, my business will tank."

"That doesn't matter. You can work anywhere."

"What the hell does that mean?"

"Only that you are a tarot card reader. You can set up shop literally anywhere in the world."

"Are you insinuating Maine?"

"Why not? I have a job there and an apartment I don't share with my siblings."

"I cannot believe you." Laurel pushed away from the table violently and paced into the front room. She spun on her heels to glare at Owen. "You're a carpenter. Carpenters can work anywhere, right? Why don't you move here?"

"I don't know if you've noticed, but we don't have anywhere to live here. I'm getting kicked out of my rental in less than a week. And tarot card reading probably doesn't come with health insurance."

"You are acting like a dick, and I would appreciate it if you would stop," Laurel said through gritted teeth.

"And you're acting like there isn't a witch here who has already confessed she's going to kill you! Give me a break. There's no reason we shouldn't be on our way off Star Island and as far away from here as possible."

"All the way to Maine?"

"Yes, to Maine! Where my powerful water witch cousins can protect you from being murdered!" Owen threw his hands in the air. "Why are you acting like that's crazy? I'm trying to protect you."

"I can protect myself." Laurel crossed her arms in front of her chest. "Look, I think you should go."

"What?" Owen repeated.

"I'd be lying if I said I wasn't furious, and I think you need to leave."

"Are you throwing me out?"

"No, I'm asking you to leave so we don't keep yelling at each other." Laurel took a deep breath. "We don't know each other well, and this has been intense. Maybe we need a breather. I need a break."

Owen's brow furrowed, but he marched towards the door and flung it open.

"Please don't work that bachelorette party. I watched you die once. Don't make me do it again because you're stubborn."

Laurel laid on the couch, staring at the ceiling.

Owen was gone, at her bidding.

She felt like garbage.

Laurel knew she was being stubborn, but she had a business to run. And where the hell did the whole moving to Maine thing come from? Her whole family was here. She could never leave her sisters. They were a team. *They* were the ones she depended on when life got supremely shitty. And he wanted her to abandon them?

Any way she looked at it, Laurel realized she didn't really know Owen yet. Her soul was playing tricks on her. It remembered him but they didn't know each other.

Lavender had been right. Laurel took things too fast. Owen was her soulmate, yes, but all that meant was that he had the power to hurt her more than anyone else on earth. She had been stupid, but for diving headfirst into an intense relationship with a stranger.

"Hey," Sage walked in, her clothes patched with dirt and grass stains. Sometimes Laurel wondered if she rolled around while planting to get as messy as she did.

"Are you going to work that party tomorrow?"

"Probably," Laurel answered.

"I'll go with you," Sage offered.

Laurel sat up and turned to meet her eyes. "Why?"

"Owen has a point."

"Please don't defend him. He said a lot of shit after you left."

"I'm not defending him. And to be honest, I don't want to hear about your fights with your soulmate. But he is right. It's dangerous for you to be on the other side of the wards now that Morana is here. I doubt any of the sorority sisters you're entertaining tomorrow would do anything other than scream and run in the other direction if Morana showed up. I'll be like your bodyguard. But smaller than you, and I won't have a gun."

Laurel snorted a laugh. "Thanks. Seriously. I think Lavender will probably yell at me and Owen's pissed. Thanks for understanding."

"I get it. I wouldn't leave my land if someone was threatening me." Sage shrugged. "All right, I'm going to shower." She nodded and left Laurel alone again.

Laurel rolled onto her side. Her anger at Owen was slowly fading into something worse.

Emptiness.

He was her soulmate, yes, but she wasn't going to stand for being with a man who wanted to control what she did.

She couldn't. She gave her word to work that party, and she was going to.

Chapter Twenty-Five

Owen slammed down the stairs of the Bay cottage, purposefully loud. He marched off the property until he hit the street, fists clenched.

Was Laurel trying to kill him?

She knew. She knew that he had watched her die and been unable to save her. He could still hear her screaming, still feel the hands of those damn guards on him, keeping him from saving her life

Why was she being so stubborn?

"Fuck!" Owen yelled at no one in particular. Maybe himself. Maybe whatever gods or goddesses were laughing at him right now. That was what this had to be—higher beings laughing at his misfortune. He'd lost his soulmate horribly, and now he was poised to lose her again. Over a stupid bachelorette party.

Owen walked home, his fuming anger slowly subsiding into an aching sense of dread. He wanted to run back. Every fiber of his being wanted to be with Laurel. Even if it was only to try, and fail, to save her. Maybe it was part of his fate. They were woven together, but never for long enough. Never to a point where they could be happy for any length of time. Only enough to give him a taste of what life could be like with her.

But she'd thrown him out.

Owen trudged up the steps to his rental. The wards Verbena had created were up, so he was technically safe there, but his safety felt hollow without knowing whether or not Laurel was going to be ok. He wasn't sure he'd ever feel secure in her safety.

Owen ate dinner alone, toast with jam and half a bag of potato chips. He needed something to distract him and suddenly the "no TV" aspect of this place wasn't so desirable.

> Owen: Hey, what's up?

> Mike: Hey, man! Nothing much. Thought you were doing no phones on this trip?

> Owen: I'm a little bored tonight. Any new jobs on the horizon?

> Mike: There's a house going up but not until August. Johnston said we'd both be on it but was respecting your vacation. Now, relax. You've got a job to come home to.

Owen did the opposite of relax. The realization of needing to leave Laurel, who clearly wasn't coming with him, hit him hard. He'd always pictured a soulmate who would love living in Maine. Hell, he came with a built-in matriarchy. Maine had everything—his job, his family, his someday piece of land perfect for a craftsman house with space for a big yard. But it didn't have Laurel.

Owen's phone buzzed, and he nearly fell on his face racing to pick it up.

"Hi, Mom," he answered, exhaling. He'd hoped Laurel was calling, telling him to come back, but his mom was an acceptable second place.

"Hello, eldest son. The last time we spoke, you mentioned you may have met your soulmate. I gave you several days of space to figure out if that was true, but I am *dying*. Any more information for me about the tarot card reader?"

"Oh." Owen grimaced. "Yeah, it's her."

"Yes! Wait. You don't sound over-the-moon happy. What's going on?"

"It's fine," Owen began.

"I should tell you that this morning I looked into a bowl of water and saw you in the Middle Ages. So, spill."

Over the course of twenty minutes, Owen couldn't control the words coming out of his mouth. He told his mom about Laurel, Amée, Morana, the Bay curse, and their fight. Owen had prided himself on keeping personal stuff to himself since he's turned fourteen, but it was clear that he needed to talk to his mom.

"Oh, Storm Chaser. You know, I'm happy you've ended up with a witch," his mother said.

"A witch who won't talk to me," he pointed out.

"You'll work it out. But I'm going to give you some advice."

"Hit me with it."

"Laurel is a witch, and you are a sonofawitch. She outranks you on magical stuff. It's just how it is. A teacher doesn't get to tell a principal how to run a school. If a painter told you how to lay flooring, you'd ignore them, right?"

"I guess."

"She gets to make the magical decisions for herself. You may have grown up surrounded by supremely powerful witches, but you aren't a warlock. Do I wish the two of you were on your way up here right this minute? Of course. If Laurel asked our family for help, I would help her in a heartbeat. Most of your cousins would too."

"Most?"

"Owen, Laurel's right in being wary. She doesn't know any of us. You're her soulmate, but she isn't a part of the family instantly. And she's a hedge witch. She's probably more powerful than most of us."

"What?"

"Hedge witches are super powerful. Visions, mind-jumping, herbal work. She can travel to a whole new realm. And aren't they healers also?"

"She never developed the healing powers," Owen pointed out.

His mom sighed. "Owen, I don't know what to tell you. Having a soulmate doesn't mean you'll have a problem-free relationship. Hell, your dad drives me insane sometimes. We work through it because we love each other. You have to talk to her. Push away your pride and have a conversation without telling her she's being stupid. And never, ever insult her line of work again. I raised you not to be an asshole. Please don't be an asshole."

"I won't." His mom was right. He had let his fear turn him into an asshole. Owen didn't want to be a jerk. He loved Laurel. And he'd hurt her feelings.

"Now, I'm going to go ahead and put you down as having a plus one for the wedding," his mom went on. "Is Laurel a vegetarian? Vegan? Please not a pescatarian."

"She eats everything," he laughed. "And yeah. I'll ask her tomorrow about the wedding."

"Tomorrow? Not tonight?"

"She said she needed a break from me, so I'll give her one. But tomorrow, I'll head over, and we can talk through everything."

"Good plan. And Owen?"

"Yeah?"

"I know she isn't keen on the idea of Maine right now, but please let her know we can't wait to meet her."

"I will."

They hung up, and Owen walked outside, parking himself in one of the rocking chairs. The ocean rushed in the dark distance, a calming presence among the upheaval.

He pulled his phone from his pocket and opened his text to Laurel.

> Owen: I'm sorry I was rude to you today. I'd like to talk to you in person, but I couldn't go to sleep tonight without letting you know that I only ever want to keep you safe. I said some terrible things out of fear today. I hope you can forgive me. I love you, mon petit oiseau. Tell me when you're ready for me to come see you.

Owen set his phone on the chair and walked out onto the sand. He kept going until his feet hit the surf. It was freezing still. This far north, the Atlantic didn't really get "warm" for another month or so. But it still felt good. Owen had never tried a winter dip in the ocean, but he wasn't sure it would be quite as torturous as it was meant to be. He had water magic in his veins.

He walked along the shoreline until he noticed the moon moving across the sky and decided to head back. He gathered his phone off the chair and headed in for bed, but risked checking to see if there was an answer from Laurel.

Laurel: You can come by around 1. I do love you, but I need to figure out what that means.

Chapter Twenty-Six

"How long is this going to take?" Sage asked. She and Laurel were standing on the porch of one of the bigger rental cottages on the island. Thankfully, they were on the Polaris peninsula and not Centauri, where Owen was staying. It wasn't that Laurel was avoiding him, but she didn't want to see him right before she walked into a bachelorette party with eight strangers.

"I'll probably be a little over two hours. It's supposed to be two hours flat, but someone always wants to chat, or has a meltdown. Or if I'm lucky, they'll offer me more money for a bit more info."

"Right. Be careful." Sage parked herself in one of the chairs on the porch. "Holler if you need a hand. Scream if someone tries to murder you." She opened a book she'd picked from the Bay witch library. Thankfully, it had the innocuous title *A Life in the Corn Fields*.

Laurel shook her head slightly, hoping to clear the murder comment Sage made out of her brain before she was expected to read tarot cards for a large group of twenty-somethings.

"The psychic is here!" she heard someone shout from inside.

"Knock 'em dead, psychic," Sage snarked.

"Rachel, Rachel!" Laurel said sternly. "Take a deep breath."

The bride-to-be's breathing pattern was quickly turning into a hyperventilating situation, and Laurel was three minutes away from calling an ambulance.

"That card...it's...no! No. I can't get that." She pointed at the King of Pentacles.

"Rachel, the King of Pentacles can mean a lot of different things," Laurel soothed while simultaneously wracking her brain for any interpretation she could think of. "It can mean new business or that you're going to tap into some intelligence you didn't know you had. Maybe you're going to learn a new language! Have you been thinking about getting a new degree?" Laurel knew she was grasping, but she needed her to calm down.

Rachel's breathing slowed. "My ex. His card was the King of Pentacles. Always. I was into tarot when we dated.. haven't been since."

"Ok. As one reader to another, sometimes a card is just a card. If I thought your ex was somehow coming back into the picture, I would tell you. Nothing else in this draw gives me that idea." Laurel was, of course, lying through her teeth. The draw basically said the wedding wasn't going to happen, but she wasn't that kind of psychic. Rachel would get to enjoy her bachelorette party without the knowledge that she wasn't walking down the aisle with the betrothed, but by December she would be getting wrecked in the backseat of a car by the King of Pentacles. In the best possible way.

"You're going to be ok. Life takes you on paths you never thought you'd find." Laurel took another step towards the future, thinking a nudge might be in order. "Have you been to the Gardner Museum lately?"

"No."

"Give it a visit when you have a moment. Staring at a piece of art can really do wonders for the soul." Laurel winked.

She couldn't say for certain that Rachel and the King of Pentacles were going to rekindle at the Gardner, but she was hopeful.

Once Rachel had calmed down and had a mimosa, Laurel wrapped up the readings. She and Sage left the Polaris peninsula, a place they rarely visited, and went home to their fortified cottage.

"Did Morana try to murder you at the bachelorette party?" Rosemary asked as soon as they walked in.

"She did not. It was a very normal bachelorette party," Laurel answered.

"Perfect." Rosemary picked up her purse. "I'm going to be late for my shift, but I wanted to make certain." She gave Laurel a quick pat on the back as she walked by. "Stay in the house."

"I will," Laurel conceded.

Sage was already bounding upstairs to change into her work clothes and with Rosemary out the door without another word, Laurel was alone.

She missed Owen.

She was being ridiculous, really. It had been just over twenty-four hours since she'd seen him. She shouldn't miss him. That was insane. She slowly walked upstairs. Owen was going to be over in thirty minutes, and she would be damned if she didn't look the hottest she ever had in her entire life.

Insane or not, Laurel had the most annoying ache in her chest whenever she thought of him. Why did he have to be such an asshole? She'd done the party, and nothing happened! She couldn't abandon her work because Morana was set to torment her. She needed to live her life. And Maine! Owen thought she was going to move to Maine? Why on earth would she want to move to Maine? Her whole life was here.

She threw open her closet and grabbed out her slinkiest black dress. It had more of an autumn vibe than spring, but almost all her clothes had an autumn vibe. It was a side effect of wearing only black and occasional dark purples.

Laurel sighed. Maine was where Owen's whole life was. His family, his job, his apartment. He probably even had friends that weren't relatives. So, if he stayed here, he'd be giving everything up.

"Fuck," Laurel breathed. Now she felt like an asshole. She slipped into her dress, added her crescent moon necklace and a pair of owl earrings. She hadn't seen Nyx in a few days and could use some love from her familiar. She would get some owl time tonight once the sun went down. It always made her feel better to fluff some owl feathers under the night sky.

Laurel heard the back door slam as Sage went to work in the fields. She glanced at the clock. Twelve-fifty. She trudged downstairs, mentally preparing herself for the conversation she was about to have. She was going to stay calm. She was going to be an adult and talk calmly with her soulmate.

And then she was probably going to have sex with him on the dining room floor before anyone got home.

Laurel went into the parlor to wait for Owen. She mulled over whether or not she should put out tea and snacks, but decided against it. They were going to talk, not have lunch.

"Laurel? Laurel, are you in there?"

Laurel froze. It sounded like Rachel, the panicking bride from earlier. How on earth did she get her address?

"I need to talk to you about my cards," she called. "Please, can I come in?"

"What the hell?" Laurel muttered. "I'll be right there, Rachel!" she called. She flung open the door.

"That worked." Morana pushed herself into the house.

Laurel couldn't breathe. Morana was in her house. She tried to yell. Her mouth opened, but nothing but gasps came out.

"Wards don't work if you let the person in," Morana chided.

"Get out," Laurel mustered.

"Um, no." She smirked. "Let's go," Morana said and grabbed Laurel's arm, digging her nails into the mark.

Laurel heard her body slam to the floor.

They were in the Hedge World.

Laurel woke up in that old hovel again, the fire burning in the corner, but this time, Morana wasn't in front of the fire. She was crouched next to Laurel, her nails still digging into her forearm.

"Let go," Laurel said, swatting her arm away.

Morana released her grip and stood. She kept her eyes on Laurel and crossed her arms in front of her chest.

"Don't try to run. I'll just bring you back here."

"What do you want?" Laurel got to her feet and rubbed her arm a few times. "You tracked me down, put some sort of homing curse on my arm, and have transported me to the Hedge World more than once this week. Why?"

"I want you to reverse the curse!" Morana shrieked.

Laurel put her hands on her hips and faced Morana. She wasn't scared this time. Something about knowing that Morana's body was in the Bay cottage living room right next to her own gave her comfort.

"You accused me of witchcraft and had me burned alive, you bitch. I cursed you appropriately." Laurel was bluffing, but she wasn't sure what else to do at that moment. The curse was unbreakable. Morana knew that. But if she had hope that Laurel did have the ability to break it, it might buy her some time.

Morana fumed and grabbed Laurel's arm again. Within moments, shooting pain flew up her forearm to her shoulder and into her chest. It felt like fire was coursing from Morana's body into hers. Laurel dropped to her knees in agony. It was like being in the flames again. The horrid heat taking over every corner of her being. She felt like her entire body was shutting down. She writhed in pain, twisting away from Morana.

"Stop!" she screamed, her hand trying to pry Morana off her. She scratched her arm but Morana held fast.

"Reverse the damn curse, Amée. If you were powerful enough to cast it, you are powerful enough to reverse it." The pain continued, spreading to her legs. This was it. Laurel was about to die again; there was no way her heart wasn't under extreme distress due to the pain.

Morana leaned down to Laurel's neck and bit her. Laurel tried to shriek but nothing could come out. She felt the blood draining from her neck, her eyes became heavy and exhausted.

Laurel's mind started to flicker. Could she die in the Hedge World? She hadn't given it much thought. Her body, her real body, was at home, probably on the floor in the living room, but the pain was so intense, it had to be real. She couldn't believe this was only in her mind.

"Can't breathe," she sputtered out.

Morana moved her mouth but kept her hold. Laurel could feel the pain slowly subsiding. It was still there, and in the forefront of her mind, but it wasn't as violent as before. Beads of sweat ran down her forehead as she tried to regain her focus. She needed to be strong. Laurel took a deep breath and shook her head.

"You're going to kill me no matter what. Might as well keep you nice and cursed for when I'm gone," Laurel spat out.

She couldn't see a way out of this. Morana was going to kill her. She already had her blood. There was nothing Laurel could do to stop her. She would kill her, then move onto her sisters. Laurel knew her soul; she was evil as Flavie, and she was evil now. Even if she knew how to reverse the curse, why give Morana the satisfaction?

Morana grabbed Laurel by the chin and forced her to meet her eyes.

"Reverse the curse or I will murder him."

Laurel's eyes flickered.

"Owen Davies. Carpenter at Yankee Construction. Lives at 62 Baxter Ave Apartment 4H, Dayton, Maine. He's a sonofawitch, but not a very strong one. Does belong to the Davies witches, but honestly, with that group, the powerful ones would probably turn their eyes the other way. The things some of those witches have done..." Morana smirked. "It would be no problem to curse him and kill him. Keep your souls from ever meeting each other again." She smiled and tapped her finger against her chin. "Or what if I curse him to die terribly in front of you? Ripped to shreds by dogs, stabbed in the chest, gunshot to the head. Over and over again and you never able to save him? Stuck in an endless loop watching your soulmate die. That would be entertaining." Morana's smirk widened into an all-out grin. "I could have a lot of fun with that. I'd want a front-row seat, of course. I would have to make sure I was reborn right alongside you. Maybe play the part of trusted friend. Then, I can move on to the other Bay witches. I'd leave the young one for Milo, of course. He wouldn't have it any other way."

Laurel felt her hands start to shake. She couldn't let that happen to Owen or her sisters. She looked at Morana. She had been powerful enough to cast that curse. Her soul still held that power. She could do it.

She had to.

Chapter Twenty-Seven

Owen parked his bike against the front gate of the Bay cottage and took a deep breath. His heart was doing all sorts of jumps against his ribs, but overall, he was relieved. He and Laurel could talk. They would work it out. They were meant to be together for the long haul, and he wasn't going to lose her for anything. He needed to accept the fact that she outranked him magically, but most of all, he needed to trust her judgment. Even if her judgment was completely bananas.

As Owen walked down the front path, he noticed the door was open and swaying slowly with the wind. His brow furrowed. Who the hell left the door open when Morana was on Star Island? He shook his head as he marched up the steps.

"Hello?" he called, peeking around the doorway.

The first thing he saw was two pairs of feet. He recognized Laurel's immediately. They were bare, her pedicure was black of course, but her skin was paler than he'd ever seen it.

"No," he breathed, running to her side. She was unconscious, her body twitching. Next to her was a woman with ice blonde hair digging her nails into the mark on Laurel's forearm.

"Is anyone home?" he shouted, hoping that Rosemary or Lavender would answer from upstairs, but there was nothing.

"Sage! Run!" Owen shouted at the top of his lungs out the back door. Sage was always on the property. He hoped she was close enough to hear him. "I need you!" He rushed back into the house, nearly falling as he clipped the dining room table, and slid next to Laurel who lay prone on the floor.

"Laurel, Laurel!" He shook her shoulders, but she was clearly stuck in the Hedge World.

Water, he remembered. He ran back into the kitchen and pulled out the biggest bowl he could find, filled it with freezing water, and hurried back to the living room.

"I'm so sorry," he whispered, then poured it over her legs.

Nothing.

He ran back and refilled it, taking the time to yell for Sage again, then poured it over her chest this time, soaking most of her body. Laurel didn't stir.

"What's wrong?" Sage burst through the back door.

"Living room!" He yelled. "I think it's Morana!"

"Oh, shit," Sage blurted, sinking beside him.

"She won't wake up," Owen panicked. "Should I throw water on her face?"

"If it didn't work on her entire body, it won't work on her face." Sage took stock of the room.

"That is Morana," Sage confirmed. "I recognize her from her picture. How did she get in here?"

"I don't know. When I got here, the front door was open."

Laurel winced and the slightest whimper escaped her lips. Her fists balled, and she started to squirm. He grabbed onto Morana's hand where she held Laurel's arm, trying to pry her off, but it was like they were fused together.

"Fuck!" Owen yelled. This wasn't happening again. This might be worse than France, at least then, he was fighting to get to her. Now, he sat like a useless piece of furniture.

"Come on, Laurel, get out of there," he whispered. Owen looked at Morana. "Maybe we can wake Morana up, get her out of the Hedge World."

Sage scooched over to Morana, wound up, and punched her in the face as hard as she could.

"Fuck!" Sage screamed, grabbing her face and falling backwards.

"What the hell?"

"She's got some sort of protection on her. I think I managed to punch myself in the face, and I've got a great right hook. Fucking brilliant witch." Sage shook her head. "Slitting her throat is out of the question now."

"Can't you, I don't know, snap her out of it? Magically? Wake her up somehow? She's trapped with a woman who wants to murder her. Can Laurel die in the Hedge World? Can she be hurt there?" Owen was starting to panic.

"Look, I don't know." Sage's eyes were wide, and she chewed on her lip. "I don't know any of this. Damn it, I wish someone else was here." She pulled her phone out of her pocket and tapped furiously on the screen.

Owen ran his hands over Laurel's face. "Laurel, I need you. Get out of there. Come on, hear my voice, come back to me. I know you can. Come back." He smoothed her hair away from her face, kissed her forehead, and pressed their heads together. "Come back to me, Laurel. You are strong enough. Figure it out, please, because I don't know what I'm doing. You're the strong one. You are a hedge witch. My mom said hedge witches are crazy powerful. I know you can get out of there. Come back."

Laurel started shaking. Her entire body was convulsing while her face screwed up in pain. A wound appeared on her neck with a line of blood trickling down from it.

"Shit!" Sage screamed.

"Laurel! Laurel!" Owen shouted her name over and over. He was beyond terrified. His fear was like white heat burning out of control. He tried to hold her still, keep her from hurting herself further. He grabbed a blanket from the couch and pressed it against the wound. Owen put his head against her chest.

"Her heart is racing. We need to call an ambulance."

"And tell them what? She's under a spell? They won't know what to do."

"Then a healing witch. Do you know any?"

Sage shook her head. "Not well. And even if I did, it would take too long to get to the island." Sage looked on the verge of tears, but then her brows furrowed. "Wait, you're a water warlock, right?"

"No. My mom's a water witch, and I have very few water-related powers."

"It's worth a try," Sage mumbled. She ran to the kitchen, refilled the bucket with water, and set it next to Laurel. "Heal her."

"What?"

"You have water magic in you. Water witches can be healers. Same with hedge witches. Laurel never cared to develop her healing skills, but maybe you can push her. Use the water, try to heal her."

"Sage, I don't know how to do this. I've never done a spell in my life. I've never even watched one, not really." Owen felt so defeated. Why wasn't he more powerful? He'd give anything to be a real water warlock right now and save Laurel.

"Owen, try. Just try. Put one hand in the water and the other on Laurel. Close your eyes. Think about the water healing her. Think about how good it feels to wash the day off when you're sick or sore or dirty. Think of every positive memory you have of water and try to transfer it into her body. You have to try. Please. Do you have any water deities that your family prays to? Or anyone your mom is close with? Call out to them. Owen, you have to do this."

Owen sunk one hand into the water and placed the other against Laurel's chest.

"Please," he whispered. "Please come back to me. You're so strong. Find your power. You can heal yourself. You can beat her. Take any power I have for yourself. I rain my blessings on you, love of all my lives. Mon petit oiseau." He paused, trying to remember how the women in his family called out to their patron. "Llŷr of the deep, watchman of my ancestors, leader of the dark line, please help her. Patron of my name, god of my blood, save this woman." He turned back to her, grasping at her chest. "Heal, heal, heal, heal, heal." He couldn't stop repeating the words, over and over again.

His hand warmed where it pressed against her, almost like he was transferring something to her. The taste of salt burst into his mouth as if the sea flowed through him.

Laurel's shaking slowed and then stilled. Owen risked a glance at her face. Where she had once looked pallid and sunken, she now was rosy and normal. She looked like herself again.

Sage peeled the blanket away from Laurel's neck, revealing a patch of dried blood, but no wound beneath it.

"You're doing it," Sage muttered. "You're healing her. You or whoever the hell Llŷr is."

"I don't think it's me," he answered. "I think he unlocked her healing powers."

Chapter Twenty-Eight

"I'll undo the curse, but you have to let go of me." Laurel said with as much confidence she could muster.

Morana slowly released her grip on Laurel's arm.

"Back up. I can't work magic with you right on top of me."

She took a deep breath. She'd give anything to have her sisters here. Or her mom and Aunt June. But they weren't here. They were eons away in other realms and Laurel accepted that. She was alone. She didn't have her cards or herbs or anything to aid her. All Laurel had was the power within her, and she had to trust it was enough.

She closed her eyes and took a breath, hoping Morana would think she was still recovering from the pain. Then she hopped into Morana's mind. She did it nimbly, barely scratching the surface. She was worried if she went too deep, Morana would notice.

Morana's mind was not a nice place to be. It was all red and slashing and deafening sounds. There were bits of pieces on the surface, flashes of other lives lived, bits of Flavie and other versions of Morana Laurel didn't recognize. There were spells and curses and symbols written in blood. Laurel jumped out only a moment after touching it.

Morana was wavering. She was grasping. She had a dozen spells in place to give her this strength.

Morana wasn't all-powerful.

But she had want on her side, a want so deep she craved it like a need. She knew about the Bay curse. She was obsessed with power; she wanted hers to increase tenfold. Morana wasn't only after vengeance. She wanted the Bay power.

"Find the light, and draw a circle around it." Laurel focused on her own body and tried to push Morana out of her mind. "Clear this space, so I may work my magic," she mumbled, hoping the nonsense words gave Morana the impression that she was already beginning to undo the curse. Laurel rubbed the spot on her arm, tracing the homing beacon. She worked her fingers over it several times, following the circles and lines until her fingers repeated it in muscle memory.

"Clear this space, clear this space, clear this space," she repeated, focusing on the mark being removed from her arm. She dug deep into her soul, pulled out some ray of light that had been hiding there and brought it to the surface. The small ember grew.

Her eyes snapped open. A burst shot through her like nothing she had ever felt before. Her nose filled with the scent of the sea.

Laurel could feel power coursing through her veins. She was healing. She was strong. The wound on her neck was gone.

She'd never felt this before; it was pure magic, there was no craft in it. There was no practice or years of study. It was from deep inside her, something passed from each version of her soul to the next. It was as if a key had turned and opened the floodgates. She was pure force of will.

She glanced at Morana.

Laurel was the stronger witch. By far. She could feel it.

She brushed the dirt off her palms and faced them outwards. She could feel everything, the Hedge World pulsing with life around her, Morana's anger and vengeance and pain pouring off her skin, she could feel Owen touching her body, his voice in her ear.

"Dissipate," she commanded. The mark on her arm melted away.

"What?" Morana began, but Laurel silenced her with a look.

She pictured the curse in her mind, a tightly woven tapestry marked with the lives of Amée and Flavie. Starting with their tenuous relationship and Amée's death, following the many lives and deaths of Flavie's soul. Evil deeds and dark lives, decades upon decades of hate and fear melded into wicked ways.

It was a terrible curse to have cast. Lain out in front of her, Laurel felt a pit in her stomach. She couldn't undo the past, but she could fix it for the future. Laurel's magic picked at the strings, found weak spots in the spell, until she unraveled it into a heap.

"I undo the curse cast by Amée on Flavie. No longer shall Flavie's soul be so punished for her deeds. The soul of Flavie and Morana will go forward without the curse of the witch Amée."

Morana's face snarled back into her smirk, but Laurel wasn't finished.

"Morana Stoch, hedge witch, I do not curse you, but I trap you here. Your body and soul are bound to the Hedge World until a witches' council decides your fate. You will not leave this realm until I lift the trap. You may harm none while here."

Laurel's mind worked quickly, designing protection wards around Morana. None could harm her, and she couldn't hurt anyone either. She tethered Morana to the Hedge World, with a new tapestry, one made of water and starlight.

Laurel swallowed a smile. She'd never worked like this before, power coursing through her like a raw wire. Her mind moved at speeds she never thought possible. She was a good witch. A powerful witch.

"You can't trap me here," Morana scoffed and waved her hand.

Nothing happened.

She waved it again, this time more furiously.

Still nothing.

"What the hell did you do to me?" she shrieked. Morana tried to dive at Laurel and grab her, but she bounced off the air and stumbled on her feet.

"Remember, harm none." Laurel exhaled. "I granted you mercy. I could have destroyed you, increased the curse tenfold. This is the only mercy I can give you. I can't risk you coming after my family. I will find a witches' council," Laurel said, and she meant it. Even if they gave her a punishment for casting a terrible curse so many hundreds of years ago, she would see an end to this.

"Get me out of here." Morana stalked the walls of the hovel, trying to find a weak point. She started mumbling words in a language Laurel didn't understand.

"I will. When I find someone to deal with you. And I'll come visit you, make sure you're not causing a ruckus here." Laurel sighed. "Live here. Leave the other hedge witches alone."

"I won't do what you say. I'll fight it every moment I'm here. I will terrorize your precious Hedge World."

Laurel shook her head. "You can't. You're surrounded by wards." Laurel shifted her hands for a moment, letting the spiderwebs of protection she had woven around Morana glow for a moment before fading.

She paused, trying to see Morana's soul. She caught bits and pieces of her past and futures, but nothing that stuck out, all darkness and blood spells. "What made you like this?"

"You did," she spat back. "Do you know how many lives I've had since I was Flavie? Six. And I always know my entire past."

"You were evil when you were Flavie." She looked further into Morana's mind. "Flavie wasn't your first life. I didn't make you evil."

Morana huffed and smirked. "Some witches are born with dark souls, cottage witch. Some of us are here to balance the light. No sense in trying to figure out why." She glanced around at her surroundings. "I won't be here long. With the amount of research I did into you, I'm sure you found out about my family. My brothers know I came here. And if you think I'm the wicked witch of the west, you've never met a chaos warlock."

"I'm sure I will. Goodbye, Morana. See you soon."

Laurel breathed.

She was soaking wet, and a heavy hand was on her chest.

She could hear a huge fuss going on around her. Several voices were there. She picked out Owen's right away, then Sage, Rosemary, Verbena, and Lavender. Sage was trying to tell a story, but everyone else kept interrupting her with questions.

Laurel rolled onto her side and slid her knees towards her belly. She wanted to be in her bed. She wanted to sleep. And eat, oh, how she wanted to eat.

"Laurel?" Owen called.

And then she felt his hands on her face, thumbs roaming over her cheeks and lips and chin.

"Owen." She smiled and fluttered her eyes open. She managed to keep her eyes on him for about two seconds before they fluttered closed again. She was so tired.

"She's awake!" He shouted but then immediately covered her mouth with his. Laurel smiled against his lips and tried to wrap her arms around his neck, but they weren't working quite yet. Owen lifted her up, cradling her against his body, and her head tucked under his chin. She wasn't sure where he was taking her, but if she was in his arms, she was safe.

Two hours later, she woke up and was immediately bombarded with questions from four sisters and one soulmate.

"Where did Morana's body go?" Rosemary asked the moment Laurel opened her eyes.

"I bound it to the Hedge World," Laurel answered. "Can I please have something to eat?"

"What?" Lavender exclaimed. "How? How can you even do that? Isn't the Hedge World...I don't know, an ethereal plane of existence?"

"I don't know how I did it, but I did." She took a deep breath. "I was dying in there and then I got a shot of power...like a key unlocked something inside of me. I dug down, and I found a well of untapped power within me. Suddenly, I was more powerful than I was when I was Amée. And Amée could work some powerful curse magic. I could see the curse laid out in front of me, and I unwove it. It was like pulling out a knitting mistake and watching the yarn unravel. Then I stuck Morana in the Hedge World. But I surrounded her with protection wards. And she can't hurt anyone while she's there. So, she's safe, no matter what might come after her there."

"That is so cool," Rosemary gushed. "I want to learn how to do something like that."

"I need to find a witches' council to turn her over to. I can't kill her, obviously. But I'm not letting her out. And cursing her again will probably end in reliving this again sometime in another life."

"There hasn't been a witches' council in the United States in over a hundred years. They kept getting killed." Lavender furrowed her brow. "But I think a few countries in Europe still have them. We could see if one of them wants to take a crack at her."

"It's better than nothing. I'll brush up on my French."

Laurel ate a veggie grinder and two lemon cupcakes and then things settled down a little. She was relieved that Morana was trapped for the time being, but the curse on her family still hung over her head. As did Morana's cryptic warning about a chaos warlock. Laurel had no idea what on earth a chaos warlock could do, but she guessed if he was related to Morana, it wouldn't be anything good.

"Do you want to sleep here?" Owen asked, running his hand over her back.

"Hell, no." Laurel laughed. "We're going to your place. And we're staying at your place until your rental is up. And then we'll figure something out. Because I want you tonight, and I want you every night of my life. I don't want to be quiet or lock the door and be embarrassed at breakfast. I want to scream your name as loudly as I want all night long."

"That sounds like a very nice way to spend the rest of our lives," Owen said, a smile spreading across his face. "I need to find an empty piece of land for sale on this island."

"What?"

"Because I'm going to build you a house. And I'm going to build it here. Clearly, the Bay witches can protect you just as well as the Davies witches could have. Maine is wonderful and everything, but I think I'd like a fresh start here. I've already got one handyman job on my resume, won't be too long until I add some more." Owen smiled. "I've got the plans nearly done; they're at my place now. It'll be perfect. I might need to add one more bedroom upstairs, but it'll be a great house for us. I've been building it in my mind for years and now I have someone to put wood to earth for."

"Owen, are you sure? Your whole life is in Maine. Your family, your work, a real apartment."

"And your whole life is here. I always had this idea that I was going to bring my soulmate into my family; somewhere familiar. I didn't know I was going to end up with a badass hedge witch with healing powers. Plus, I couldn't ask for a better place to live. Surrounded by the ocean and lots of north Atlantic storms to sense? It's perfect."

"If you're sure. I know I was bitchy about Maine, but it's got to be lovely."

"We'll visit. Imbolc and maybe Mabon?"

Laurel's heart did the loveliest thud against her chest. She leaned against him and wrapped her arms around his waist.

"Imbolc and Mabon sound great. I love you, Owen Davies."

"I love you, Laurel Bay. Let's get out of here so I can get you out of those clothes."

"Sounds like a perfect plan to me."

They turned towards the front door, hand in hand, ready to leave, when a pounding stopped them in their tracks.

Laurel opened the door slowly.

"May I help you?"

A police officer she'd never seen before stood in the doorway.

"Good evening, ma'am. I'm looking for Laurel Bay."

"That's me," she answered.

"Have you by any chance seen Morana Stoch lately? Her brother contacted me. He said she was coming here to visit you but hasn't gotten in touch with him for a few days and that was unlike her. Have you seen her?"

"I'm sorry, who are you?"

The man smiled warmly. "Sorry about that, I'm Officer Evans. I'm the new sheriff on Star Island, just started two weeks ago. Haven't had the chance to make your acquaintance yet." He stuck out his hand and Laurel took it, then offered it to Owen.

"Owen Davies."

"Nice to meet you both. So, have you seen Ms. Stoch?"

"Who the hell is at the door at this hour?" Rosemary called as she walked in from the kitchen. "I swear to all the goddesses—"

Rosemary stopped talking. She dropped the bundle of thyme she had in her hand and stared at Officer Evans.

"Oh, fuck," Rosemary said.

The Hedge World

Morana paced the cabin.

It had been her solace, the dark little corner of her soul. Stupid, selfish Amée had turned it on her, made it a cage.

Not Amée. Laurel Bay. The hedge witch had been much more powerful than Morana anticipated. Laurel Bay was a tarot card reader. Regular humans did that shit. She never would have come alone if she'd known the limits of her own magic in comparison to that damn Bay witch.

She huffed and searched the boundaries. They weren't hard and fast. Nothing like the curse that had been laid on her hundreds of years ago. Morana rolled her neck a few times. With the weight of the curse lifted, her magic had to be stronger, right? She could break through these wards, get out of the Hedge World, and finish what she started with the Bay witches.

She tried to conjure her door, the dark little exit that would deposit her back into the Bay house. What a fucking sight that would be! Morana bursting out of the Hedge World and raining hell on their entire family. She grinned at the thought.

Hell, Laurel's blood had been delicious. She hadn't thought herself a blood witch, but Milo was right. There was nothing like the taste of power. She had four more witches between her and more power than any witch had ever wielded. Once she had the power of five Bay witches in her soul, she'd be unstoppable.

It was a good thought.

She closed her eyes and concentrated, but no matter how hard she pulled at it, the door wouldn't come.

A voice traveled toward her, singing softly on the evening air. She perked her ears and opened the door to the cabin.

"Hello, there," Morana called to the visitor. "Would you give me a hand?" She tried to keep her voice sweet, her tone light. The witch, a young thing with braided hair and big brown eyes, took a few tentative steps in her direction.

"Are you alright?" the other witch asked.

"Yes, I only need a moment of your time." Morana reached for her. If only she could make contact, dig her nails into the skin of this other witch, she could hitch a ride back to the human world and—

A sharp pain traveled up her arm and into her chest. She shrieked and shrunk backward into the cabin, and the other witch scurried away like a frightened mouse.

"Fuck!" Morana shouted. She wasn't going to hurt that witch. Not really. Just a bit of a puncture to her arm to help Morana get out of the Hedge World. How did the damn wards know that?

She shuffled towards the fire and sat down with a huff. She could break these wards. She had all the time in the world. The blood of the Bay line wasn't going anywhere.

Not that she needed time. Ivan and Milo knew where she went. They'd know what happened when she didn't come back.

She grimaced thinking of the shit they'd both give her, bested by a Bay. Didn't matter though. Her brothers were powerful warlocks. Stronger than they should be.

Morana only had to wait and see what happened when a Bay witch encountered a couple of warlocks. She stretched her legs out long and grinned.

They'd come for her.

Thank you for reading! Did you enjoy? Please add your review because nothing helps an author more and encourages readers to take a chance on a book than a review.

And don't miss the next book of the *The Witches of Star Island*, BEWITCHING ROSEMARY, available now. Turn the page for a sneak peek!

You can also sign up for the City Owl Press newsletter to receive notice of all book releases!

Sneak Peek of Bewitching Rosemary

"Whoever might be out here, listening in on this slightly drunk garden witch's musings," Rosemary began as she clipped some thyme, "thank you. You know I don't hold much stock in good and evil; no one sees the villain they are. But you kept the Bays safe, and we are grateful."

She rubbed a few soft leaves between her fingertips until the earthy fragrance drifted through the air.

"Perfect," she hummed. The three glasses of wine she'd downed in the last hour had her feeling deliciously magical. It was a good night for spells, and acts of gratitude, especially after the day the Bay sisters had. Her younger sister, Laurel, had been attacked by the witch Morana as she tried to steal the Bay's magic. Laurel had nearly died before managing to trap Morana in the Hedge World. Gratitude was in the forefront of her mind.

Rosemary headed back into the house down the white stone path. She loved this walk—wildflowers creeping between the stones, her herb garden in the distance. The air was warm and breezy against her skin, carrying the scents of mint, basil, and chamomile. Summer on Star Island had a wild sort of magic about it that Rosemary loved. Her plants were at their strongest, and so was she.

Laurel would be heading out soon—out of their house and into her new life with Owen. The prophecy had started; each of their soulmates were coming and Laurel's happened to show up first. The book of their young adulthoods was closing, and Rosemary couldn't be more excited. She'd wished for her soulmate since she was sixteen, dreamed of what he'd look like, and even what he'd taste like. She wanted to know what it would be like to wrap her legs around his hips and show him everything she'd learned—and see what he might bring to the table. Or the shower. Or the earth under the full moon. She couldn't wait to tell him everything about herself and learn everything there was to know about him. It was like waiting for the best sort of best friend. One who she'd fall madly in love with.

In the kitchen, Lavender, the oldest Bay sister, had a beef and carrot stew simmering. It was a bit heavy for summer, but there was nothing like a dangerous afternoon to put a true hunger in one's belly.

Rosemary was about to sneak a quick taste when a heavy knock at the door made her jump out of her skin. It was very late for a social call on Star Island. The population liked to keep old-fashioned hours in every sense. After the afternoon they'd had, Rosemary steeled herself. Another magical battle could be on the horizon.

"Who the hell is at the door at this hour?" Rosemary called as she walked into the dining room. "I swear to all the goddesses—"

She stopped talking and the bundle of thyme she had been holding slipped through her fingers and bounced on the floor.

"Oh, fuck." Her entire body felt like it was on fire, and her fingers and toes buzzed so violently she thought they might vibrate off her body.

Rosemary took one look at the police officer taking up the entirety of her doorway, turned around, and walked straight out of the parlor. She didn't stop as she marched into the kitchen, out the screen porch, and past the herb garden. She kept going into the darkness to the deeper parts of their property, because there was no way this was happening.

Rosemary Bay, garden witch and sex magic enthusiast, was not soulmates with a cop.

Yes, he was handsome. His face was perfectly constructed and would be welcome buried between her breasts. The bright eyes that didn't leave her face could probably bore right into her soul. Even beneath his beard, she could tell that he sported a jawline that could cut glass. Yes, her heart slammed into her stomach and then her throat and then against her ribs the moment she saw him. Which paired with the full-body explosion of heat and electricity was an undisputable sign of a soulmate. And finally, yes, he was the size of a small tree and could probably carry all one hundred and seventy-five pounds of her without breaking a sweat and transplant any tree or shrub she wanted moved without complaining of back pain.

But no.

No amount of tree transplanting or bosom-nuzzling would change the cold, hard fact that Rosemary was not suited to the idea of having a cop as her partner. Forever.

She kept walking, paying little mind to the fact that her abrupt exit in the middle of a visit from local law enforcement probably looked suspicious. There was also that pesky detail that her sister, Laurel, had just bound an evil witch to another realm and therefore made her an accessory to a missing person case. But that did not stop her from stomping away from the house.

"Rosemary!" Lavender hissed into the darkness.

"Walled garden," she yelled to her sister and did not slow her pace.

Rosemary continued on her way, following the loose stone path lined by her perfectly chaotic wild flowers. She took a few deep breaths. The flowers should help her calm down, or at the very least help her to regain some sense of self. She was a garden witch; she was most powerful when surrounded by *her* garden. She needed those plants to start working for her.

The Bay property had several different gardens tucked and spread throughout their land, courtesy of Rosemary. The herb garden, rose garden, walled garden, as well as a few other collections of aesthetically pleasing groups of blooms were Rosemary's territory. But while she may have sown the seeds, blessed the ground, and poured her love into the plants, once the flowers got started, there was no stopping them. They had their own wild, inherent magic. Rosemary just gave them a little push.

She walked under the arch into the walled garden and found her favorite bench, the one with the archer carved into the side, forever shooting an arrow into the night sky, and sank down until she hit the cool stone. It was one of her favorite places on their property, and she was a strong believer in a comforting environment helping a person through a hard time.

Her soulmate was here. And somehow, after a month of being ready for him to come and fifteen years of waiting impatiently for him to show up, she was unbelievably and completely unprepared.

"What is wrong with you?" Lavender broke into her thoughts. "It looks extremely suspicious that two of us disappeared into the night when the new sheriff came asking about Morana. Are you trying to arouse distrust?"

"Did he follow you? The cop?" Rosemary kept her eyes buried against her hands, not yet ready to face her sister.

"I doubt it, but I wouldn't yell anything, just in case."

"That cop," Rosemary paused and took a deep breath, "that man in our parlor talking to Laurel about Morana Stoch, is my soulmate."

Lavender burst out laughing.

"Stop it, Lavender, it isn't funny," Rosemary spat. She crossed her arms over her chest and grimaced at her sister.

"Funny? No, it's damn hilarious. Your soulmate is in the parlor, Rosemary. *Your* soulmate. You've been talking a big game for the last month. Hell, you've been doing it for years. 'Once my soulmate shows up, we'll spend three days between the sheets. I can't wait until he gets here so we can have sex under the full moon. The second I see him, I'm attacking him like a spider monkey. We're going to do so much sex magic,'" her older sister mocked her. "Look at you! Just as scared as Laurel was. And you didn't even have the decency to talk to him first, just immediately hid in the garden. I would have thought you'd be crawling up him right now or dragging him to your bedroom. Or worse, taking your clothes off in front of all of us." Lavender chuckled.

A few weeks earlier, their younger sister Laurel's soulmate, Owen, had appeared on Star Island. It took her a little while to be accustomed to the idea of her soulmate suddenly in her life, and Rosemary had teased her on more than one occasion.

"Lavender, my soulmate cannot be a cop." Rosemary gestured wildly with her hands. "Do you know how many hallucinogens I currently have growing on our property? Seven. I did Witch's Eyes two weeks ago. I go to the Women's March every year in Boston. I'm a registered member of the Green Party. I cannot be soulmates with a stick-in-the-mud cop!"

"Just because the majority of the cops on Star Island have arrested you for public indecency doesn't mean this one will be like that. Maybe he'll love having a crazy little nudist as a life partner. And wait, you are growing illegal substances on our land and didn't tell me? Are you insane?"

"Lavender, focus. There's no one more well-versed in botany on this island than me. Unless this new guy used to be on a drug taskforce specializing in mind-altering drugs of the pre-modern period, he won't recognize anything. And pot is legal now, so I can't get in trouble for that."

Rosemary wasn't a *heavy* drug user. She smoked pot once in a while and saved the stronger stuff for spells. She grew everything; it was in her nature. She had an entire garden of baneful herbs tucked away in a corner of the land no one used, and they were far more dangerous than her patch of Witch's Eyes.

"Do you want to go talk to your *soulmate?* Get his phone number and send him a dirty text? Ask him out to dinner? Or go back to his place and fuck him senseless, considering that was what I thought you would do as soon as you saw him?" Lavender leaned against one of the magnolia trees and absentmindedly ran her hand over the bark.

"No. I think I'll sit out here for a little while." Rosemary closed her eyes and blew out a breath. What a mess.

Lavender nodded. "I'm going back to the house so I can answer any questions he might have. Hopefully I'll come up with something believable about why you disappeared into the garden on my walk back." Lavender rubbed her fingers against her brow. "I'm so tired." She sighed, then turned and walked under the arch and disappeared into the darkness.

Rosemary tipped her head back and stared at the stars. She wished it was daytime. She needed to garden, and not just cut a few flowers and rub a few herbs between her hands. Rosemary needed to move bushes, plant a few new trees, and maybe redesign an entire new garden. She had been considering putting in some peonies in a spot just outside the walled garden. She could probably take a quick trip to the mainland this week and grab a few tubers to get it started. A big project would help her accept the fact that her soulmate was probably a pretty buttoned-up police officer. Maybe he'd surprise her and be really into landscaping. She could hope.

She whimpered. Someone being a cop didn't necessarily mean he would be a rule-follower, right? She grumbled. Cops enforced rules. It was sort of their life's work.

It wasn't like Rosemary wanted a criminal for a soulmate. She followed ninety-five percent of the laws in place. She just wanted someone to get into a little mischief with. Or someone that would turn a blind eye to some of the questionable things she did. Like aiding her sister in trapping a witch in the Hedge World.

Oh well. She would have to figure out a way to make it work. Because there was no way Rosemary Bay, garden witch and sex magic enthusiast, was tamping her spirit.

"Oh shit." She laughed. After all that, she had forgotten to get his name. So, for now, her soulmate would be known as tall, bearded cop.

When Rosemary finally ambled back to the house, tall, bearded cop was gone, as were Laurel and Owen. They'd headed to Owen's rental for the foreseeable future with a promise to text in the morning. Lavender and Sage were both sleeping, but Verbena was at the dining table taking notes.

"I didn't expect you to still be here." Rosemary pulled out the chair next to her.

"Well, you know Lavender and Sage turn into pumpkins if they stay up too late. Besides, I wanted to make sure you were okay."

"Just some disappointment that manifested as panic. I'll be fine." Rosemary paused. Verbena sat beside her, but she couldn't ignore the fact that her sister felt hundreds of miles away.

"Related," Rosemary shook out her hands a bit to clear her thoughts, "do you have any houses on the market right now that could use a few new trees in their yards? I'm going to be gardening all day tomorrow, and I don't know if Sage would appreciate me transplanting her entire apple orchard. I need to do some heavy work."

"Not particularly. I do have a house with a fifty-percent-dead pine out front that could use some serious pruning. Care to hack away at dead branches?"

"Better than nothing. Text me the address. I'll be there in the morning." Rosemary settled into her seat, wondering if she should make a cup of tea or eat an entire cake. It felt like that kind of night.

"I'm going to head home," Verbena said, pushing in her chair and grabbing her purse.

"You could stay?" Rosemary offered. "We still haven't touched your room, you know. Sage and I are fine sharing."

"Thanks, but, you know me, I like to keep my routines. Helps keep me sane." Verbena forced a smile. "Try to get some sleep tonight. It's going to be okay."

"I know it's going to be okay." Rosemary mustered a small smile in return. "I was just hoping it would be extraordinary."

After Verbena left, Rosemary made herself a cup of tea. There was no cake to be found in the fridge—a true tragedy when living with a baker—so she settled for a chocolate chip cookie the size of her palm. The tea, Don't Let the Bedbugs Bite, was one of her own creation. She and Lavender both dabbled in the tea world, and this one was a simple blend of chamomile, vanilla, and orange, plus a little bit of spell work.

Rosemary finished her tea and cookie, then headed to her bedroom. She carefully opened the door, to not set off a deafening creak, and tiptoed past the already snoring Sage. Their twin beds were situated on either side of the room, just as they had been for nearly thirteen years. Their room still looked like a couple of teenagers lived there, each with their own style. Sage's wall was sparse, only a *Farmer's Almanac* calendar hanging on it, while Rosemary's had close to thirty small pictures pinned up with thumbtacks. Between their beds was a dwarf clementine tree and a lush fern. Neither wanted to be too far away from plants while they dozed.

Rosemary slunk out of her dress, a simple pale green sundress with permanent dirt stains around the edges, and pulled on an oversized T-shirt and boxer shorts. She climbed under her covers, fidgeting with the pillows and tossing around until she got comfortable. She finally settled on her back and stared at the dark ceiling.

This was not the way she pictured spending the night after seeing her soulmate for the first time. She had expected a lot more passion, a lot less clothes, and a lot less fear.

This wasn't like her. Rosemary didn't back down from a challenge. She grew in-ground succulents in the north Atlantic, for Gaea's sake. She could handle anything.

She decided right then it *was* going to be okay. Maybe it was her fate to draw him out of his shell. Maybe he needed to break free from society's constraints. Tall, bearded cop just needed a wild witch by his side, and in no time, she'd have him sky clad under the full moon, a student to her every desire.

Hopefully.

Don't stop now. Keep reading with your copy of BEWITCHING ROSEMARY.

And sign up for Colleen's newsletter to get all the news, giveaways, excerpts, and more!

Don't miss book two in the _The Witches of Star Island_ series, BEWITCHING ROSEMARY, available now, and find more from Colleen Delaney at www.colleendelaney.com

With a curse on her bloodline and a soulmate she didn't expect, Rosemary Bay is set to have a summer to remember on Star Island...

A garden witch who adores meddling in things related to love, Rosemary Bay has been ecstatic with the idea of meeting her soulmate—the other half she's known over past lifetimes but has yet to meet this time around. But when he shows up as Sheriff Asher Evans, looking for a witch her sister banished to another realm, Rosemary panics. Her days are full of spells, curses, and magical danger—how is a human cop going to fit into her life?

Asher Evans came to Star Island to escape the pain of his past, but when a missing person's case leads him to the Bay Cottage and he meets Rosemary, his life is turned upside down. Yes, she is beautiful and enigmatic, but why on earth does he feel like he needs to protect a woman he just met?

When a villain from their past life shows up on Star Island, Rosemary and Asher's happiness will be tested by a centuries' old curse, an unavoidable destiny, and a metal warlock determined to keep them apart.

Please sign up for the City Owl Press newsletter for chances to win special subscriber-only contests and giveaways as well as receiving information on upcoming releases and special excerpts.

All reviews are **welcome** and **appreciated**. Please consider leaving one on your favorite social media and book buying sites.

Escape Your World. Get Lost in Ours! City Owl Press at www.cityowlpress.com.

Acknowledgments

One rainy June night in 2019, *Cringe* by Matt Maeson came on the radio and changed my life. So, thank you to Q101 in Chicago. You helped me birth an entire world of witches during a summer storm alone in my car.

To my husband: first and foremost, this book, and every book I've ever written, wouldn't exist without your support. I could not have written a better partner to share my life with. I'm so happy we ran into each at that party and I made you walk me to my car for "safety reasons." And to my four adorable children, you aren't allowed to read this until you move out of the house. And then never tell me you're read it. Actually, just don't read it. Maybe I'll write something you can read one of these days.

To my dear writing friends—Jen, Abigail, Tova, Katy, Desirée—thank you for fielding all sorts of questions, day and night, reading drafts, and cheering me along on this writing journey. Without you, I would have been an overwhelmed mess. To Abigail in particular, you will always be the first person who one of my books made cry. I hope there are a long line of people behind you someday.

To my OG writing friends, the girls from Katharine Hall—Kristen and Misti. Fate put us in the same dorm as eighteen-year-olds and I'm so happy that over twenty years later (ahem) our friendships are going strong. Thank you for reading my LOTR fanfiction in 2003. Maybe someday there will be fanfiction about Laurel and Owen living in an AU and fighting orcs.

To the team at City Owl—Tee, Tina, Yelena—thank you for believing in this story and me as an author. I will forever be grateful for your support and dedication.

Lastly, to every single reader: you've made my dreams come true by reading this book. When I was eight years old, I won a poetry award and I've never looked back. My teenage self promised she'd get her first tattoo when I published my first novel. Time to start looking at Bay Leaf designs.

About the Author

COLLEEN DELANEY is an author, librarian, gardener, and occasional baker. She likes being outside in every season except winter, which she prefers to enjoy from a window. She currently lives on the shores of a Great Lake with her husband and four time-consuming children.

www.colleendelaney.com

instagram.com/colleendelaneywrites

x.com/cdelaneywriter

tiktok.com/@colleendelaneywrites

youtube.com/@ColleenDelaney

threads.com/@colleendelaneywrites

About the Publisher

City Owl Press is a cutting edge indie publishing company, bringing the world of romance and speculative fiction to discerning readers.

Escape Your World. Get Lost in Ours!

www.cityowlpress.com

facebook.com/CityOwlPress

x.com/cityowlpress

instagram.com/cityowlbooks

pinterest.com/cityowlpress

tiktok.com/@cityowlpress